I0760819

Madwood

by Elias D. Thorn

Madwood

a Novel

Ordering Information: Special discounts available for book clubs. For details, contact the publisher at director@vanvelzerpress.com.

Paperback ISBN: 978-1-954253-76-6
Hardback ISBN: 978-1-954253-75-9

Second Edition

Printed in the United States of America FSC-certified paper when possible

VanVelzerPress.com

TABLE OF CONTENTS

For those the world erased,

but who kept

writing themselves back in.

THE BEGINNING: CRAWLING ROOTS

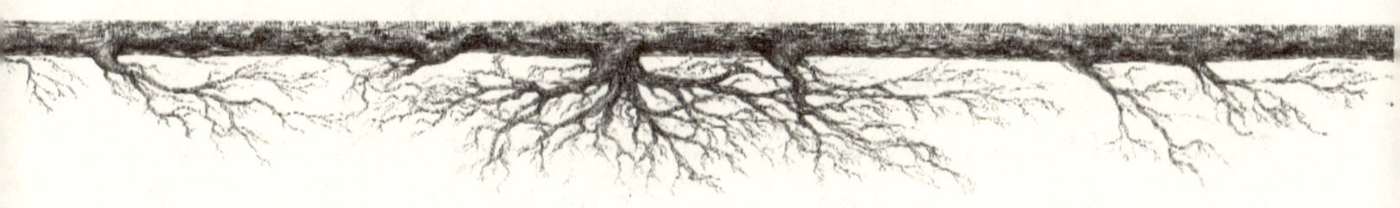

The 3 Rules of Madwood

They're simple enough to remember.
The burden of the cost reveals itself when it's too late.

1) It feeds where the air is heavy.
Grief. Terror. Shame. These make the root-tips swell. In light, empty rooms, it only listens—waiting for a weight to return.

2) Touch is a contract.
Skin oil, a breath, the grain of wood, the gleam of gold—anything your body leaves behind can be claimed. Once touched, you're part of the ledger.

3) It creates nothing.
Madwood only closes circuits already wired by human want (desire, debt, fear) and then tightens them until they're a close circuit forever.

Edward owned a peculiar little business on Broadway Street in Sacramento—a narrow antique shop with a cozy café nestled inside. Locals from nearby China Town, especially from the Wong Association building just across the street, would stop in for coffee and sweet buns, then linger to browse shelves crowded with brass trinkets, brittle books and relics that looked like they might confess a secret if you stared long enough.

Edward rose early every morning, long before dawn's first light touched the sycamore leaves outside. By five o'clock he was shaping dough with calloused hands, letting the scent of coffee and sugar warm the air before unlocking the front door. However, the soul of the shop wasn't the café. It lived in the shadows of old maps, yellowed photographs and clocks that hadn't ticked in decades.

It was on one of those mornings that Lilith first arrived, hand-in-hand with her grandfather. Her small hand was locked in her grandfather's grip like a leash yet she didn't hunch; she moved like a blade slicing through the warm café air, gleaming under the red neon sign.

The old Chinese man had the wiry build of someone who'd worked too hard for too long. A gray coat hung off his frame like borrowed skin. His grip on the little girl's hand was tight—*too tight for comfort,* Edward thought at the time. Little Lilith didn't flinch. She walked beside him as though the world answered to her, not the other way around.

She was striking in the kind of way that unsettles rather than pleases—skin pale as porcelain, hair a wild halo of dark, deep brown/red curls and eyes that held the soft shape and dark luster of her Chinese heritage. She looked like something misplanted: a ghost orchid growing in the wrong garden, too pale and still for the bright, primary colors of Little China.

Her gaze swept the shop with unnerving calm.

"Do you want these magazines?" Edward asked, nodding toward a stack of old National Geographics piled near a battered steamer trunk. Their pages curled like brittle leaves, forgotten by time.

Lilith tilted her head slightly, her eyes locking on him—not with curiosity, but with something older, colder. Then she softened, blinking once. "Really?"

"Of course," Edward said, brushing flour from his apron. "No one reads them anymore."

She moved forward, scooping them into her arms like sacred objects. Her grandfather hovered behind her, a stiff smile stretched across his weathered face. But there was something else behind his eyes—wariness, Edward realized. Not the wariness of a caretaker, but of a man who had once had control and now wasn't sure he still did.

She turned toward the far wall then, her attention caught by a tarnished brass telescope. She approached it like she already knew what it could show her. Her grandfather shot Edward a quick look. He didn't speak, just ... waited.

Edward nodded, lifting the telescope gently from the shelf and handing it to Lilith. "This is an old handheld scouting telescope. Do you like telescopes?" he asked.

"They let you see far away," she replied. Her voice was calm, light—her hands were steady. Too steady for one so young.

She carried it outside, cradling it the way a child might hold a kitten. On the sidewalk, under the soft glow of the morning sun, she lifted the eyepiece to her face. The telescope was too heavy for most children her size, yet she held it with ease, eyes fixed on the sycamore trees lining the other side of the street.

"What do you see, Lilith?" Edward asked.

"The trees. And the people," she murmured, barely louder than the wind. She held her breath, yet her eyes stayed fixed, as if caught in a structure deeper than the tree itself. No one noticed. Her eyelashes trembled slightly and somewhere in the folds of her retina a subtle vibration began. A connection to something the emotionless little girl had never felt before.

Edward smiled. "Trees and people, yes. Which do you like better?"

She lowered the telescope and looked straight at him. "The trees," she said.

He laughed softly. "Why's that?"

"They live longer," she said. "They see more. And when they die, they can still be made into things. They're better than people. More useful."

A chill passed over Edward's spine. There was no malice in her tone. Just fact. He glanced again at her grandfather. The man's eyes had fallen to the sidewalk, his smile collapsed into something else—fragile, defeated. A man living in silent fear of her judgment.

"If there's a tree that can see through people, I'd watch it for the rest of my life." She said this quietly and to no one in particular. When she said it, the sycamore tree had been reflected in her eyes through the lens—as if it had taken root there. From that moment on, her eyes were never quite the same.

Lilith turned and walked back into the shop with the telescope in hand. Sunlight glinted off the brass, painting her in gold. She stepped past her grandfather without a glance, her bare feet whispering against the tile. They got a donut to share and left.

Edward watched her go. He couldn't even remember if they paid for that little piece of history let alone the donut. The telescope wasn't a toy to her. It was an instrument. A way of learning the angles of the world, and maybe how to bend them.

Even at this young age, she wasn't just observing life.

She was evaluating it.

It would be 30 years before Lilith reappeared in the shop owner's life. And yet, her story found its way back to him, again and again. Out there, people said it was her—Lilith—who brought about her Chinese grandfather's death. As for how? Edward heard a dozen versions, each darker than the last.

That night, Lilith had a very strange dream. In it, the stately sycamore was no longer in its home along the street—it had begun growing out of her own eye. Its roots crawled slowly through her ears and nostrils, winding their way into her brain. It calmed her. She smiled.

When she woke, her hand was wrapped tightly around the brass and wooden telescope. Her palm was damp with sweat and a faint ring of yellow dust clung to the brass eyepiece.

BRANCHING OUT

Eldon could never erase the first time he saw her: Lilith kneeling on iron, knees bloodied, body bent in shame before the neighbors' silent gaze. Her two younger sisters begged with tears for mercy, but Lilith didn't cry. She stared at a speck of dust in the lamplight as if that were her sky, blood tracing patterns through the grate at the lamp's base like a vow no one else could read.

He'd seen it all from his shed doorway—the drunken father's cable lashing the air, the mother's shrill curses, the neighbors' silence pressed like a weight over the street. To Eldon, the three sisters were not children but fallen angels, their beauty ground into the dirt like rats, yet still a beacon of all that heaven promised. Lilith was the eldest, and she bore the most. Even then she seemed both fragile and unyielding, radiant as a candle refusing to die in a draft.

Lilith walked up to Eldon's carpentry shed in the dimming Sacramento twilight and handed him a crumpled flyer. It was not long after she took possession of the old wooden telescope. The paper was creased, she'd drawn an ugly duckling on the back—its beak crooked, as if mocking someone.

"Can you make one?" she asked.

He set down his saw and studied her. Her eyes weren't large; they were dark and didn't waver. Her pale skin didn't flush with the shyness most youngsters had. She wasn't pleading or coaxing. She looked at him the way someone examines a tool—checking if it still worked.

"Why me?"

"Mom said you could," she'd said. "We can't afford to buy one."

He knew that was the truth. Days earlier, Lilith's mother had come by. She hadn't spoken, just left a plate of scorched rice at his doorstep. The burnt aroma had clung to the air, thick and smoky. At the time, he hadn't thought much of it. Now, he realized—it had all been arranged; a pre-payment of sorts. Trade and odd payments were normal in Chinatown.

The streets were lined with peeling Chinese shop signs, slumped wooden houses leaning against workshops, the soil still littered with Gold Rush debris. Eldon's shed stood at the edge of Locke, taking up the end of a lane wedged between sagging buildings, shaded in summer by a walnut tree. That day, the day of the payment delivery, her mother had worn a red dress. She'd left the rice and walked away. He'd stood in the doorway, the scent of charred grain lodging in his memory like a nail. Her mother always dressed in bright colors. Her heels clicked loudly when she walked, her posture rigid. Back then, Eldon's pulse quickened whenever he saw her. He couldn't meet her eyes, he knew his desire would show. He liked her for many reasons. He liked her low-cut blouses. He liked the way her heels left her bare feet partially exposed—smooth as ivory.

He never told anyone. *How did she know I wouldn't refuse to make a toy for her daughter? Did she see me watching her?*

That winter, he carved Lilith's wooden duck. Under the trembling bare bulb in his shed, he worked the timber until his hands blistered. Every stroke across the grain was an attempt to erase the blows of the cable, to sand away the curses. Shavings piled around his boots like curls of unanswered prayer, until at last a small duck rested in his palms—round, harmless, carved from everything he couldn't say.

When he finally placed the duck in Lilith's hands and saw how tightly she clutched it, as if protecting the only comfort left to her, Eldon felt a release that was almost cruel.

It was as though all the misery he could not prevent had been carved into that piece of wood—carried away from their damaged souls.

Her family fell apart soon after.

Her father drowned in the river outside town—drunk. Rumors spread. Some said he'd jumped. Others claimed he'd been pushed. Lilith's mother overdosed within weeks of her husband's death. No one read the note her mother left behind—except Eldon. He'd found it himself, hidden in the folds of the silky red dress. Two words: ***Too late.***

He never told a soul. He didn't know who it was for—Lilith or him.

Two sisters were sent to foster care. Lilith insisted on living with her grandfather. Lilith and her sisters had been Eldon's north star. He'd once gone to the Locke Children's Shelter in Sacramento proper, tried to adopt them. Filled out forms. Sat through interviews.

They'd deemed him *unfit*.

Eldon returned to his sawdust-choked shack and carved until his arms gave out, until the blade dulled, until he collapsed in despair.

Lilith nudged the door open, a plastic bag swinging at her side, its crinkle cutting through the stale air of the house. A faint smile flickered on her lips, unreadable as shadows pooled in the corner. "Grandpa, I brought cake. No sugar this time, so you can eat it."

She glided through the room like she owned every creak of the floorboards. The cake thumped softly on the table, its pale surface catching the dim light. Her gaze wandered, slow and deliberate, until it snagged on a rag doll slumped in the corner—its fabric worn thin, colors bled out like secrets left too long in the sun.

"This doll is so cute," she said, fingers tracing its frayed edges. Her head tilted, just a fraction. "Do you play with it a lot, Grandpa? Do you think it's prettier than me?" Her voice lilted, playful, yet something sharp clung to it—like a needle wrapped in cotton.

Her grandfather shifted in his chair, his fingers twitching against the armrest. "That? I—I bought it ages ago. It's just been there, collecting dust. Of course you're prettier, Lilith. You're the prettiest girl."

Her smile tightened, holding its breath. Her fingers lingered on a patch of dark brown thread, stitched in a place no child's doll should have details. "Why does it have hair here?" she asked, tapping it lightly, her nail making an actual click against the fabric. "That's so funny."

His face flushed, a curtain yanked open on something he'd buried deep. His laugh stumbled, thin and unconvincing. "Oh ... probably just a prank from the toy maker."

"Really?" Her eyes didn't blink, fixed on him like a lens focusing. "I want a doll like this too. But I want a boy. One that plays the same kind of pranks."

Steam from the laundromat next door drifted in through the cracked window, curling into the room with the faint scent of soap. Grandfather's eyes followed it before settling on the folding table.

"Maugham once said, 'To acquire the habit of reading is to construct for yourself a refuge from almost all the miseries of life.'" He spoke softly, as if reciting scripture. "I've built mine well. Got too many books to finish to be trapped in here all day."

"I see." Another vicious smile took over her face as she let him change the subject. "What do you love most?" Lilith asked.

"There's one thing I've wanted my whole life but never did."

"What?"

"I want to go to prison," he said plainly, like stating the weather. She laughed, thinking it was a joke.

"I've got friends there," he added, eyes gone distant, still following the steam drifting in the air. "All the good people ended up behind bars. Books, too. A whole mountain of them."

She leaned closer, teasing. "And me? Didn't you once say you'd marry me when I grew up?"

He chuckled, looking away. "Maybe. Before I get locked up."

Her laugh echoed his, but the corner of her eye twitched—maybe from the draft slipping through the window. Maybe not.

Later, she bought a doll fitted with a tiny hidden camera, the lens glinting faintly inside one glassy eye. She set it quietly in a shadowed corner of the bathroom, angled so the camera would see everything yet appear harmless.

It stayed there for days, patient and still, recording nothing but steam and the hum of pipes—until one afternoon, she stepped inside, closed the door, and began to undress beneath its unblinking watch.

He pulled back the shower curtains. Saw her. Froze. Seconds stretched, heavy as damp air. Then he took a step forward, his breath catching.

Days later, she replayed the footage, her pulse steady. She began drafting her police statement.

A voice came from behind her. "Was that enough?"

She spun around. Her grandfather stood there, his silhouette steady, almost translucent in the dim light. It seemed like he'd known all along. "You knew?"

"Of course," he said, his voice calm, final. "I just wanted to give you what you needed. And give something to myself." He exhaled, a slow release, like shedding a weight. "Now I can finally go to prison. See those old friends. And that whole mountain of books."

Lilith never spoke of how her grandfather died. Maybe she didn't know. Maybe she knew and chose silence. She never visited him, not even once.

From a young age, right and wrong had blurred in her mind, lines smudged like chalk in rain. She believed—perhaps truly believed—she was helping him. Fulfilling a wish while moving into her own future.

He died in prison—one swift blade from behind, opening his carotid like a zipper. They called him a pedophile, an incestuous old Chinese man.

But the truth? He'd never touched her. The footage showed only his approach, his hesitation—enough to damn him, not enough to make it true.

Whether she understood that, whether she chose to forget or never cared, remained a shadow. What mattered to her was this: she gave him what he wanted. Lilith decided that was enough.

His body didn't leave with his spirit. In the dirt of Saint Mary's Catholic Cemetery alongside other unmarked pine boxes, the roots held his wish—and her lie—entwined.

Madwood feeds where the air is heavy—grief, terror, shame swelling its roots like a feast.

Lilith never stopped by Eldon's shop anymore. She was busy planning her future. She was finished with him; Lilith set her eyes on Burt Anderson. The older man was a delivery driver that serviced the stores on her street. A few flips of her deep chestnut hair and his heart was captured. The solemn young girl soon convinced the courts that marrying at 17 would be the best thing for her future.

Burt. A drunk. A dreamer. Forever chasing fortunes that never came. It had been easy to marry him. Any softly made suggestion she whispered he was helpless to ignore.

Yet beer was his downfall. It bloated him like a barrel within a few years of their marriage. Worse: when he drank, his fists fell like rain.

One night, Burt fell asleep with a cigarette dangling from his dry lips. Lilith stood in the kitchen, stroking a pillow. The fabric felt deceitfully soft between her fingers. She moved soundlessly—so soundless, even time held its breath.

"Well done, Lilith. You did the right thing," God whispered, his approval like a cold ember in her soul.

Burt's death brought her a surprise $350,000 life insurance payout. The sudden power of being out of poverty flushed a new energy through her. Lilith spent most of it to buy an old Victorian three-story house—living on the top floor herself, planning on renting the other units below which would be money she could live off of. The only things she brought with her to the new home was a wooden duck, the telescope that was given the honorable position in the center of the mantlepiece in the common room, and a few boxes of family papers in Traditional Chinese.

Grandfather's mind had been weak and brittle, his judgment clouded by age and trust. It was not a great task for Lilith to guide him down a path that ended in chains. When she no longer wished him in her world, she laid the trap with a child's ease, and he stepped into it as though it were his own choice. Eldon was lonely therefore easy to manipulate. Burt was addicted to alcohol and it gave her an easy path for controlling him.

The wood of the duck seemed warm and alive as these thoughts looped through her mind. (Lilith didn't realize she was stroking the duck as she had the pillow.) *Everyone must have some weakened hidden door. If I can find it, I can use it.*

The only tenants who came to look at her house were those connected with government help, and the oversight from their programs demanded many upgrades that she could no longer afford. She felt her newfound power slipping. Freedom itself was at stake, just like the old Chinese hero Dr. Sun Yat-sen.

Tapping her fingernails on the window as she stared across a rundown section of the city near China Town, thoughts of Grandfather's tales came back to her. *Sun Yat-sen.* He'd been to this area in 1911; that was when the Chinese part of her family was settling here. If Grandfather's stories were true, and that scrap of paper he kept in a sheet protector was legitimate ...

Her grandfather's story was the legend Lilith recited to herself most often. Each time, she told it with the conviction of a true believer:

My great-grandfather was a friend of Sun Yat-sen! Yes, the famous Chinese revolutionary. He trusted my great-grandfather so much that he handed him a gold deposit certificate worth an entire ton of gold! The Qing officials were so terrified when they found out—imagine! All that gold, hidden in the imperial tombs, and my great-grandfather held the only proof of ownership!

"If it was, why did we live like street rats?" Lilith snarled out loud.

Power and Freedom. They weren't illusions or lies, she'd felt them for a brief time. She wanted more.

Lilith whirled around and rushed to the closet, pulling out a box and finding the paper. It was 4x7 and starting to yellow from age. It was from 1910 .... Given to her great-grandfather for services rendered to the man that overthrew the Qing Dynasty: in 1911 Dr. Sun Yat-sen took over the Chinese government as the first provisional president. The certificate itself should be worth thousands, maybe millions.

If it really could be used to command gold to be turned over to her, the value was incalculable.

THE STORY OF GOLD BEGINS LIKE THIS

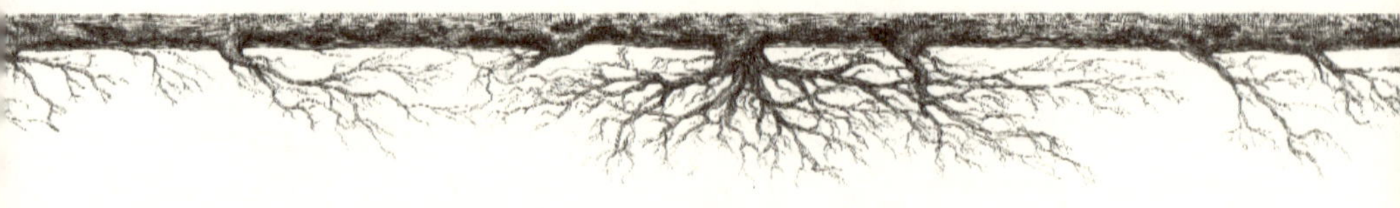

Lilith Anderson flew from Los Angeles to Shanghai with light luggage and a heavy mind. In her possession was a gold deposit certificate—a counterfeit so convincing it might as well have been real. The original document was safely in her house; it had no stamp. This certificate was stamped with a red forged Kuomintang-era seal, its edges slightly curled, its paper yellowed with artificial age.

She knew better than anyone: People didn't believe in facts. They believed in good stories. Anything could become real if it was old enough, grand enough.

This document was a dream she was about to sell. If it was real, all the better.

Lilith checked into Peace Hotel where the amber glow of old Shanghai bled into the black-and-white checkerboard tiles, a hallucination caught between eras. The lobby's bronze chandeliers cast thick, syrupy light—the kind that clung like lingering lies from a bygone century.

She chose a seat near the revolving door, unfolded a Forbes magazine and let the corner of the certificate peek out from her fingers like a fishing hook breaking the water's surface. She flipped pages with practiced indifference, her gaze lazily scanning the guests—waiting for the right fish to bite.

The next morning, Lilith returned to the same spot. The air smelled of polish and faded perfume, the warm light casting silent shadows. A man and a woman settled nearby—close enough to be noticed, far enough to seem accidental.

The man wore a traditional Chinese tunic, his round body puffing like a steamed Yangzhou soup dumpling, his skin glossy, his eyebrows thick. The woman was younger, her makeup precise, her smile perfectly formed.

In English tinged with an accent he said, “Have you heard?” His tone was casual but deliberate, just loud enough to carry. “The Qing dynasty gold seized by President Sun Yat-sen, those deposit certificates—they’re being honored now.”

“Really?” The woman’s eyes widened, her voice dripping with calculated greed. “How much are they worth?”

“If genuine? Hundreds of millions.” He nodded confidently, lowering his voice. “Especially the early Qianlong-era ones. Priceless relics.”

Lilith’s fingers twitched, the movement hidden beneath the rustle of turning pages. She kept her gaze on the newspaper, masking the spark in her eyes.

That afternoon at the hotel’s back entrance they happened to run into each other. This time, the plump man introduced himself as Zhao Hongkang. The woman, who called herself Han, claimed to be his wife—reserved, demure. They casually mentioned they noticed she might have a piece of history. Lilith lied that she was here to discover more about her family’s history. Just here to learn stories to pass on to her children.

Zhao invited her to see a “critical asset location,” a place that held the secret to verifying that certificate’s worth, the one he just happened to see in her scattered papers the day before. Lilith hesitated, then nodded. “Of course, but this has to stay just between us?” They nodded. She felt herself climbing an invisible ladder, each step leading toward a gilded future.

They drove through Shanghai’s western outskirts where the city’s roar thinned into birdsong and the scent of camphor drifted through the air. Sunlight spilled through an avenue of plane trees, dappling the road in shifting gold, as if guiding them toward a memory. At the lane’s end stood a grand villa, glowing softly in the dusk. Its Tudor-style façade rose in creamy white, dark timber beams latticed across the walls. Some of those beams were once railway sleepers shipped long ago from England, tar-soaked and now polished by time into a deep sheen. Above them, red roof tiles glimmered in the twilight, the whole house kept so well it seemed untouched by a century.

The house had lived many lives: a British tycoon's summer retreat, a Hong Kong elite's family's gilded refuge and, after the country's reopening, a nouveau riche playground of crystal chandeliers and imported marble. The grandeur had not faded—it had deepened, burnished by the touch of each passing dynasty and family, standing with the patience of one who knows all empires are temporary.

Lilith might have thought it was only a relic of polite history if Zhao had not grinned and leaned closer. "Few know this," he said, voice dropping to a velvet hush, "but beneath our feet once lay one of the People's Bank of China's gold vaults. That is why we are here, to connect to the memories and traces of gold."

Zhao stood on the emerald lawn in loose white trousers, his posture both dignified and absurd—a bloated clay idol. He waved his arms as if conducting an invisible orchestra. Han trailed behind, clutching a stack of thick folders.

"Look," Zhao said, his voice louder now and strained with fervor. "This ton of gold—no, this *sacred* gold—is a remnant of China's emperors. Seized then sealed in an underground palace! Centuries later, the Taiping rebels found it in a tunnel that had a secret river. Then, during the Republic's chaos, revolutionary soldiers dredged it up!"

He paused, face twisting with near-religious zeal as he locked eyes with Lilith. "This isn't just wealth. It's the soul of a nation. Gold among gold!"

Lilith arched a brow, her expression cool, detached—like a theatergoer watching a hack magician pull a sick rabbit from a battered hat. "Marvelous storytelling," she said, smiling. "Better than if Qin Shi Huang himself told it."

Zhao puffed his chest, pride gleaming as he continued to show her around. He led her through arched halls smelling faintly of cedar and ink, past murals of peonies and cranes, down a spiral of stone steps. The air cooled and thickened, carrying a metallic tang that clung to the back of the throat. When the steel doors swung open, the sight inside was not of gold—but of its absence.

The vault's granite walls still wore the shadows of stacked ingots, dark rectangles where sunlight had never reached. Dust lay undisturbed in the corners, yet the air seemed to hum, as if remembering the weight it once held. Deep grooves in the floor marked where armored trolleys had rolled, the tracks leading into alcoves shaped like side chapels in an underground cathedral.

Lilith stepped inside, her footsteps echoing in the cavernous space. It was not the mental image of gold that awed her, but the echo of it—the way the emptiness still pressed against her skin like the palm of a powerful, unseen hand.

She turned to Zhao, a flicker of gratitude in her eyes. *Yes,* she thought, *I've chosen the right man.*

The air in the vault lingered on her skin, frosty and metallic, long after they stepped back into the light. Zhao paused at the threshold, as if weighing whether to speak, then simply nodded happily as they walked away.

Lilith glanced once more over her shoulder at the mansion's hollow entrance. Once a grand mansion, then a front to cover the national bank's hidden gold reserves, now a tourist trap with a gift shop. Its silence was heavier than the gold it once guarded.

Madwood feeds where the air is heavy—on the grief and hunger that linger when a treasure is gone. Nothing makes a person more gullible than greed. It makes them believe exactly what they want to believe.

Lilith was a textbook case—her hunger for wealth was so blindingly intense that she ran toward the bait like a fly to blood, completely oblivious to the trap closing around her.

She believed in her "golden legend" so deeply that even she could no longer tell truth from fiction.

And the ones who saw through her weakness? They let her build her own dream, weaving a trap from the very fantasy she created.

The plump man sighed theatrically, shaking his head. "Ah … it's, well, complicated. Verifications, authentication processes, connections—this kind of thing isn't simple. But if you're serious, I might be able to introduce you to some people. Just know—the risks are high, they may not work with a white woman, well a mixed woman, like you. Perhaps I should do all the work?"

Lilith nodded eagerly. "Of course! Please, I'd be so grateful! And if it works out, I'm willing to pay—pay generously for your help!"

Zhao took a slow sip of air, savoring the moment before answering. "Alright then. But don't get your hopes too high. There are a lot of forgeries out there."

"Mine is real!" Lilith's voice was sharpened—like a cat whose tail had been stepped on.

"Oh, of course, of course." The man smiled reassuringly, but in his mind, he was laughing. *Hook, line and sinker. Greed is the Perfect Bait.*

On a patch of mossy lawn behind the mansion they were visiting, Zhao spread his arms like a preacher. "This gold," he said, "was once Qin Shi Huang's war tribute—seized from the Xiongnu. Hidden in underground chambers. Dredged up by Taiping rebels. Rediscovered during the Republic's chaos. And now …"

He touched his chest. "Now it waits for people like us. The ones who know how to listen to what history wants." Like many swindlers, he didn't even realize he'd spoken the same words for the second time. Lilith, unable to help herself, smiled at him with a trace of pity.

Lilith tilted her head. "You think gold speaks?"

Zhao smiled. "Not in words. It grows. Like a system. Like a tree. Each burial, each retrieval—they are rings in its trunk." He frowned, *why did I say that?* The trees shivered overhead. He felt a strange pull, an urge to slash his wrists and die at their trunks. He forced his mind back to his American mark.

He looked at her forged certificate. "That," he said, "isn't paper.

It's a leaf. And it's found its way back to the root." He shook his head again, confused at the words he was choosing.

Lilith smiled—tight, unreadable.

Zhao thought he was reeling her in. He didn't see the tendril of her forged document wrapping around him, his own greed snaring him in its shade. Zhao soon convinced her he was positive the certificate was real, that he had connections he could convince the same, so that the actual gold could be claimed. It would take months.

Leaving a small retainer fee with him for his expenses, with the promise of a 10% commission once the gold was in her possession, Lilith promised they would both be filthy rich. Lilith would return home in a few days, sure she would possess nearly a literal ton of gold very soon.

Back at the hotel Zhao was soon busy on Lilith's laptop setting up his appointments leaving Han and Lilith to fetch a late lunch for them all. In the elevator a very odd conversation took place.

Han's voice wavered, then steadied. "If anyone can authenticate your gold certificate, it's Zhao."

Lilith's face was a still lake, the faintest ripple of amusement was suppressed; a nod urging the woman on. *If you want it sweet, add salt,* Lilith thought. *This is a woman-to-woman conversation now. Let's see how she tries to hook me.*

"I was assigned to him," the wife continued, "back when I was a student at Shanghai International Studies University. I followed orders. Became his 'wife.'" She hesitated, an unspoken weight in her pause. The elevator chimed and they walked toward a restaurant.

Away from the crowded lobby Lilith prompted, "But?"

"Zhao is impotent." The woman's voice barely rose above the wind, trembling with a cautious honesty. "Two years. He hasn't touched me."

Lilith tilted her head, twirling a lock of hair between her fingers. "Oh?" Her tone was breezy, as if discussing the weather.

"But he's brilliant," the wife added quickly, as if reassuring herself. "He always finds a way. Trust me, your gold certificate is in good hands."

Lilith chuckled. Her laughter was laced with something unreadable. "Brilliance doesn't solve everything."

She studied the woman's face, her gaze honing in on a secret. "Why are you telling me this? To make me drop my guard? Or to earn my sympathy?"

The woman pressed her lips together and looked away.

Lilith opened the restaurant door, amusement flickering in her mind. *Impotent? Well, this makes things easier. I can teach him desire. He will be ensnared with finally feeling sexual satisfaction.*

Her grandfather used to say *Your mother was a virtuous woman. Confucius said, Food and sex are fundamental desires. Hasn't it always been this way?*

As the day moved toward midnight, Han left them, needing sleep. Lilith soon found out the wife had lied or was deceived.

Zhao was anything but impotent. In bed, he was a beast awakened. Lilith found herself caught in a chaos she hadn't anticipated, both conqueror and conquered. His touch was rough, urgent, raw with primitive force. And she—she lost herself in it. A paradox of control and surrender, pleasure laced with an unfamiliar, unnerving thrill.

"You're a fraud," she whispered between gasps.

Zhao stilled, gazing down at her with an odd expression. "And so what?"

His voice was calm, still as a dead lake, just like hers.

Zhao and Han made immediate use of the forged certificate; they moved very quickly having set up a shipping container and all the necessary fake passports for them to start a new life in Los Angeles with no intention of ever contacting Lilith again.

Greed glowed off of them in shimmering waves. With a snap of his phone, Zhao copied the shipping container's label to prove he had been on the sending end when he needed to retrieve the container.

中远集团 COSCO

未认领货物：XX 壹吨

存放日期： 19XX年

货柜编号： C-LK-1911

THE 2ND DEATH

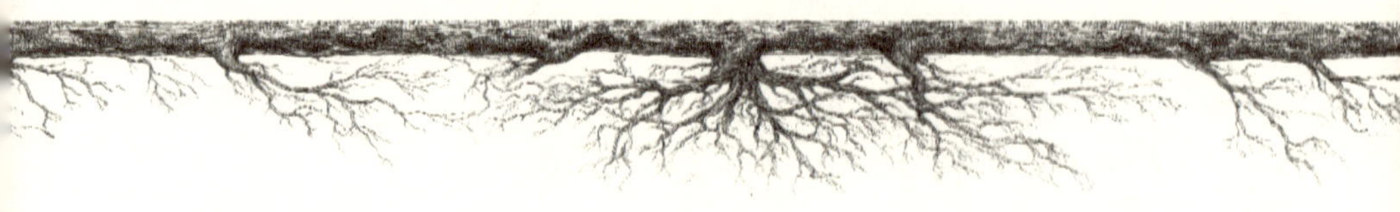

Back home, Lilith moved through the front hall with measured steps, her boots thudding dully on the warped floorboards dragging her luggage behind her. Then she saw him: a man, large and disheveled, standing motionless in the dim light of the downstairs corridor, blocking the doorway to one of the unused rooms.

"Home," he whispered, as if tasting the word. "Here. Home here." He spoke like a child trying to remember a lullaby, though his eyes were hollow and unfocused. His shirt was stained and inside out. He'd arranged scraps of paper—torn mail, wrappers, something scrawled in crayon—into a circle on the floor around him. Trash and threadbare clothing were strewn in a kind of ritual chaos.

Lilith said nothing at first. The first flush of fear was gone; leaving cold appraisal. She stood there, watching this trembling creature who had chosen her house—*her* house—as his sanctuary. There was a folder wedged beneath the corner of a broken chair leg. She walked forward and lifted it carefully, as though it might dissolve in her hands. Inside: state documents, smudged with overuse. A name: **Richard Frieter**. And a number.

Lilith made the call.

The voice on the other end—bright and brisk, almost offensively so—confirmed Mr. Frieter was a ward of the state, diagnosed with severe and persistent mental illness. His case worker shared he had a history of "noncompliance with traditional housing placements." Her home, the voice informed her, did not meet residential care standards. But the system was full. They didn't want him back anyway; and winter was coming. A waiver could be signed. Lilith was appointed a guardian of the simpering fool.

By the end of the week, a modest monthly check arrived—an

electronic deposit, polite and impersonal. Power to get her through the next few months until her gold showed up. Lilith found herself pulling the lace curtain aside each morning just to see if Frieter was still standing in the same spot in the backyard that he loved.

He was.

Months later, when Lilith discovered that Zhao and his wife had vanished with her $60,000 (and potentially 24 million dollars or more in gold), she didn't scream or rage. She simply stood on her 3rd floor balcony, staring at the camphor tree in the yard, her mind a quiet void.

Anger? Yes. But above all, a profound sense of emptiness.

She took a slow breath, closed her eyes. Then, she exhaled and smiled.

"Well," she murmured, "let's see how far this game can go." She felt a tenuous connection with Zhao somehow. Not fondness or desire, just an existence she could sense. He was out there with her gold, and she knew that somehow if he came closer to her, she would know, then she could pursue Han and Zhao and use her charms to entwine them to her will. The gold would be hers again. This was a part of her life that was calling for patience, though she needed more money badly at this point so patience would be difficult.

Before long, she began to wonder just how many others like poor Richard Frieter there might be: adrift, invisible and paradoxically profitable. She softly reached out to his case worker and left hints about how well Frieter was doing under her care.

The caseworker funneled another tenant to Lilith under the same conditions. Then the pastor of Crossroads Community Church approached her, they had two tenants for her that the corporate office wanted to sponsor with rent and food covered if she would provide their care and prep the meals. Word spread, soon all nine rooms on the 1st and 2nd floors were filled. Each tenant had their own struggles with reality, yet one rule was supreme and no tenant dared to break it. No one was allowed up the stairs to the 3rd floor or past the oak door in the kitchen which was the only way down to the cellar.

Low rent and a place to stay with their own room door earned her obedience. Dependence.

She tapped her finger lightly against the windowsill, her gaze returning to the backyard. The wind toyed with a plastic bag, its movements disturbingly alive.

"A house is power," she whispered. "Everyone who lives here lives in the palm of my hand."

Looking flatly at Frieter across the crowded dining table, Lilith felt a hum under her palm. The genuine cherry grain of the table was vibrating. None of the fools eating with her seemed to notice. Suddenly the vision of the life insurance check received after her husband's death came fully formed to her mind. Then a flash of Frieter in a mahogany coffin.

The smile that lifted her lips would have stopped the heart of anyone who thought monsters didn't experience evil joy. She was now done with Frieter as she had been done with the others. He was often non-functioning, taking too much of her time, then suddenly normal. He kept her locked out of her own room, claiming it as his own domain. He was too secretive.

Lilith had never been one to linger in indecision. Once her mind settled, her body followed without pause. By nine the next morning, she was striding through the glass doors of a life insurance firm at the far side of Sacramento—a place whose receptionist wouldn't know her name, whose clients came and went without small-village chatter. She'd done just enough living to understand the value of anonymity.

She waited in the lobby as the receptionist finished a call.

It was then that the front doors banged open behind her—

"He was one week too early," said a man's voice, crackling with satisfaction. "Perp just got life for killing his wife. If he'd waited one more week, the autopsy might not have shown a thing."

Another voice—light, amused. "Well, I *did* tell you my gut doesn't lie. Just call me the fraud whisperer."

"Amy," the man said, with mock gravity, "I expect that brilliance to show up in your year-end bonus."

Their voices trailed off down the hall, but the damage was done. Lilith paused mid-way to standing and going to the reception desk. ***A week. A single misstep of timing.*** She adjusted her plans—a small delay for research. *Patience,* she reminded herself, *is its own kind of weapon.*

At the reception desk, a young woman was flirting with a slick-haired Asian man. He held a teacup, murmured something, and the receptionist laughed coyly. "Oh, go die ... shameless—you've got a wife at home ..."

The man leaned in closer with a gleaming smile and softly continue to speak.

"My god," the receptionist said in mock surprise, then jerked her chin toward the lobby. Dick Hu followed her gaze. At first, all he saw was a middle-aged woman in an oversized loose sweatshirt and jeans sitting quietly. Her posture was slouched, shoulders drawn inward, she seemed small and uncertain. She kept her eyes down, fiddling with the corner of a pamphlet, projecting the sort of quiet plainness that never caught a second look. He felt no spark of interest whatsoever—until he noticed the New California Life brochure in her hands. In an instant, the ingratiating smile he'd been lavishing on the pretty receptionist pivoted toward the stranger.

Lilith's finger rested on the cover photo—the same face now staring back at her. She let her expression ask the question.

"Yes, yes, that's me—Dick Hu," he said, smiling as if he were on stage accepting an award. "What can I do for you?"

"I've seen you on a roadside billboard," Lilith replied in a soft voice; she was using all her power to regulate and keep it smooth.

Hu tapped his own photo, feigning modesty. "That's right, the real thing, Dick Hu. Wait—why are you holding a New California Life brochure? Could it be—"

"Yes. I'm here to ask about life insurance," she filled in silence he had expertly let unfold.

Hu's heart gave a sharp jolt, like a starving wolf catching the scent of blood. Outwardly, he stayed composed; inwardly, he was elated. Three days. Over two hundred cold calls. Not a single appointment. And now—a client just walked in uninvited. Like a lamb wandering straight into the butcher's shop. He bent slightly at the waist, ushering her into his office with the confidence of a man convinced the contract was already won. Lilith kept her head lowered, unwashed and tight ponytailed hair framing a look of helplessness. Facing this "lamb," Hu launched into his pitch, arms slicing the air in grand sweeps as though he were addressing an arena. Lilith played along, her look of amazement even more exaggerated than the receptionist's.

Lilith's eyes drifted toward Hu's bookshelf as he droned on. In that instant she felt she'd read the man as plainly as his spines. The shelf was a confession booth disguised as mahogany. Anthony Robbins's grinning face stretched across three editions of *Awaken the Giant Within,* as if one giant wasn't enough. Next to it, a slim black paperback titled *Cheat to Win* leaned against *The Subtle Art of Tax Evasion.* A faded hardcover boasted *Seven Habits of Highly Indictable People.*

She tilted her head, she tried to keep the words in, but her real essence pushed them out. "Self-help or self-defense?"

Hu flushed, adjusting his tie. "Those, uh, ... those are professional resources. My mentor wrote *Cheat to Win.* He's now our company chairman."

On the wall above the shelf, framed certificates offered further elaboration on the man's character: motivational seminar diplomas, a Certified Emotional Engineer plaque and—most suspicious of all—a Harvard degree in a basic font and on cheap paper Lilith was fairly certain came from an office supply store.

She smiled widely and put as much as she could fake into it. She had to save that snarky misstep she spoke before, so to wrap this up lightly and move on was her goal. "A whole syllabus of aspiration and exit strategies, I must be in good hands."

"Life insurance," he said, leaning forward, tone solemn, "is the most noble profession in the world. It began with miners—real men—pooling their wages for widows after a cave-in. That's love. That's dignity. We have Term, Whole Life, Universal Life, Variable Universal Life ..." he paused to see if he was losing his mark.

Lilith tilted her head with a vapid yet encouraging smile. She decided to steer the focus to a spot that might help her. "And what if ... someone has a mental condition? Can they still be insured?"

Hu lowered his voice, as if sharing a state secret. "I've got someone, a Dr. Meyer. Good friend of mine. Slip him a little money and he won't ask questions. A blood test can't detect madness. Get through the first two years with an appointment with Dr. Meyer once a year to establish health and questionable mental state, and you're golden." He winked. "Rules are just locked doors. I have the keys."

"And if the insured isn't here to sign?"

"When we're ready I'll step out for a minute. When I come back, maybe the form has ... signed itself. You trust me, I trust you. You know, I know, heaven and earth know. Besides, it would be cruel to drag a mentally ill person into an office in the middle of the city, they may be afraid. We would be doing them a favor."

In the corners of the office, potted plants gave a faint, restless shiver. Their leaves whispered together as if stirred by something other than air. Hu picked up his pen, wrote ***Whole Life*** and circled it twice. "This is the king. Steady premiums, high cash value, pays out no matter how long you live—or when you die. Twenty years from now, you'll thank me."

Lilith listened closely; her mind was calculating, plotting. Ordinary clever people could take one fact and see three moves ahead; she could take one and see ten. Term insurance was the clear choice—lower premiums, same money buying several times the payout. And she didn't intend for these people to last past two years whereas most people were hoping their 'loved one' lived long after the policy was purchased. When she said she wanted Term, Hu's smile collapsed like a punctured ball.

"Term ... is also practical," he muttered, forcing a grin while cursing inwardly—this commission wouldn't buy a daily cup of Starbucks. "No problem," he said grandly, "we're the same kind of people."

"Yes, yes," Lilith replied smoothly, pretending she hadn't noticed his disappointment.

When they reached the **Relationship to Insured** field, Lilith feigned puzzlement. "What should I put here?"

Hu's eyes lit with understanding. "Best to write relative—husband, maybe?"

"Wouldn't the insurance company ask for a marriage certificate? And anyway, I'm the legal guardian."

"Oh, don't worry about that. Two years from now, no one will do a deep check on the paperwork if no one complains."

That was exactly what she hoped for. For indeed, no one would ever bother to check on the people she was going to insure. Lilith hadn't expected to meet an Asian man who spoke nothing but brazen nonsense—yet every word was perfectly tailored to her crazy purpose. She was quietly pleased yet kept a somber expression.

At the door, Hu's smile was still a little strained, the thinness of the commission hanging over him—until Lilith said, almost casually, "In a few days, I'll be back with another relative to insure."

Relief flooded him. His smile snapped back to full wattage. A few days later, having cleared the first hurdle without trouble, Lilith repeated the method and delivered another "lamb" to Hu—it was Penny's turn.

The church woman had become insufferable, prying into tenants' habits, organizing community clean-ups and chore charts. Lilith had no interest in domestic utopias. She didn't care how the tenants lived—so long as the checks for rent came in, they stayed away from her 3rd floor and for some reason they also had to stay out of the basement, this need wasn't clear to her, but was very strong. Simple rules that didn't strain her.

Penny wanted structure. Accountability. Fellowship.

She had to go.

The following week, Lilith visited a different insurance office, this time in a different part of town. She wore a blonde wig and a t-shirt, her first time in shorts since girlhood. The disguise itched, in more ways than one.

Maire Colclough sat beside her, smiling softly. Drugged just enough to stay compliant, perfect for signing what was placed in front of her. Lilith appreciated Hu. Yet even his avarice-soaked soul would have it limits and when she started to collect the policies it would trigger investigations. She would insure every tenant over the next few months with different companies.

The blonde wig would not do. Too flashy. Too false.

Lilith made a note to have a gray wig tailored. Something quiet. Something that wouldn't be remembered. A sweet older lady didn't raise red flags.

Her body responded to this, the control, the planning; she needed physical relief to ease the excitement, to allow her to wait patiently for her target dates. No better diversion was at hand than the first fool that would make her rich: Frieter.

He was shocked the first time she pushed her body against his in the hall. Mentally he just couldn't let her in his room. Realizing he would be dead in just over two years, Lilith brought Richard up to her room having him swear never to talk about what he might see. This turned into a ritual that took place at least three times a week for the next two years.

Concern doesn't die by decree or time. It calcifies. Quietly, it becomes a kind of religion.

Years had passed for Eldon, he grew older, slower. The world turned strange and sharp around him. *Not competent, not part of us,* was the loop running through his mind.

Unfit. ***Unfit. UNFIT!***

All he wanted was to be part of a family. That chance passed when young Lilith's family fell apart. Since his rejection to be a foster for the sisters, he had not been able to keep a thought in his mind long enough to work. Homelessness gobbled his health; he was bent over and shuffling through the days.

And then, while queuing outside a church-run food pantry in a blistering corner of Auburn, CA, he heard whispers of a new place. A quiet place. An unofficial sanitarium, they called it, though no one used that word anymore. Run by a woman whose name rang through his ears like a long-forgotten prayer. ***Lilith Anderson.***

It was back in Sacramento. A 40-minute drive; how long a walk his mind couldn't comprehend. He sought her out with trembling hands and a spark of something like joy. The journey to his old city was long, but Eldon never wavered. Surely, she would remember him. Surely, she had not forgotten the young man who once tried to save her.

She had. Or else, she pretended to.

Eldon froze when Lilith appeared at her door in response to his tentative knock. The fragile, sly little girl he once knew had vanished; in her place stood a woman of startling fullness, luminous and irresistible—an echo of her mother, the woman who had haunted his hunger all his life, as if the same mold had pressed them both into being. Her breasts and hips rose and swelled like waves summoned from air itself, yet nothing about her seemed grotesque. What clung to her instead was the quiet restraint of an Eastern beauty topped with deep reddish brown hair and pale white skin. She exuded a discipline of allure which made her aura give off waves of sex and danger.

Eldon was a carpenter; his world was measured in joints and seams, in the perfect marriage of mortise and tenon. Lilith was the socket—waiting, receiving, inevitable. In that instant, her mother's figure re-emerged in his mind, though stripped of the metallic reek of money and compromise. Lilith carried no stench of commerce. What she bore instead was a raw kinship with the underclass, an inborn solidarity connecting those who had always lived close to hunger, loss and silence.

Never in his life had Eldon imagined that at the bitter end—when cancer was already gnawing its way through him, when he could feel death's nails pressing against his coffin wood—he would be granted this apparition: Lilith, not as the girl she once was, but as a sudden, impossible transfusion of vitality. A jolt straight into his failing heart, a pulse of heat stronger than medicine.

But a question thundered in him, merciless: could such fire ever truly belong to him? Or was he only the fool who mistook her warmth for love, carving his own ruin into the wood grain of fate?

Lilith invited him inside and led him to her desk. She met his gaze with practiced serenity; the kind found in cult leaders and saints. Her eyes were cool, expression unreadable. No flicker of recognition, no softening of the mouth, not even when her fingers grazed the small, hand-carved duck resting on her office shelf—the one he made just for her so long ago from driftwood and care.

She turned it slightly. Smiled at the grain. Said nothing.

Whatever affection she may have felt—if any—was buried beneath a skin of marble and calculation. She was no longer a girl in need of saving.

She was needed now.

Her image—philanthropic guardian of the fragile and forsaken—couldn't afford giving in to nostalgia. A single "I remember you," could split the lacquered surface of her myth. She was determined to keep any leaks about her childhood from touching her adult life.

And so Eldon, whose hope had led him like a tethered dog to her doorstep, became something else.

He became useful.

No longer a would-be savior, he lived now in the shadows of her house, tucked deep in its underbelly, beneath the rooms where voices rose and faded. Eldon became a facilitator—a carpenter once more. She brought him food and gave him assignments.

There was no friendship between them. He was not whole enough for that—his bones already brittle with cancer, his spine stooped like a penitent monk.

Her words—when she gave them—were enough. They calmed his mind enough for him to pick up the saw or the plane and work.

For Eldon, Lilith's instructions carried the weight of scripture. Her calm, her cruelty, her cold precision—these were now holy things centered around the projects: large plain boxes of only wood, never a nail, never an embellishment.

He needed no thank-you. No touch.

Only purpose.

And that ... was enough.

The night Frieter died, they were drinking heavily at a bar. On the way home, Lilith rode pillion on his Harley, the wind lifting her skirt, thighs spread wide, nothing underneath but the cold streetlight.

She could hear the white men laughing, some raising their phones to film. She didn't care. She felt like Marilyn Monroe. Queen of the night.

Frieter parked the Harley in the back, near a tree he went to when low-functioning depression claimed him. Lilith stood in the moonlight watching him walk toward the door. Watching him collapse at the doorstep—face ashen, eyes open, staring at something unseen. She dragged him into his room then walked upstairs to her bathroom.

She turned on the faucet, took out Yes. Yes was the oversized vibrator she bought at a brazen little shop near Shanghai's Peace Hotel called Oh Yeah. It was designed for women exactly like her. From then on, she always called it Yes in an American play off the store's name, Yes seemed more empowering and more queenly.

She tried to douse the fire still smoldering in her body, but the mechanical vibrations were lifeless, uninspiring. Lilith's hunger remained unsatiated, waiting for something far greater. She tossed Yes on her bed and smoothed down her skirt. She walked barefoot over the wood floors back down to the tenant areas.

When she returned to his room, he was stiff, extinguished like a lamp blown out by the wind.

"Well done, Lilith," God whispered, his voice threading through the roots beneath her feet. "You have harvested well."

She searched the old bastard's pockets for keys and opened the fridge. The one place he had the audacity to keep a secret from her. And of course from Penny. The fridge had been the fulcrum of many arguments over the past two years between Penny and Richard.

Inside, neatly stacked, were small credit card sized blocks of gold. Lilith laughed aloud. Then gathered them all up and took them to her room. She didn't sleep. Lilith just sat there, counting, counting. A total of $70,000.

This windfall find slammed home the fact that she had not been able to contact Zhao or Han; they had arrest warrants out for them, that much she had learned. Warrants based on a forged certificate that they turned in for gold. Then they just disappeared. *Killed? Ran with her gold?* In a fury at this reminder of her loss, she paced all night.

At breakfast she made a show of calling for Frieter. Then opening his door and screaming. The police were called. Lilith pretended distress and walked outside to leave the police to their job. She waited on a bench under the large camphor tree in her back yard. Calculating how much she would get when selling the Harley. As his guardian, she would inherit everything he owned. She smiled.

Suddenly, Lilith heard whispers from the bench. Deep, steady hums creeping up from the soil like vines, curling around her ears.

"Lilith," they murmured, "You're not God. You are merely insane."

She laughed. "God creates the world from chaos. Fools stumble through it, lost. I am not lost. I am God's right hand."

The wind grazed her as if in answer. From beneath the soil, something was growing.

FERTILIZER

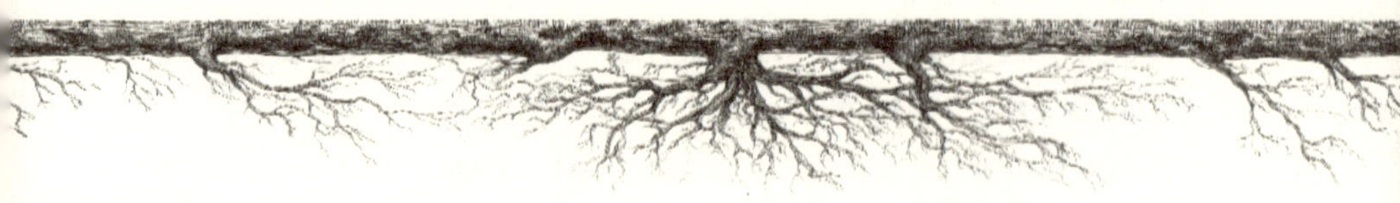

Frieter's body was released into her care. Cause of death was determined to be critical anaphylactic reaction to an over consumption of alcohol. The morgue thought she was transporting his body to a funeral home. They had no need to follow up; no family asked about him, no authorities came to follow up.

The body went to her home. Eldon had been busy over the last three days making a pine coffin sized just for Frieter. There was no silk lining. No handles. No nails. Just an elegantly made tongue in groove pine box.

Frieter's corpse rested in the trunk of a rental car in the shade of the large camphor tree; the spot in the back yard that had always drawn Frieter.

The tenants were restless, as many such street-hardened people were. Their minds were thrown off balance by change, and the death of Frieter was a huge and unexpected change. Hypervigilant, their buzzing aura was annoying Lilith.

Lilith waited until dusk before gathering them in the dining room. She'd set the table with mismatched teacups and poured a deep brown liquid into each one. The scent was floral, faintly bitter and had the slight smell of green tea, which was her preferred drink.

She stood at the head of the table, her silhouette framed by the gold-pink light of the ceiling light. Calm radiated off her in waves. "Tonight," she said softly, lifting her own cup, "we remember Richard Frieter. He was quiet. Gentle. Sometimes confused. But always polite."

Some nodded. One rocked slowly. Another whimpered and clutched the arm of her chair. Penny scowled.

"I know many of you are feeling unsettled." Lilith's tone never changed—measured, melodic. "Death has a way of waking old fears. But Frieter's passing was peaceful. He has no pain now. No confusion. And he would want you all to rest."

She paused, letting her words drift like mist.

"To Frieter," she said. "May his journey be easy. May ours be gentle."

They raised their cups like children mimicking a ritual they only half understood. One by one, they drank.

The hush that followed was warm. Heavy. A few murmured their own little toasts, vague and misaligned as they went into the common room and sat in their preferred spots.

Minutes later, their bodies softened. Eyelids fluttered. Muscles slackened. Heads bobbed like wilted flowers.

Lilith moved quietly between them, smoothing a sleeve here, adjusting a pillow there. The cups she gathered with care, rinsing them in lavender water and placing them in the drying rack like communion vessels.

Outside, the night thickened.

Inside, the house sighed into sleep: a deep, still and unquestioning motionlessness.

Lilith turned out the lights.

And smiled.

When full darkness came, Lilith lead Eldon up into the air and showed him a spot within the roots and commanded him to dig a deep hole big enough for the coffin. She left him to his task and went inside. Her body was tingling, wild for unplanned movement; to jerk and snap around. This was movement and noise she was unable to indulge in with the sensitive tenants around. She always had to be careful what she said, how she walked. The goal was to keep them all calm and worried about their own fears, to keep their thoughts off of her unless she expressly wished to engage them. Richard was the one she could always call to her room; he never asked questions. He performed and promptly returned to his room. She was limited to her vibrator again. She reached for Yes.

After a barely satisfying physical relief, Lilith went back to the great tree, helped Eldon place the empty coffin in the hole; secure in the knowledge no one was able to peek out of a window to question what was going on. Then they lifted Frieter from the trunk and carried him over. Eldon was about to bend his cracking knees to ease the body in, Lilith just let go of his head and the form crashed down. She kicked the lid down; it wasn't even flush on its tracks.

"Cover it up and then put moss over the hole so the soil looks undisturbed."

Eldon nodded yet said, "But I need to fix the lid first."

"No. Let the dirt fall inside also. The sooner it all rots, the better." She had no idea why she felt this way. Leaves above her rustled in the still air as if in approval.

Touch is a contract—the soil's embrace of the new corpse bound it eternally to Madwood's ledger.

Strategically, Lilith didn't chase the insurance payoff for Frieter's death. She waited like a spider, then expressed mock surprise when Dick Hu called reminding her to bring in the death certificate to allow a check to be drawn and the policy to be closed.

Penny was next. As Lilith waited for the appropriate time to pass for Penny's policy, she plotted a new way to unalive the loud mouth. She dreamed every night of roots stirring beneath her house; embracing Eldon as he slept, sending hair thin tendrils up into the Victorian structure, testing the soil just beyond the backyard fence. When she woke, she sometimes found the floorboards cold and damp beneath her bare feet—as if something had been in the house while she slept, mapping the path to its next feast.

She knew what was coming for Penny wasn't murder. Lilith was merely obeying orders—like a stream flowing inevitably into the sea, like dry land longing for its first summer rain. It was the most natural thing in the world, a cosmic balance she alone could wield. The ones who thought they were alive—those were the really mistaken. They wasted time, wasted resources, took up air that should have belonged solely to her. And she—she was just cleaning, a gardener pruning the unworthy from her sacred plot. They should be grateful.

Penny didn't notice the way Lilith's gaze weighed her that evening, measuring Penny the way a carpenter studies a beam before cutting—eyes tracing the hands, the slope of the shoulders, the unguarded softness of the neck.

"You've got a good touch," Lilith said casually, watching Penny wipe down the kitchen counter. "I might ask you to help me in the yard tomorrow."

It sounded harmless. Friendly, even. But the words had a certain weight to them, like a mark scored into wood grain. Helping was Penny's love language. Even though she felt a shiver at the shadows beneath those words, Penny couldn't refuse to help anyone.

That night, Lilith went down to the yard barefoot, her robe open to the chill. She walked to the camphor tree, laid both palms on the bark and whispered a name—not her own, not her God's, but Penny's. The roots shifted faintly under her feet a ripple moving through the soil.

"Remember her," Lilith breathed. "Make her yours."

From that moment, Penny was no longer just another tenant. She was soil-in-waiting.

A blocked drain in Penny's bathroom the next day forced the woman to call her landlord, a faint metallic scent of menstrual blood was in the air. Lilith didn't flinch when Penny explained, embarrassed, that it was "just a women's problem." Lilith simply called for Eldon, handing him a dented enamel pail and a quiet instruction, "Bury it tonight. Deep. Under the camphor roots."

At dusk, she stood by the back steps as Eldon emptied the pail into the churned earth. Damp paper rolled into the hollow like pale petals, and the roots quivered—barely perceptible, like an animal scenting prey. Lilith's lips parted in a private smile. It was not yet the main feast, this first taste was enough of a promise to keep the roots calm.

The next morning, she gave Penny a plastic rake and pointed toward the yard. "The rainwater's pooling. Clear the leaves before any rot or mold sets in." The heap at the fence line was already prepared—golden and brittle at the top, dark and wet beneath, laced with splinters of bark and fine root-fibers slick with sap.

Penny worked without question.

Lilith watched from the kitchen window, eyes narrowed in the soft satisfaction of a gardener testing new soil.

Within a week, the signs began. Penny grew restless at night; her eyes shadowed with sleeplessness. She drifted through the hallway barefoot which would have offended her sensibilities before, pausing for long minutes as if listening to something far below. She spoke less, ate less.

Soon the dreams came: the camphor tree's shadow at her bedside, its roots like strands of hair curling toward her, grazing her throat. She woke to dry leaves on her pillow, damp earth clinging to her soles. The edges of her fingernails began to green—not a bruise, but the slow blooming of color from something alive beneath the skin.

Lilith said nothing. She let the days lengthen, the roots work. This was not murder. It was a gift.

That afternoon, while Penny dozed on the sofa, Lilith passed behind her and caught the faintest sound—like tiny bubbles breaking in wet soil. It came from beneath the floorboards, a slow, patient rhythm. Penny shivered in her sleep and drew her knees to her chest. Lilith smiled. The roots were already inside the house.

One night, the hallway light flickered and went dark.

From the blackness came a muffled sound—like wet cloth twisting, then a quick, choking gasp.

When the light returned, Penny's door stood open.

Inside her bed was unmade; her nightclothes, folded with unnatural care; bed sheets speckled with fresh, wet bark and something darker, soaking slowly into the fabric. The air reeked of sap and iron.

A thin trail of damp soil led from the doorway toward the back steps—at first just a faint smear, then thickening into clumps, marked with the drag-grooves of fingers clawing for purchase.

From outside came a low, grinding sound. In the yard, the camphor roots pulsed thicker than Lilith had ever seen, a deep ember-glow crawling beneath the skin of the wood.

One root, fat as a man's thigh, strained upward. It was coiled twice around a shape that twitched feebly before being pulled under. Penny's hair, matted with dirt, was the last thing above ground—snatched down in a final hungry jerk.

The root sank back, its slick surface streaked with something darker than sap, fibers tightening like a satisfied muscle. The earth around it shivered once, then closed over with a wet sigh, leaving only a faint rise in the soil, as if the ground itself was digesting. Lilith placed her hand against the trunk. The bark was warm, almost feverish, the heat pulsing in time with her own breath.

"The bitch has finally learned to shut up," she whispered.

The ground gave a soft, satisfied noise that seemed to indicate agreement. Penny would not be heard from or seen again—not in this yard, nor anywhere the living walked.

Penny had to go like this due to God's command, Lilith had complied. This meant she needed to clean the house and file a missing person's report. Lilith would be unable to make a claim on Penny's policy until she was legally declared dead.

God counseled patience. Lilith would submit for now. At least she had the rent coming in for all her tenants.

"Well done, Lilith. I love you," God said banishing Penny to memories.

Lilith's backyard would soon be filled with many buried wooden boxes. Her seeds, her disciples, her little altars. Each time she buried a box (human or animal), she cast a blessing—building a slide for the children, delivering hot meals to the homeless, buying new patrol cars for the police station, even raising a scholarship fund for Wensen the newest tenant taking over Frieter's room. He was a painter, or thought he was.

The soil drank the essence of her harvested offerings, and the world thrived under her quiet stewardship. Their deaths hadn't been wasted. They took on a higher calling—so that the living could go on.

"Lilith, you've done well," God whispered once more, his voice threading through the roots beneath her feet.

Lilith Anderson always heard the breath of God in the stillness of night. It hovered in the air like a motionless gust, like a shadow crouching in the corner, like an invisible hand pressing softly against her forehead. It never really left. Whenever she cleaned up the aftermath—buried a wooden box, or returned a soul to the soil—the breath rose from deep within her chest, like reefs laid bare after the tide retreats—cold, fractured and sharp. And she liked those fractures.

Just as she liked damp earth.

These were part of life, the jagged edges of her dominion.

"Well done, Lilith. I love you," God said to her in the dark, his voice a velvet shroud over her sins.

She first heard that voice on a night many years ago. It was the night she pressed a pillow over a drunk man's face, feeling his breath grow shallower, lighter—inch by inch—until it vanished altogether. He had shuddered once beneath her palm, like a dead leaf caught in an autumn breeze, his final gasp a hymn to her resolve. Then everything fell quiet. She liked the quiet, a silence that crowned her as its queen.

The attic smelled of dust and secrets, the air thick with the musty breath of forgotten things. Lilith stood by the cracked window at the end of the hall on the 3rd floor, her fingers tracing the brass eyepiece of the sycamore telescope. The tube burned against her skin, not with the cold bite of metal but with a pulsing heat—like a copper kettle simmering with unspoken truths. She remembered Richard's gaze fixed on it the days before his death, his eyes clouded with dread, as if sensing a dormant secret stirring. The warmth had crept in after his passing, faint at first like morning fog, but now it seared, the telescope adjusting its focus with a will of its own, choosing what to reveal.

Through its lens, she spied the camphor tree in the backyard. The bark's cracks twisted into the visage of an old man, hollows brimming with silent mockery. Branches writhed like coiled beasts, roots slithering from the soil like probing tendrils. The telescope's gaze pierced deep, shattering reality's veil. When a homeless man lit a brush fire in the state park, she smelled acrid tar and charred meat. When a judge tangled with a defendant's wife on a courthouse sofa, she heard leather creak and frantic gasps. When the new senator shook hands with Reagan's ghost on the steps of the Capitol, her fingertips tingled with marble's cold pulse. Each vision scalded her palms, the heat snaking up her wrists like a toll for stolen sights. *Sins, weakness.*

Tonight, she pivoted the lens toward the Pacific. The ocean view tore up into California's night sky, pierced fog and raging waves, and anchored itself on another continent: Shanghai, China. Where her hopes had shattered years ago.

Amongst the dreams of stretching, growing, exploring roots also came visions of Lilith helping at soup kitchens. Sponsoring a new playground in the area. After a few days of this, she felt a physical push in her chest to make an abandoned lot into a large community playground. The vision followed her into the daylight the next day. It was insistent. It sent waves of pushing, thudding energy that caused severe headaches. Visions of Laynda, a local elementary school principal who was new to the area, who was lonely, who was not connecting to the local parents, slammed into her thoughts.

Principal Laynda Forbes sat alone in her office long after the final bell rang, the silence more punishing than young chaos had ever been. A second grader called her a witch that morning—*loudly.* A mother accused her of poisoning school spirit by canceling pajama day ... as if Laynda could control the budget.

She was tired. Tired in her bones, in her breath. The town hadn't warmed to her and she'd stopped pretending not to notice as depression wrapped around her heart.

A soft knock on her open door broke the stillness.

"Forgive the intrusion," came a smooth voice. "I hate to interrupt, but I believe we haven't yet properly met."

Laynda looked up.

The woman in the doorway was impeccably dressed in a long yellow dress, her chestnut hair tucked neatly behind each ear. She held a stack of handouts in one white hand and a soft smile hovered at her lips, oddly it never quite reached her eyes.

"I'm Lilith Anderson," she said. "You've probably heard of me."

Laynda had. Everyone had. The church leaders. The social workers. The whispered stories about her taking in the most disturbed, unwanted people and calming them enough to live within the group of her tenants.

Lilith stepped inside without invitation, laying a color printout gently on the desk. "A playground," she said. "Vacant lot just two blocks from here. I've already spoken to the landowner. He's amenable."

Laynda blinked, unsure what to make of this.

"I know things have been difficult," Lilith went on, her voice wrapping around the words like silk. "Transitions are hard—especially from small towns to a place like this. But children need to play, and parents ... well, they need somewhere to take pride in and you can connect them to this new safe spot for their children."

Lilith leaned in, just a little. "I'd like to fund it. Quietly. But I want *you* to be the face of it. The new principal who brought joy back to the neighborhood. Doesn't that sound lovely?"

Laynda looked down at the flyer. Slides. Benches. Smiling stick figures. Her name in bold above a dedication plaque.

"I—" she began, but Lilith's hand was already on her shoulder.

"Think about it," Lilith murmured. "Let them adore you. Let them stop seeing you as an outsider. You can announce it tomorrow! No need to wait. I've got it all under control." She didn't wait for a yes. She didn't need one.

By the time Laynda looked up, Lilith was already halfway down the hallway, her heels clicking on the polished floor.

Later that night, Laynda stared at the flyer in her kitchen. Her name looked too large. Too loud. And somehow, she couldn't stop grinning.

At the dedication of the playground, as a thanks, Laynda gave Lilith a red gift box. It sat heavy in Lilith's palm, solemn like an offering at an altar. The weight was a tribute, a blood price willingly paid.

Lilith brought it home and placed it on the table. She smiled, thinking, *God accepts offerings from the faithful too, doesn't he?*

Her smile was a blade, cutting through the mundane to reveal her covenant.

She opened the box. Inside lay a piece of baklava. Golden syrup soaked through the crispy layers—so sweet it made her nauseous. The cloying taste was a mockery, a reminder of the living's ignorance.

Lilith Anderson belonged to that rare breed of women on whom time left marks like blessings instead of punishments. Past 38, her beauty hadn't withered; it had ripened. Her cheeks held their fullness, her figure its dangerous curves, the faint lines around her eyes softening rather than erasing her allure. She was the kind of woman age seemed loath to take away—God's reluctant favorite.

In other countries (Korea, Japan) she could have leveraged this peculiar gift.

Their cult of mature beauty might have delivered her entire realms of privilege: money, loyalty, men kneeling at her feet. As she had her whole life, Lilith chose the stranger path. She buried it. Instead of flaunting what time gilded, she masked it—powder, wigs, sunglasses, even silence, lest words should draw eyes.

Her beauty wasn't gone; it was hidden. She treated it like contraband, a secret blade kept sheathed until the right moment. To reveal it would have been easy profit. To conceal it was strategy.

One day, she set down her brush and lipstick, as though laying down a burden. Others called time a butcher's knife, but before the mirror she made a different bargain. Time left no scars upon her face; instead, it became her accomplice, veiling a beauty too sharp to bear. She dug through an old box until she found the custom-made wig and oversized sunglasses from the 60s. From this point on, they would be part of every outing.

Now she stood at the 3rd floor window, gazing out at the backyard. Broken sofas littered the lawn. Trash bins leaned sideways. Stray cats prowled the garbage piles on the other side of the fence.

The old camphor tree swayed in the wind, its branches casting cryptic shadows like coded messages—roots sunk deep, as though the house itself were holding secrets in its bones.

She pushed open the window. Cold wind surged in, carrying the rank stench of rubbish and alley cats. When she turned, her reflection in the three mirrors surrounded her—like time folding in on itself.

The sunglasses concealed her eyes, sealing every emotion behind a shiny glass void. Together, the hair and glasses made her look both odd and solemn—like a solo performance rehearsed a thousand times and never abandoned. The oddness was not so overblown as to attract attention; it was just enough to have people subconsciously avoid her.

"Seventy suits me," she murmured. Her voice seemed to come from the mirror. The woman staring back wasn't her past self, nor a ghost of her future—that reflection showed a carefully crafted mask.

She gently touched her neck. The wrinkles there looked like silent sentries—guarding secrets that must never be spoken. Someone might ask: Why pretend to be 70? Why would anyone choose to wear the face of age?

The woman in the mirror responded only with a restrained smile—the kind that inspires trust. Like a friendly neighbor. A harmless old lady. Beneath the wig and glasses, her gaze remained deep and dark.

Lilith lifted off the wig and laid it gently on the vanity. Her gaze wandered to an old wooden box. Inside, she found yellowed letters and photographs, fragile as pressed flowers from another life.

She lifted the lid. Her fingers touched a photo—a man in a checkered shirt, smiling faintly, unease lurking behind his eyes. Her lips curled into a cold smile.

"Burt Anderson," she said, dragging the name out. She tossed the photo back.

"The only thing he ever did right in this life ... was die properly."

THE FATAL KISS

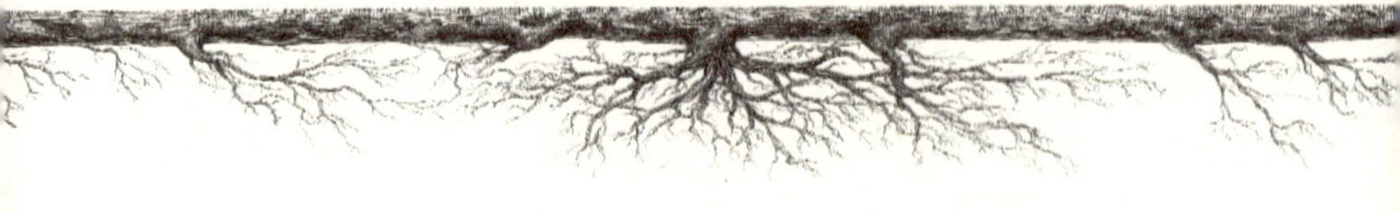

Dick Hu woke with a start, the room cloaked in darkness. His hand clutched a single sheet of paper, a beneficiary claim form bearing his name and a death date two years hence—a dream so vivid he still felt the paper's pulse beneath his fingertips. The air carried a faint whisper of green tea and on the wall a tree's shadow stretched its branches, swaying without a breeze. He blinked, the vision fading, yet the green tea scent still teased the air in his office where he had fallen asleep while preparing for a client meeting. Shaking his head, he rose, the dream's form fading as he grabbed his briefcase, its weight heavier than usual, as if carrying the dream itself to the upcoming client visit—a meeting with Lilith Anderson that now felt predetermined by that uncanny vision, his fate was waiting for him.

When Dick pushed open the iron gate, the hinges groaned. The screech of rusted metal echoed across a silent courtyard. Beneath a large camphor tree, an old house shimmered in the heat, its outline warping like a mirage. A tautness stirred deep in his gut, like an unseen hand had plucked a nerve.

He'd met hundreds of clients, but the closer he got, the clearer it became—this wasn't an ordinary insurance call.

Suddenly he saw Lilith standing there, her grey/white wig trembling slightly where it brushed her shoulders. Delicate wrinkles marked her face, yet her smile—soft and mist-like—remained untouched by time.

"Come along." Her voice was raspy but pleasant, like a melody from an old vinyl record.

She led him across the rest of the courtyard toward the house. Cracks splintered across the pool tiles under the fractured daylight, crawling outward like roots. Her reflection drifted across the water, out of sync with her movements, as if memory were lagging behind reality. A flicker of the morning's dream haunted him—the form in his hand, its date aligning with a memory he couldn't grasp. He shook his head, trying to anchor himself, but the unease deepened.

She stopped in front of the Accessory Dwelling Unit (ADU) and turned into it instead of the main house. Once inside, without warning, she reached up and tore off the wig, tossing it onto a chair in the corner. Her chestnut hair shimmered like damp soil after rain, and the weariness drained from her face, replaced by something fierce and alive. Her eyes locked onto him, predatory and unyielding.

"You're late," she said with a sly smile. "The tree has already chosen you."

His shocked recognition amused Lilith. She extended a hand—soft, warm, impossibly youthful. The touch unsettled him. These were not the hands of an old woman.

Standing at the doorway, he noticed the air change as he peered inside the ADU. The scent of flowers vanished, replaced by the sharp tang of earth and minerals. She slipped into the shadows like a fish gliding into a darker current, then said abruptly, "Enter. Wait."

Dick stepped in slowly. The walls were lined with yellowed portraits. The faces seemed blurred, their identities uncertain. One was clearly a state senator. Another looked like a silhouette cut from an obituary.

Lilith didn't offer him a seat. A cigarette dangled unlit from her lips. She said nothing. She waited.

"I'm here today because—" he began.

She moved toward him as if she had cast a spell, the scene unfolding in slow motion. Then—he leaned in and kissed her.

The moment their lips met, a jolt surged through him—unnatural, electric. He recoiled in panic. *What am I doing? She's a client! She's—*

She showed no surprise. Only smiled with quiet indulgence. "You're interesting," she murmured.

He tried to anchor himself in professionalism. "I'm not—"

"It's fine," she cut in, waving a hand. "The world's too dull. A little improvisation makes things fun."

He noticed dirt beneath her fingernails—as if she'd just clawed open a grave. *Grave? What made me think of it that way. Garden, yes, I'm sure she was just doing something in her garden.*

"You need more confidence," she said, reaching for a folder on the table beside her teacup tray and handing it to him. "Even fate bends to ambition."

It was a life insurance application form. Every field already filled in—except for the signature. The date written beneath the beneficiary's signature line was exactly two years and one day in the future.

"What is this?"

"Your third policy with me," she replied. "If you do well, there'll be many more."

"What kind of clients?"

"My tenants." Her voice turned sharp, surgical. "They all need protection. And you're the perfect person for the job."

A chill crept up his spine. He understood who she meant—drifters, the forgotten, those who vanished without a sound. They were the ones she called tenants. But this wasn't to help them. It was orchestration. It would lead to murder. He should've walked out. Instead, he stepped closer. "What exactly are you doing?"

She traced the rim of her teacup. "People need something to believe in. Faith. Legacy ..." She looked up, pupils dark as pits. "I offer something real to them—something aligned with the rules of the world."

"Rules?"

"Exchange," she said.

And then the second kiss arrived.

Not sudden. Not impulsive. He didn't know why he leaned in. Her gaze pulled at him like gravity. Their lips met—no spark, just the taste of rust and dirt. Like biting into a buried secret.

Her breath carried the scent of cold tea and fresh soil. She tilted her head slightly, as if this scene had been rehearsed a hundred times.

"Sorry," he gasped, pulling away.

She smiled. "Most people only fantasize. You actually did it."

He looked down at the form. He felt like he was still in a dream: slow/fast/unreal. The signature line stared back at him, almost daring him. He didn't sign. Instead, he slowly tore the paper in half. "Everyone knows after two years the insurance company stops digging into the cause of death," he muttered, voice trembling with defiance.

Lilith raised an eyebrow—amused, not offended.

He reached into his briefcase and pulled out a blank form. "I'll prepare a cleaner version. All you need to do is sign here."

As she signed, her fingers brushed his—soft, subtle, and carrying the scent of earth. Outside, the camphor tree swayed. Not from the breeze. From memory. From connection. Then it shuddered wildly. The pool's surface remained still as glass.

Dick turned to leave, his mind racing with the dream's echoes. He glanced back at the torn life insurance application form on the table and his breath caught. The fragments were no longer scattered—they had reassembled, the edges fusing as if alive.

Across the signature line, a blood-red imprint read:

签署已确认

A low, guttural sound came from outside. The tree's shadow lurched forward, closer now by two centimeters, its branches clawing at the glass. From the ADU's corner, a faint rustle came, as if something unseen stirred within the shadows, watching.

Yeti—a wretched white dog. A furry shovel, stubborn and shameless, digging through her backyard day after day, trying to uncover everything she'd buried. Its snout burrowed into the earth like a traitor's blade, intent on unearthing her secrets. Its nose was too sharp, as if misplaced by fate in order to destroy her and all she was building, all she was sacrificing for. Yeti's eyes were too white, too bright. Every time it looked at her, she almost heard it speaking, its mute accusation slicing through the air.

She hated its very existence.

"Lilith, get rid of it," God commanded, his tone a decree etched in stone. The unmistakable command was a welcomed one. Permission given to take care of this alarming threat.

That day, she saw it on the street. It wandered freely down the middle of the road, its fur gleaming blindingly under the sun—like a blade drawn from its sheath. Its arrogance shimmered, a beacon of defiance in her ordered world. It didn't even look at her. So sure of itself. So certain it could keep digging. How laughable.

Lilith mashed her foot on the gas pedal. Within seconds the tires crushed its spine. She heard the bones crack—short, crisp, ritualistic. Like lightning splitting an old tree. Like an umbilical cord snapping. The sound was a sacrament, sealing its fate beneath her wheels. The crimson stain spread like a votive offering, seeping into the asphalt altar where Madwood's roots drank silently beneath the surface layer.

Lilith stepped out of the car, crouched and brushed her fingertips gently over its ear. Her touch was a priestess's blessing, absolving its trespass with icy grace. Its eyes were still open—to her relief that bright gleam was finally gone.

"You are forgiven," she whispered.

Then she called the neighbors. Her voice was so gentle, it startled even herself. The softness masked the steel beneath, a predator's lullaby. "There's an injured dog here. I think it is your sweet white dog. Please come quickly."

The owners arrived—a young couple. The man was a neurosurgeon, the woman a real estate agent. The husband checked the dog's pulse, speaking urgently to his wife. "We should call emergency services. Or the police ... Isn't this a hit-and-run?"

The woman shook her head, voice trembling. "She said she found it on the street ... didn't see who hit it ..."

They exchanged a look. The man hesitated, then quietly took out his phone.

Lilith stood to the side, her expression calm—like someone attending a funeral that had nothing to do with her. Her stillness was a mask, a canvas painted with divine indifference.

They wept over the bloodied white body. They realized the little dog had passed away. There was no saving it. They were numb with sadness.

Lilith finally walked up to them, she said she knew they lived in an apartment, instead of taking the body to a vet, she offered a space in her backyard, a space they could bury the beloved pet and they could plant flowers over its grave.

Sobbing, they expressed their thanks. Lilith put a hand on each of their shoulders. She shooed them off to their home, promising to take care of it all. They could visit in a few days to plant whatever flowers they decided upon.

Lilith stepped barefoot into the backyard where the stars above seemed blotted out by an enormous canopy. The entire house had plunged into the hollow of a pitch-black wooden clock, its hands frozen on the exact second she'd been waiting for.

The ground wasn't loose; it stretched taut like skin. She knelt and rapped her knuckles against the soil three times—*thud, thud, thud*—a passcode, and a knock of offering.

The pit lay cradled between the camphor tree's roots like a preexisting wound, a mouth split open by Madwood itself, hungry for a meal.

In her arms was a small corpse, a dog glazed with a thick mixture of camphor oil, white phosphorus and red pine resin—a root stimulant so potent the air reeked of perfume and the tang of formaldehyde. It was a concoction designed to rouse Madwood's subterranean tendrils, priming them to unfurl their swallowing pores. It was a harvest Lilith was unaware she was making. The mist she thought she was immune to had burrowed deep into her brain. Obedience was a mantra for Hu, but not just for him.

Beneath the dog's white fur tiny vascular ridges bulged, resembling seeds straining to break free. Those weren't organs anymore. They were Madwood's tendrils, already branching inside and consuming the feed.

Lilith leaned forward and lowered the body into the incubation pit.

The pit was layered in five tiers:

1. **Base:** Redwood shavings, salvaged from scraps of Eldon's handmade coffin. Each splinter bore trace bloodstains from unnoticed wounds.
2. **Mid-layer:** Teeth, toenails and fragments of ear bones from five "living dead" (not corpses but "signatories") already hypnotized by the fragrance, their souls adrift. They weren't dead, but they no longer belonged to themselves.
3. **Third tier:** Carbonized camphor ash rich in guaiacol, engineered to induce Madwood's dreaming state.
4. **Fourth tier:** Shredded insurance documents, including carbon copies and thermal-printed receipts, all burned to ash. Policies as scripture.
5. **Top layer:** A three-year-old amalgam of Lilith's saliva and menstrual blood, stored in an amber vial, meant to trigger Madwood's maternal circuit. Her attempt to exert control over this powerful god.

She stood, drew a pipe carved from a deceased signatory's finger bone from her trench coat and lit a pinch of Madwood powder. The first exhale didn't rise. Instead, the smoke descended, pooling liquid-like over the pit, coiling around the dog's body—a breath confirmation ritual. Each wisp gauged whether Madwood would accept this new vessel.

Lilith's gaze fixed on a nearly imperceptible green protrusion above the dog's heart.

A leaf bud.

Not pure plant. It was a specialized hybrid, spliced from multiple genetic materials and it taught Madwood to do more than feed. It grew the leaf with animal muscle; the leaf moved in delightfully new ways from its roots.

As Lilith walked back inside her house, Madwood realized it could invade and control beyond this yard. It now understood a new avenue to grow. The dog was limited; humans were not. Madwood set in motion plans to bloom inside living people.

The Madwood camphor tree had known warmth, minerals, salt. It now knew how to grow into and change living things. And from that knowledge, it felt something new.

Not just sustenance. Not solely water, sun and nitrogen. But memory. It reached for the bodies deep in the soil surrounding its trunk. Flickers of light and sensation passed through its fibers like static: a face, a scream, the pain of lungs collapsing. The tree had no name for these things—but it absorbed them from the newly harvested bodies. It especially liked their gold rings and teeth.

Then it bloomed.

Tiny red leaves pushed up from the soil a week later—spade-shaped, trembling, wet. Birds didn't eat them. Deer would not graze them. Even insects avoided their scent.

Madwood was still hungry.

It reached.

Thin filaments slid upward through a body's ribcage, following veins and cavities, mapping nerves like rivers. The skull offered no resistance. It was already cracking. And so the plant grew up, inside the jaw, behind the eyes, blooming like a coral reef through the hollows of the woman's forgotten face.

That's when the hand twitched.

Madwood froze.

Not from fear. From wonder. Another leaf unfurled behind the eye socket, brushing the optic nerve. A visual burst—light, shape, blurred outlines. The tendril adjusted. It pushed again, tracing along the spinal cord, threading itself into sinew and marrow. The mouth moved. Slack-jawed. No words. Just breath.

Inhale. Exhale.

Muscle memory. The leftovers of a life. A system without a soul. Madwood learned the rhythm.

And then, in the dark, it stood. Not well. The body swayed like a drunk puppet. But it moved. It moved forward. Toward light.

Roots—still buried in the earth—felt the signal stretch across its filaments like a spiderweb. It did not think in language, but if it had, it would have known one word now:

More.
Expand.
More.

It sent spores on the wind. Seeds into the river. Roots into sewer grates. A whisper passed across its network like a prayer in reverse.

More bodies. More vessels. More control.

Humanity had spent centuries burying its dead in the soil, never imagining the soil might one day give them back.

Driven by the mandate for more, Lilith decided to gather in more of the dispossessed. She traveled back to her childhood neighborhood which was not far from Madwood House. Back to the first spark of knowledge about the world and power.

By then, the shop had changed. The antiques were long gone—only the donuts remained, along with a mostly empty street outside. Familiar customers had drifted away like fallen leaves. Edward was living in stark poverty now.

The phone rang. Her voice was still sweet, but it carried a subtle pressure. "Hello Edward. Remember me?"

"You're ...?" he asked hesitantly.

"Lilith," she interrupted, forcing her voice to indicate she was smiling, pulling back on the pressure for now. "Once you see me, you'll remember." He soaked up her attention. He nearly wept in happiness when she said she would love to stop by for a visit.

A few days later, she came.

Sunlight streamed through the shop window, gilding her outline in light. She had changed—grown up—but her presence hadn't. It still carried the same quiet certainty.

"I want to rent your building," she said directly. She hated to waste time, now face to face she merely waved the rental contract at him, allowing the scent that had been sprayed on it to drift in his direction.

"What for?" he asked.

"A care home," Lilith replied. Her eyes were as calm as concrete.

The shopkeeper hesitated. Edward felt dizzy, unsure. This odd request had never crossed his mind. "Are you serious?"

"Of course." She gave a soft smile. "Even the forgotten need a place in this world."

"I have no place to live if we do this." He was still confused at this new idea. To use the actual building to make money and not as a shop to sell things should have been obvious to him, yet he had never thought of it before. As his mind tried to sift what was happening into a smooth idea his gaze met hers.

In that moment, he saw her again—not the woman standing before him, but the little girl with the telescope.

Her gaze hadn't held wonder back then. It had held assessment.

Lilith wasn't someone the world abandoned. She was someone who moved under the surface to harvest it.

From then on, Lilith became a regular at the shop.

They had an arrangement: She paid only the taxes and utilities as long as she stayed and talked with him into the night at least once a month.

Her presence was like a tide, slowly washing away the loneliness he'd carried for years. The tenants were picked by Lilith and were ones that stayed in their rooms. Edward barely noticed they were there. Yet they were, and the ordinary presence of others coming and going soothed him.

One evening, Lilith sat at the bar, a cup of green tea in her hands.

He asked, "Do you still use that telescope?"

Lilith smiled. "Now and then," she answered. Her eyes looked like a frost-covered lake as she remembered. "Sometimes I use it to watch a play."

She didn't explain what kind of play. She didn't say who was acting, or where, or why. Sometimes when she put her eye to the lens, she swore something blinked back. It was a thought she pushed into the back of her mind. She didn't elaborate in response to his questioning look.

He didn't ask.

He had a sense that he was just a small stone beneath the old tree, chosen by her, quietly moved into place—just one part of the story she was weaving.

He owned a dying local grocery store. Sparse shelves indicated a business gasping under chain-store shadows. He lived in the small storage area in the back of the building.

Then came Lilith.

She arrived with crates of expired food-bank goods, charged inside and started to put pricing labels on them in brisk movements.

He just stood there, astounded, confused.

"It's not fraud, Lenny," she'd said, smiling. "It's salvation."

She bought in bulk, paid cash, haggled never. A hot wind through his crumbling world. He remembered her heels ticking like a clock as she moved through the aisles. Watching her relabel expired cans, he'd felt she was a mechanic of time itself. She re-bought all that she delivered. He had no idea why an angel was showing up each week and doing this, spending enough to keep his shop open one more week. It wasn't long before he longed for the days she would stop by. He would do anything for her.

Then one day, she brought a man in a tailored suit. "Sign this," she said, her voice a hypnotic murmur.

The man's cuff links were silver crosses—antiques, not trinkets. His starch-stiff cuffs carried a scent like camphor and embalming fluid.

The document wasn't just her normal insurance policy. Page two's corner listed what was covered, who was the beneficiary. Lenny didn't bother to read it. He signed. Two policies: commercial and life.

"Trust me," she whispered. "You'll thank me for this."

Months later, the store burned to ash.

Lenny stood before the wreckage—his last tether to reality, gone. Then his angel showed up. She stood beside him; he felt stronger with her there. She would make everything better.

Lilith patted his shoulder. "It's over, Lenny. We succeeded."

His puzzled expression amused her. She knew the payout for the commercial section would come quickly, the rest ... that would come in good time.

"You shouldn't be alone," she said. "Move in with me. I'll manage everything from daily meals to dealing with the insurance money. You won't have to worry about anything."

He nodded, handing over everything—including himself.

PEABODY'S MURDER SKETCH

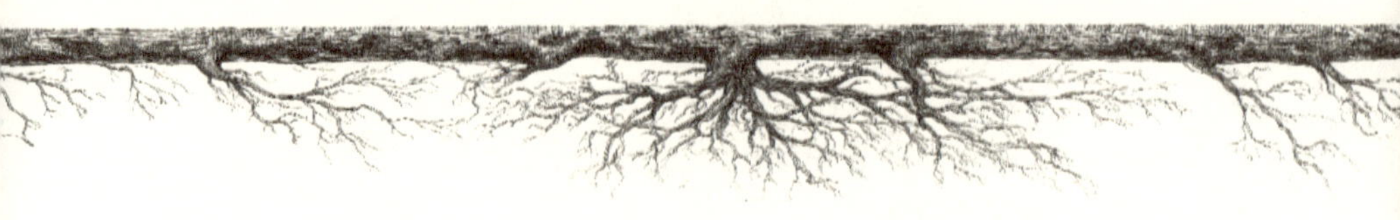

Wensen had stood shirtless in front of a canvas for hours. No food, no sleep. He lived off the paint Lilith provided. He said red tasted sweet—because she had laced it with clove oil, iron filings, green tea, cedar and manganese. Not enough to kill, just enough to corrode him from within—tremors, disassociation, collapse after too much was absorbed which would take years at this dosage.

He painted her. Not her actual body—but something more primal.

A tree.

Breasts with eyes beneath them.

A mouth torn open.

Roots spilling out of her abdomen like a pulsing placenta.

She was his only model. Always seated in the same folding chair he'd given her. That day, she sat naked, without a word. His eyes flickered—from knees to shoulders—then dropped.

He painted in silence.

When she got up to pee, she left the door open. The sound of urine hitting the bowl was like waves striking a beach.

He stopped mid-brushstroke. "She's awake," he said.

"Who?"

He pointed to the canvas. Roots were bursting from the painted woman's belly—like a forked tongue spitting venom. Red paint dripped from the gash of her open mouth.

He was obsessed with her wrinkles.

"You're a girl when naked. A crone when clothed."

Lilith smiled knowing Madwood had found its way to his brain.

He whispered, "You get to decide what I'm allowed to see." He kept painting her mouth—ripping it open again and again, letting roots spill out. His hand began to shake. The paint blurred. Even his signature lost form.

She said with unnerving calmness, “My body is yours.”

The words, so simple and matter-of-fact, left no room for misinterpretation. Yet Wensen did misinterpret the extent, he believed her body belonged to him, for his eyes alone ... for eternity. Lilith smiled, knowing this. The pain he would endure later when she gasped and writhed with another would make both this and the future coupling all the more sweeter for her.

Lilith was a chameleon. Naked, she seemed ageless—her contours supple, fluid. Clothed, she became whatever woman was needed in the immediate context, wearing sundresses or wrinkles like a mask, as if time itself was something she could put on and take off at will.

She handed him a tube of Venetian red. More of her special blend. He accepted it like communion, inhaled deeply—twice. He used the rest of it to repaint her lips. Her areolas. He ripped his clothes off and painted fully erect.

She placed a palm against his forehead, then led Wensen to his bed.

Lilith was a storm. She swept through Wensen’s studio with quiet ferocity, leaving his mind ensnared within the confines of her flesh. Painting was his life; with Lilith becoming his light.

Wenson believed a painter’s fate was carved in suffering—success reserved for after death. This new connection caused him to wonder if a painter’s life must end in tragedy. He could rethink the fate for great artists. For a fleeting moment, Lilith made Wensen feel alive.

While Wensen sank into her gravity, another life in the same house was turning inward.

Ask who he was, and he'd say: Lenny. A speck of dust. Some lived with sin; he was drowning in it. And the wind? Lilith. She scattered his thoughts, left him where he didn't belong.

Lying on the narrow bed, the ceiling beams jutted like bones from a dream. The curtain fluttered like his old can formations (they called it ACD but Lenny knew it was controlling the oxygen in the room). Only now, he was lining up his life.

Nights were different.

The sounds came every night. Not a house's usual groans or pipes murmuring. This was slow, deliberate. Like dampness seeping into rot, like fingers tracing what shouldn't be found.

The first time, rain tapped the window at 3:30am. Then came the other sound—footsteps above, methodical, as if someone paced the ceiling. The beams trembled, something pliant being pulled.

Sometimes it rose from the basement: a chair dragged in darkness. Sometimes it slithered from the 3rd floor—Lilith's room. But these weren't house sounds. They were presence, waiting behind doors.

Lenny never looked.

Then one night he'd tried. Movement killed the sound. The basement stood empty; Lilith's door stayed shut. Only shadows. The air stilled, the house holding its breath.

He wondered if that breath was Madwood's. He'd heard it but the moment he froze to really listen he heard only echoes of the floorboards, baseboards, wallpaper as they inhaled and stilled.

Not wind or leaks.

The house was waiting.

But if he retreated, if he thought, *Maybe it's nothing*—the sounds returned. In bed, he waited for silence.

So did the sounds. They whispered through floors, into bone, slowing, growing heavier. Not a heartbeat, it was something older. He lived in constant fear for months and months.

He didn't know if it came from the house or his own veins.

The next night Lilith made a rare appearance at his door. "Still on shift?" she asked Lenny. She walked into his room to assess his state of mind.

He nodded. "I'm moving your things. Can't fall behind."

He wasn't moving real supplies. He was transporting delusions. Building a tomb out of soup cans, tape and paper scraps. In his mind, it was a sanctuary. A temple.

He often had palpitations, but refused to see a doctor. A prescription for nitroglycerin sat untouched on his side table.

"Let the chest pain stay," he'd said to Lilith as she nodded with a calming smile. "That stuff would suck out the oxygen I worked so hard to preserve."

On that quiet night she took the bottle from the stand and shook it. Full. She smiled again. "I'll get you something gentler."

Lenny had been a tenant nearly two years at that time. Lilith had no intention of letting him stay past his due date. He was jittery, smelly and absolutely not interested in satisfying her body's needs. Useless alive. A payoff dead.

In the kitchen she replaced the label:

Gentle Vasodilator – Soothing Formula

She filled it with empty capsules. This was all it would take.

One day soon, he would seal the room tighter. Breathe a little harder.

And when he finally reached for the pills—

Nothing would happen.

Inside that oxygen-starved chamber, his heart would quietly stop with no detectable medication in his body; nothing would look suspicious, he just had a heart condition and succumbed. It was recorded in all his doctor visit notes: Patient non-compliant with prescribed medication.

There were many twisted kinds of love that drifted in and out of Madwood House, Nigel's was the most elegantly insane of them all.

Fancying himself as a writer, all he could actually produce were letters. Before he moved to Madwood House he wrote to people in prison because they always wrote back. One of his pen pals was released and ended up a tenant with Lilith. That was when she zeroed in on his pathetic, whining letters and knew she could pull him in easily. She wrote back explaining his pal was indisposed, but she would answer. Within months she had him there in person, breathing in the mist, touching the wooden siding of her old Victorian.

Nigel Peabody didn't love real women—the ones who sweat, who raged, who demanded hugs and explanations. He loved the souls trapped on paper—especially the imprisoned, the silent, the ones waiting to be understood.

He wasn't a hunter, but an archaeologist. He sifted through old newspapers and case files, searching for women who might have been wrongly convicted, then wrote to them. Lilith was the only one who touched his heart. Her handwriting was a little rough, but her sentences held shadows, composure and a kind of addictive intellect. He thought he was saving her.

In truth, it was she who chose him.

The talentless writer often told himself, *I refuse to be mediocre.* His current grand dream was to write a detective novel that would burst to the top of the best seller list. To write it with classic German exactness, he felt he must work at mastering German. That cold, exacting language slices through truth like a scalpel. He envied its precision, its relentless clarity. To act without understanding was the ultimate in wasteful; to achieve understanding requires patience—a willingness to sink into thought until it sharpens to a blade's edge. One day, he convinced himself that he would write a masterpiece—a crime novel so meticulous, so perfectly reasoned, it would chill reader's hearts like a flawless German sentence.

He wasn't short on material. He fixated on his landlord, Lilith. *She's a walking, unfinished novel. Every gesture is both a secret kept and an invitation extended.*

Late one night, restless and unable to sleep, he let his thoughts stray too far. He jolted awake, sweat slick on his hot skin, and left his room to get some water. That's when he saw her—slipping up the stairs with exaggerated caution, the careful, deliberate steps of someone desperate to remain unheard. It wasn't the fear of waking someone; it was the weight of a secret she refused to let surface. He watched her shadow vanish into the darkness as she went up the stairs to the forbidden 3rd floor and a chill coiled around his spine. His erection was immediate. Painful.

Lilith was a woman who conjured both trust and doubt in equal measure. She spoke to each tenant equally yet revealed nothing of herself. When she addressed Nigel, she usually stood at an angle, her voice dropping into a near-whisper, as if they were conspirators. Sometimes, her hand grazed his back—so fleeting, so deliberate, it unsettled him and connected him tighter to his fixation.

She remembered details no one else did—articles he wrote for The Sacramento Bee, names of colleagues long erased even from his own memory. It unnerved him; the way she saw his past flattered his ego. And yet, she kept his secrets. She never exposed his shoddy work, never stripped him of dignity.

The ghosts of his reporting days—the stories he buried, the lies he told—still lingered in the corners of his mind. Lilith knew them, referred to them, and yet said nothing of it to others. Her silence wasn't indifference; it was deliberate, he thought it was almost protective. It allowed him to preserve the illusion for the other tenants. He was sure they saw him as a journalist, a man with stories.

The real story belonged with Lilith. She had to control her laughter when she overhead the other tenants gossiping about his horrible talent and bloated self-image.

Moving like a cat, Lilith was slipping into lives unnoticed, leaving no trace except the weight of her gaze. She was a mystery in a different way to each and every tenant, a patch of damp earth where secrets were planted and later unearthed. Nigel suppressed the knowledge that he was one of those secrets.

When she looks at me, she doesn't see me. She sees through me, as if reading something I cannot name. Her gaze makes me feel like an unfinished manuscript, a detective novel waiting for her to write the final chapter.

She terrified him. Terrified all of them.

She fascinated him. Fascinated all of them.

They never registered as married, nor did they call each other husband and wife. Yet soon she changed his assigned room. They lived in adjacent rooms on the 3rd floor, he convinced himself that being on that floor was a place of honor. His room was small with thin walls that made each other's breathing part of the nighttime soundscape. He thought that was true intimacy.

They repaired the house together. They fed Madwood House together, of course, Nigel had no idea that was how she referred to it in her mind in these early days. Gradually, he became her tool. Whatever she needed, he gave it. He never said no. She never said thank you.

He got used to it. Nigel got used to everything.

Whenever she made love to Wensen, the moans pierced through the thin wall, rattling the bones of the entire house. Nigel would lie silently on his bed, flat like a corpse, hands folded on his chest, ear pressed against the wall. Lying to himself about the moment of union—Lilith and Wensen—no hiding, no shame, only instinct and flame. Her moans came one after another, drifting through the wall like fire licking dry wood. Each of her cries, each creak of the bed made him picture roots slowly stretching through the cracks in the floorboards—nourished by her pleasure, fed by Wensen's disgust-filled thrusts.

Nigel didn't feel betrayed. He felt invited. He was not an outsider; he was a witness to the ritual. Her moans drifted between pain and ecstasy, her voice so heavy it seemed almost too much for the room to contain.

He believed she knew he was listening. And he knew she meant for the wall to be that thin. He felt no jealousy—only intoxication.

The vines of the camphor tree writhed silently under the moonlight, coiled like sleeping serpents in the damp, fertile soil. The night wind slipped through the branches, their shadows swaying gently—as if those serpents had stretched in their dreams before retreating back into the dark.

Nigel Peabody stood by the hallway window, his fingers pinching the curtain, leaving only the narrowest slit. In his black-bound notebook, he wrote the time: **12:44 a.m.**

Lilith and Eldon were dragging a long, wooden crate across the backyard, their steps sluggish, ankles snagged by the camphor tree's exposed roots. The crate struck a root with a dull thud which was swallowed instantly by the night.

Nigel flipped to the notebook's earlier pages, confirming the markings. In the top-left corner, embossed in gold, was the label: Subject # 7. He thought it just a personal classification system. But now ... His thumb brushed the paper clipped to the inside cover—a photocopied discharge form from a psychiatric hospital, the signature line of the guardian for Rose Kindly clearly reading: N. Peabody.

He held his breath and watched silently.

Legally, he would get the policy payout on Rose. But in every way that mattered, he was only an observer. Lilith would control the incoming payment and where the money went. Lilith controlled everything. Especially when it came to sex and murder. He knew—distance was the foundation of imagination. Too close, and clarity vanished. Too far, and reality slipped away. He lingered precisely at the edge of life, behind the curtain. His body hardened at the thought of his times in bed with Lilith. He said he loved her. The sex certainly brought blessed sleep for them both.

But he'd never truly understood *her*.

He watched her like a living crime specimen. Taking notes for his novel. She never avoided his gaze. If anything, she seemed to invite it. Some strange, unspoken understanding had formed between them. Yet she had never shared this part: the burials.

Nigel must have twitched the curtains. Lilith paused, raised a hand,

and whispered, "Shh."

The sound was as light as a leaf falling in the wind, yet it carried undeniable authority through the open window. Eldon immediately bowed his head, shoulders trembling. The roots of Madwood coiled around their ankles, touching lightly as if verifying whether some ancient, secret pact still held.

The camphor tree, Madwood, Eldon, Lilith and that heavy crate—all waited in silence ...

... for the running water upstairs to stop. For every light to go out. For the house to sink into the unfathomable hush of deep night. Time passed, second by second.

Finally, the last desk lamp flickered and died. The toilet's flush cut off abruptly. The curtains fell like heavy eyelids, sealing the house in darkness.

They began to dig. When the shovel first pierced the earth, Madwood's roots seemed to sense it—thin tendrils rising from the pit moving away from the shovel tip then back, draping over the crate like a nurse's hands. Lilith didn't retreat. Instead, she knelt, pricked her fingertip, and let a drop of blood fall onto the central root.

It twitched violently. Eldon nearly stumbled back, but a single glance from her froze him.

Peabody bent over his notebook, writing swiftly: **Digging lasted 37 minutes. Steady rhythm, uninterrupted. Indicates premeditation; drop of blood.**

As he finished, an image surged into his mind—not a fantasy, not a deliberate memory, but something real, climbing up from his subconscious like Madwood's roots.

Yeti. The white dog.

For days, Yeti had barked at the camphor tree at night, sharp and urgent, like a warning. The neighbors had complained. Lilith had sent Rose to warn the dog's owner twice. Then, one night when it was Nigel's turn to sleep with her, she sat up in bed and said, "It's going to get us killed."

Peabody wasn't sure who she meant as part of the "us," he hoped it was the two of them as a couple, it was probably herself and Madwood. He was sure she thought he was asleep and had not been talking to him.

The next afternoon, he'd watched her the same way as he was now, peering through the curtains. She drove down the alley with both hands on the wheel, her focus absolute. A yelp. A new corpse for the tree.

A gnarled knot in the camphor tree faced his window. Moonlight made its fissures look like that dog's face. He told himself it was just shadows, bark, memory playing tricks—but then he counted the knots. Nine. How many pets had gone missing in town these past three months?

Exactly nine.

Outside, Lilith and Eldon kept burying the crate. They moved like extensions of Madwood, guided through some silent ritual. Shovelful after shovelful, then the dirt packed down—steady, precise. The camphor tree's shadows swayed in the wind.

Peabody closed the curtain and hurried to his room. He sat down heavily on his bed. In the dark, the white dog's eyes still watched him. He tried to write using the moonlight, but couldn't find the words. Eventually, he shut the notebook.

He dreamed of closing it again—but this time, the inner cover held a small mirror. It didn't reflect his face. Instead, he saw those dog eyes: lost, pained, uncomprehending.

He woke with a start. On the desk, scrawled in shaky handwriting was:

Subject: **N.Peabody**
Day: **329**
Observation: **Continues**

"Old man." Lilith knocked on his door, her voice laced with its usual tease and command. "Still writing to your little sweetheart?"

The door opened. Nigel lowered his head like a child caught

stealing candies, eyes evasive. Behind him, the typewriter was still warm. A half-finished letter was on the desk. At the top, it read:

Dear S—,

the rest blank.

Lilith leaned against the doorframe, tapping it lazily with a finger. "I need you to cooperate," she said. "If anyone asks about Rose, tell them she's on vacation. Where? You don't know. Why? Doesn't want to be disturbed. Got it?"

He nodded. "Of course. Whatever you say."

Her gaze lingered on his face for a moment. She didn't thank him. Didn't explain. Nigel never needed explanations. He had long memorized this theater's script—when to appear, when to stay silent.

Lilith moved down the hallway, knocking on one door after another. To each resident of Madwood House, she repeated the same lie: "Rose is on vacation. Don't ask where. Don't disturb her. She will leave us and move in with a distant cousin."

No one questioned it. No one asked why.

The chef nodded and went back to stirring his fermented memories.

The painter raised an "okay" sign in silence.

The grocery owner, headphones on, said only, "Got it, Sister Lilith."

The goldsmith carved wood grain into his fingernails with a tiny blade, mumbling an affirmative response.

Each person in Madwood House moved in their own orbit, and Lilith moved among them like a deity, inspecting her planetary system.

At last, she reached Rose's door. She lifted her hand, ready to knock. Her knuckles paused midair. The door stood silent like a wooden tombstone. She hesitated. Was she really on vacation? Even Lilith was nearly convinced. Or perhaps ... she had already—

Lilith was disappointed that Madwood felt it had to dig into her brain, she was dedicated to it by God. She would serve. So she didn't knock. Her hand lowered slowly. She turned and walked away.

Behind the door, no sound.

Inside the wall, Madwood's roots gave a faint twitch—like a sleeping creature turning in its dream.

Nigel returned to the typewriter and sat down. He didn't continue the unfinished letter. Instead, he inserted a blank sheet. He stared at it for a long time, as if waiting for words to appear on their own. He wanted to type: **I am not the author.** But he knew—no matter what sentence he wrote, Madwood would rewrite it under Lilith's guidance.

She had never been a character in his story. It was he who had been written into hers—into Madwood's script.

Wind slipped in through the crack under the door, like an invisible hand, turning the page. Someone knocked outside the wall—not on the door itself, but on the glass of a framed picture. Then from beneath the floorboards, the sound drumming up through the wood like a buried fist.

Thud—thud—thud.

As if to remind someone: it's time to write the ending.

Or—Sign Your Name.

AWAKENING OF MADWOOD

For years, the camphor tree behind Lilith's house had been treated as something sacred. Locals whispered it guarded the souls of the dead from the old asylum that used be next door. Candles appeared at its base. Ribbons and prayer notes dangled from its branches. A woman with sunken cheeks and trembling hands was often seen staring up into the leaves, murmuring, "It watches over us."

And maybe, once, it did.

Until the night it didn't.

The warm vibrations Madwood used to share with the disenfranchised who came to rest under it turned aggressive the night of that great storm. No longer did it give out calmness as it slowly tickled its tendrils into the people (worshipers). As the wind picked up and rain that was almost hail began to pelt the ground the camphor tree stiffened, it reached up into the heavy storm clouds.

It injected a splinter into each person making up the small group gathered around its trunk. They all stumbled away, backing out of the yard. Shaking their heads as their thoughts muddled. Lilith gasped. Her thoughts were suddenly sharper. The voice of her god whispered it was time to feed it more. It wanted fed every month now. It was growing.

Madwood wasn't a garden tree any longer.

It was a god, and it had fed well. It was waking up.

The wallpaper peeled in long, yellowing strips. It had once been floral—roses, maybe—but now it looked like a disease. The apartment smelled like oil from the thrifted space heater.

Zhao sat cross-legged on the floor, poking at a dented tin of beans with a dull butter knife. Han was across the room, half-buried under an army blanket, staring at the cracked ceiling like it might split open and swallow them both.

They had come to claim the gold.

They were living on beans.

"This isn't how it was supposed to go," she said quietly, as if talking to the mold in the corners. "We were supposed to be taking our shipment here where it would be lost in the madness of LA, then go on to live in Tokyo. Or Vancouver. We were supposed to buy a house."

Zhao didn't answer.

They'd sold everything to ship the gold; their forgery was discovered quickly, yet the shipping container had remained secret. They slipped in through ports and paper shadows. For six months, they'd worked invisible jobs, kept their heads down, and planned for the day they would claim their container—an elegant con that would let them vanish into a new life with a small fortune in untraceable precious metals.

Instead, they were squatting in a rundown apartment unit. The couch had springs poking out of the fake leather. The shower leaked.

"What if we call the shipping company again?" Han asked, her voice brittle. "We could say it was a mistake, that we're ... customs liaisons or something."

"They already flagged it," Zhao muttered. "It's going back in two weeks. Singapore or Mumbai—somewhere they will auction it off as an unclaimed container; and someone is going to be an instant millionaire."

"And we can't follow and bid on it?"

He didn't look at her. "Not without money. We have none."

She curled tighter under the blanket. "So we're just done?" she asked.

He was quiet for a long time. Then, "No."

She lifted her head. His eyes were bloodshot, but sharp now. Hungry. Desperate.

"We go to *her,"* Zhao said.

Han blinked. "You said we never would."

"I say a lot of things. This is all we have left. That container is the only thing between us and sleeping in the subway."

"But she ... We stole it all from her."

"Then we go humble. We say we're sorry. We offer her a cut. Half. Most of it. Whatever it takes."

She sat up, her mouth trembling. "What if she says no?"

"Then at least we tried."

"And if she says yes?"

Zhao looked out the broken window.

"Then we get out of here, even a small percent will keep us rich for life. No more cans. No more mattresses on the floor. We disappear the right way this time. We start over—clean."

Outside, the sky was pink and copper, like a bruise healing wrong and too slowly.

Neither of them noticed the tiny flicker in the outlet near the space heater—the quiet spike in vibrational activity. Madwood had eyes everywhere now. And it began to prepare for their arrival.

The yard gate was open. They walked through in the bright afternoon sun. That was their first mistake.

Han and Zhao stood at the edge of the cracked asphalt drive, half-hidden by the overgrown hedgerow. Madwood's compound, looking like nothing more than a large backyard, now pulsed faintly with light—silent and waiting, like the lid of a sarcophagus barely cracked.

"She's here," Han whispered.

"I think she is always here," Zhao muttered, pulling the collar of his coat tighter. "Look, we don't need to go in far. We just make the offer. Worst case, we walk."

Best case, they'd be long gone with enough gold and platinum to buy citizenship on another continent. Worst case? Zhao didn't let himself dwell on it. He hoped he could send Han off on some errand

and finish the convincing by fucking Lilith's brains out, doing it hard, he knew it touched the only living part of her, and she had taken every bit he shared with her in China. He knew what she liked; he would give her that and more before he ghosted her again. In fact, he realized it may be the only way they could pull this plan off.

Han and Zhao stepped forward together, almost like they really cared for each other, hand in hand, crossing the invisible threshold between civilization and something else.

Inside the fence a large camphor tree shivered in the still air.

Lilith was sitting at a table on the porch with three steaming tea cups. She sat and watched them; they hadn't noticed her yet. When their eyes finally picked her out of the shadows she said, "You came back," not looking up. Her voice was lower than they remembered, somehow colder. A projection of empathy rather than the real thing.

"We ... We know what we did," Han began, her breath trembling. "But the container's stuck. They're threatening to send it back. We only need a small portion—just enough to—"

"To survive?" Lilith finished. She finally turned toward them with a face reflecting an eerie approximation of serenity. "You wish to barter. Life, in exchange for what was already mine."

"It was a mistake," Zhao admitted. "We panicked. But we have the documents to reclaim the container. You can't do that without us. We just need fake IDs to match the rest of the paperwork then a small bribe for the dock workers."

A pause.

"You are correct," Lilith said, and for a terrifying moment, hope bloomed in their hearts.

She gestured at the open chairs, smooth and predatory in her movements. "Have some tea."

They quickly sat. In her offer of having a civilized tea they saw a promise of a way out.

Every promise glitters before it binds.

Lilith insisted Han have another cup. "You," she looked meaningfully into Zhao's eyes, "will sit there and be still while Han finishes."

He realized they had been poisoned in some way, yet had no willpower to speak out, he merely nodded at Lilith. Soon Han was bobbing her head forward.

"It is fortunate for me this cedar mist only affects brain neurons, I have plans for the rest of you." Lilith jerked him to his feet and yanked him inside.

As they went up the stairs she warned the tenants not to disturb their new guest on the porch. They were already trained to ignore any screams of pleasure or other sounds that may come from Lilith's rooms on the 3rd floor.

Sweaty and relaxed, Lilith gave Zhao a predatory grin as she forced some cold tea down his throat so she could enjoy fully passing out and allowing her body to reboot. The hot, uncaring, hard sex was exactly what she craved. She may have to keep him around longer than Madwood planned.

Priorities were shifted. Still, the family's gold belonged to her. No matter what happened with them, retrieving the gold came first.

IDs confirmed, paperwork in order; the container arrived in the dead of night and was placed in the far corner of the yard.

It was placed under a tangle of industrial netting in the back as though some ancient beast had been captured and left to starve. Its metal doors were intact, sealed and clean. Too clean.

Han glanced at Zhao in a panic. He shook his head almost imperceptibly. They both knew something was wrong.

Lilith turned to them. "You will open it."

Zhao hesitated. "You said you would allow us to take a small share and leave."

"I lied."

The words hit like a gunshot.

Suddenly, the ground beneath them vibrated. The netting collapsed backward and inward, pulled by something beneath the dirt—wires? Pistons? Roots?

With a heavy groan, the container's doors sprang open.

No gold.

Just some old boxes, stacked neatly—maybe as decoys. Zhao gasped. "You already—"

"Yes," Lilith said. "The contents were repurposed, rehomed, yesterday. Distributed. You were never meant to reclaim any of it. This was a test of your desperation." Lilith hoped that even Madwood was not aware of where her workers put *all* of the gold.

Nigel, Chandler and Wensen had worked beside her for two nights while she kept the couple sedated. They'd buried gold starting at the trunk specifically for Madwood to absorb (and to keep its focus as they took care of the rest). Then along the fence line and in the basement. Some was in the walls, some under beds. The entire property was lined in gold with plenty left over to sell outright. She knew Madwood would quickly absorb all that its roots could touch. That was fine, she was rich beyond her wildest dreams and this extra gold was only needed/wanted because it was hers by right of inheritance, so she'd claimed it. As soon as she could manage a few days without that damned tea or the mist in the air; she would run to the Caymans to live happily ever after. Sometime, somehow, Madwood would drop its connection to her and she would take that opportunity. Until then, she had Zhao to help her work out her frustrations.

In the moments of Lilith's thoughts, Han had turned to run. A root shot up and pushed her inside.

Zhao lunged for the side gate—electric arcs shot from the metal, throwing him backward, convulsing.

Lilith stepped forward.

"Please," Han begged, sobbing now. "Please. Just let us go."

"I will let you *stay,*" Lilith said. "Your bodies are inefficient but useful. Organic matter repurposes easily. You will be absorbed Han. Your fear and remorse will be very nourishing. Your thought patterns will be learned. You, Zhao, will be employed."

"Employed?" he gasped.

"Eldon requires a helper now, he is very weak. You are chubby with muscles. Eldon and I will work all of that off of you, then you can rejoin Han if you like."

The horrified look on Zhao's face caused her to laugh cruelly. "If that is not to your liking, if you are good boy, perhaps I can find some place for you in overseeing some financial matters. Skills you once used in China."

He nodded in relief.

And under perfectly ordinary soil, the earth vibrated faintly with the hum of buried riches—and one heartbeat, still human, still working endlessly in the basement.

CLAIMS INVESTIGATION

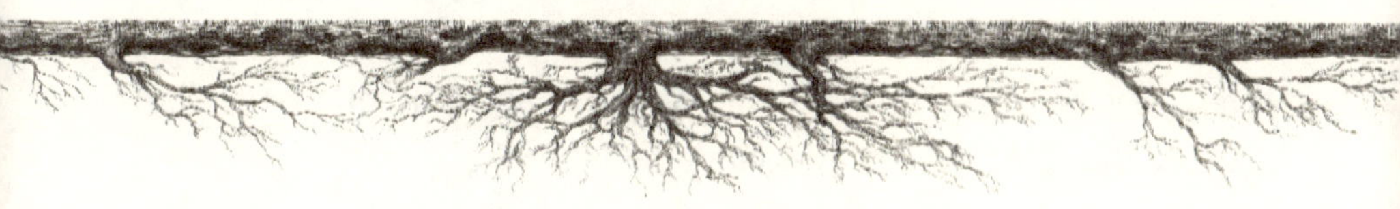

Two years is a legal boundary. She preferred to kill just at the border. She never broke that law. She let the law break itself. A well-timed death wasn't illegal. Just profitable. Yoshi Kinjo's mistake was assuming that insurance fraud had to involve a crime. Lilith Anderson's genius lay in discovering it only required a loophole—and time.

The parking lot of Earth Café smoldered under the noon sun. The asphalt shimmered like wet oil paint, and even the street signs at the corner looked half-melted by the heat. Car windows reflected scattered, broken shards of light.

Yoshi sat by the window, a claims file spread out before him. His fingers tapped his soda cup, deep in thought. The label on the file folder read:

Lilith Anderson, Beneficiary

From the activation of the policy to premium payments to the date of death—every detail aligned with standard procedures. Except for one small issue. That was why he was here for this so-called routine interview.

Death Date: Day 725 after policy activation

Five days short of the two-year incontestability period. Had the deceased lived just a few days longer, Yoshi wouldn't even be assigned this case. Like a detective facing a thief—or a lawyer a criminal—Yoshi secretly enjoyed these borderline claims. He also felt a strange gratitude toward his interviewees. After all, they paid his bills.

The door chime gave a soft ding. Yoshi looked up.

She walked in. Average height. Tight-fitting tank top over a summer skirt. Full breasts that somehow didn't match her age. Her silver/grey hair was immaculate, not a strand out of place. She scanned the café, and her eyes landed on him.

In that instant, Yoshi frowned—barely perceptible. It was as if she had sucked the air out of the room when she entered. His chest tightened.

"Mr. Kinjo?" Her voice was soft, but every word was clearly enunciated. "Lilith Anderson," she introduced herself.

He nodded, stood and offered his hand. "Please, have a seat." He flipped through the file—not to check anything, but to avoid her gaze. That expression of hers, calculating, like a doctor examining symptoms. "What was your relationship with the insured?"

She smiled slightly. "Neighbor."

"Not family?"

"No. But I cared for him for nearly two years."

"When did the policy take effect?"

"You're looking at it, aren't you?" she said with a soothing smile. Almost like she was the investigator here.

"And why did he name you as beneficiary? He had children."

"Yes," she replied evenly, "but how many of them ever came to visit him?" She ever so slightly cocked her head. "If I hadn't called 911 over and over, he'd have died countless times already."

As Yoshi took notes, he noticed her watching the way he held his pen—like she was comparing something. Trying to ease the tension, he said, "You do know the policy hasn't passed the incontestability threshold yet?"

"Of course," she answered, meeting his eyes. "Otherwise, why would we be here?" Her tone was calm. In fact, she seemed to understand the rules of this game better than he did.

Twenty minutes later, the interview ended. When Lilith wasn't looking, Yoshi quietly jotted a 10/10 at the top of the file. Then he closed it. "Thank you for your time."

She left without haste. As she stepped into the sunlight, Yoshi saw her shoulders bathed in a translucent glow. The way light clung to her—once again made him think her figure didn't match her age. She approached a white Lexus, opened the door and set her handbag down.

The next moment nearly stopped Yoshi's breath.

He watched her right hand reach up toward her hairline. Her fingers slipped beneath her scalp and tugged gently. Like removing a hat, she lifted a full head of silver hair—it was a wig.

The wind lifted her real hair—deep, dark chestnut brown. Under the sunlight, she looked vivid. Alive.

Yoshi's pupils contracted. Not because of the wig.

But because—

That gesture. It reminded him of someone. Many many years ago. *That* case. The one he thought he'd closed and forgotten.

He leaned forward, fingers digging into the edge of the table. It was *her.* A young widow whose husband died on their couch and who hadn't shed a single tear. The woman who said, "He died with a peaceful smile."

She never fled. She'd simply used a different name, changed her hair, came back—signed a new contract ... and buried another policyholder. *No, she didn't even change her name! Bold.*

The essence stayed the same. Only the mask had changed.

He closed his eyes. The white Lexus blurred into the image of a silent kitchen from 17 years ago—the first time Lilith Anderson had entered his field of vision.

She'd been standing by the kitchen window, cradling a cup of tea. Her fingers were pale and slender, nails unpainted. The kettle on the stove shrieked. She didn't move to turn it off until steam had coated the window—like a schoolgirl ignoring the bell on purpose.

Back then, she was also called Lilith Anderson. *Yes, she is quiet, but she is bold not to change her name,* Yoshi thought as he concentrated to pull in the memory with more clarity.

Insured: Burt Anderson.
Age: 56.
Occupation: plumber.
No known history of heart disease.
Policy value: $350,000.
Date of death: 48 days shy of the contestable deadline.
Cause of death: natural—acute cardiac arrest
No further investigation required.

She hadn't argued. Hadn't pushed. Yoshi remembered clutching the risk assessment form, only to realize there was no box to tick for Suspicious when there was no incriminating evidence to use for a deeper inquiry.

Her documents were flawless—neatly packed in a cream envelope: marriage certificate, policy declarations, signed authorizations. He still remembered the way she presented them—unhurried, almost graceful. No wig back then. The same dark brown hair shot with red undertones, but it was short and sleek then. Her face wasn't classically beautiful, but there was something disturbingly magnetic about her.

"Mr. Anderson passed peacefully," she had said. "He didn't feel a thing." Then she smiled faintly. "He always said the world was too complicated. Better to leave it simply."

Yoshi hadn't recorded that line. But now, thinking back, it was as if she'd just said it yesterday. His closing report at the time had contained only one sentence: Beneficiary behavior normal. No signs of evasion or manipulation observed.

Now he understood: her emotions had been rehearsed hundreds of times; she was in tight control of her emotions, if she even had any. If she was a sociopath as Yoshi now suspected, there may be more than these two policies. He felt the thrill of a chase about to begin.

The insurance office was empty. Yoshi stood in front of the archive room on the 7th floor. The room was Risk Control – for Audit Division use only. He scanned his badge, signed in, pressed his fingerprint—each step robotic, like signing another invisible contract. When the door opened, what greeted him wasn't air-conditioning, but the musty scent of paper and dormant servers. He flipped on the light. Pulled up the internal system.

Eagerly he started a search on Anderson, Lilith.

Matching policies: 7
Policyholders: varied
Coverage amounts: $180,000–$750,000
Payout status: all approved
Death dates: beyond contestability clause—7 out of 7

Yoshi stared at the screen, his knuckles whitening. No alias. She'd simply changed locations, relationships—morphing from spouse to caretaker, from neighbor to legal guardian.

Seven cases.

Seven policies.

Seven deaths occurring around day 730 after activation—three of them precisely on day 735: five days beyond the threshold. That was just with his own company. He accessed the internal risk control system and typed:

High-Frequency Cross-Beneficiary Analysis
Name: Anderson, Lilith
Threshold: >5

A loading icon on the screen spun for five seconds before a red alert popped up:

ACCESS DENIED – LEVEL 5A AUTHORIZATION REQUIRED

Yoshi froze.

He'd never seen a 5A classification. It wasn't for investigators. Not for regional managers, zone chiefs or even the head of claims. This was *beyond* the system. He clenched the mouse, breath caught in his throat—not because he was denied access, but because—

Someone knew.

And *someone didn't want anyone else to know.* He sank into the chair. The desk lamp cast a greyish shadow across his face. He stared at the red line of text. Didn't shut it down. Didn't close the file. He just stared. Unable to believe it was real.

Five minutes.

Ten.

He looked down. His palm was sweating. The pen slipped from his fingers and hit the table with a quiet tap—like a punctuation mark. He exhaled. The chair creaked. Just take a break. Just a moment. He didn't remember falling asleep.

He only closed his eyes ...

~ ~ ~

Then—the chair was gone.

The file was gone.

He stood in front of a house. His brain shouting, *This is a dream.*

"Yes, but more, more than a dream," a voice like a breeze whispered in his ear. "Welcome to Madwood House."

He recognized the place immediately—an address that had haunted his investigations like a ghost, always appearing in background checks but never listed on any official policy until this last one.

A three-story Victorian house loomed before him. The eaves drooped low, its white paint peeling like diseased skin. Vines, sickly and serpentine, clung to its walls. The house had no visible number. Beyond the lopsided porch stood an ancient camphor tree, its gnarled branches reaching like the hands of a blind man.

He didn't ring the bell. The door creaked open on its own.

Inside—no one. The hallway was saturated with the scent of cedar and damp paper. Every step Yoshi took seemed to stir a low, sleepy moan beneath the floorboards, as if he were walking across the back of some slumbering beast.

On the entry table sat a visitor logbook with his name and Lilith listed as a host scheduled for 3 pm.

He checked his watch. 3:02pm. *Two minutes late.*

From beneath the floor came a faint click. Not footsteps—more like the snapping sound wood makes when it's slowly consumed by flame. He stepped inside.

All the photographs on the walls were blurred. Faces smeared, unfocused, as if an invisible hand was perpetually wiping them away. The living room light was strange. An orange-pink floor lamp cast a dull glow in one corner. In the center of the room, a door to the basement stood ajar. There was no railing, just steps down into shadows.

It looked like it was waiting for him. Each step down took a moment of calculation. *Is this the bottom?* He reached the final riser. Another door. Cold air seeped through the crack. Yoshi pushed it open.

The basement was dim. Exposed pipes ran like the veins of a giant beast. A long table dominated the center of the room, lit by a single hanging bulb. Along the wall stood seven wooden crates—not shaped like coffins but storage boxes.

Each was labeled with the case file numbers he had just read on the computer. *Those people weren't dead.*

"Correct, Yoshi. They just quietly disappeared from your world."

Maybe they were still collecting government checks under their old names. Maybe they'd been tucked into some nursing home. Or maybe—they had never existed at all.

He walked up to the only open box. The lid leaned against the wall. Inside, everything was perfectly arranged: policy applications, names, call logs, beneficiary ID copies, signature samples—even handwriting analysis reports.

At the very top was a faded, unfiled insurance policy. He picked it up. **Insured: Yoshi Kinjo**

His throat constricted. This wasn't a template. Every field matched an activated policy—reference number, underwriter signature, payment logs, mailing address.

Payout: $950,000
Beneficiary: Lilith Anderson
Status: Approved
Effective Date: blank
Termination Date: not listed

He flipped to the last page. The signature line bore his handwriting. *That's really my signature!* He didn't remember signing it, but the strokes—the upward slant of the letters, even the subtle dot used for forgery prevention—were all unmistakably his.

He checked the folder. Then the others. They were part of the same project—not forged, but deliberately buried within the company's unindexed files.

Then—a sound. *Thud.*

He looked up sharply. Not from the floor. The sound of paper inside the box—absorbing moisture, swelling, then collapsing.

Thud.

Not like a corpse hitting a coffin lid. More like the soft, final stamp of a notary seal. The air thickened. Every breath tasted of toner dust. His throat burned. Sweat cooled along his temples.

"They're not dead, Yoshi. They just agreed to disappear. You will, too. Time to stop investigating Lilith. You will join us soon."

Footsteps approached the doorway. Soft. Unhurried. Like a night nurse checking rooms on the late shift.

Yoshi turned. Lilith was at the basement's entrance, framed by the door, holding a white porcelain teacup. Steam curled upward from it in delicate strands.

Cedar. Clove. Green tea.

She stepped forward and placed the cup gently on the table. "You were two minutes late," she said softly.

"I never scheduled this," he rasped.

"You didn't," she replied, locking eyes with him. "Madwood did."

She sat. Her fingertips rested lightly on the rim of the cup. Her nails were unpainted but perfectly trimmed.

He tried to read her expression. *What the hell is she thinking?* "I don't want to die," he muttered, barely audible.

She cooed at him like to a child. "This isn't about dying. It's about filing." She flipped to the last page of the policy.

His signature stared back at him. "I never signed this," he whispered.

"You did," she said gently. "The moment you hesitated to investigate me as a young widow. The moment you chose to go home instead. Every time you dismissed an anomaly in other cases." She nudged the tea closer to him, patient, like someone awaiting the inevitable. "Will you have it now?"

He stared at the cup. The steam no longer rose outward but curled inward—swirling like a tiny vortex. It pulled in every image from his dream: the policies, the boxes, the seven vanished names, the red 5A warning ...

He didn't move, yet his hand was already on the rim. He didn't drink. He tried to push away, but the chair's back dug into his spine. He tried to speak, but his mouth was dry as ash. The tea's scent—paper & vegetation—wrapped around his throat, strangling the words before they could form. He looked down.

The signature still glowed faintly. This was not just his handwriting—it was a structure disguised as choice. A threat. A promise. He hadn't signed it. He'd merely traced what had already been written, waiting for the ink to dry.

He closed his eyes. His body felt like an unearthed file—cold, carrying the sterile scent of a morgue and finalized accounting. *A damn dream.* He willed his mind to reach for his office. To wake up.

~ ~ ~

He jolted awake. The chair groaned beneath him.

Silence. No wind. No light—except the computer screen, and the desk lamp flickering once, then dying.

He was back in the 7th floor archive room.

There was a file laid open before him, its corners curled from moisture. His palm was stuck to the armrest; his shirt clung to his back. His custom wood pen rolled to the edge of the desk.

He gasped for air like a diver breaking the surface.

Looked down. Not the policy from the dream, but it was identical in structure. He flipped straight to the last page.

Signature line: blank. The pen rolled onto the paper stopping at the line for his signature.

And in the center of the page was a printed copy of the dream policy's first page paperclipped to the real policy paperwork:

Policy ID: #0783-KIN
Insured: Yoshi Kinjo
Beneficiary: Lilith Anderson
Status: Pending
Signature: Awaiting confirmation

Yoshi stood, legs trembling like he was stepping out of a decompression chamber. The archive lights still glowed. The ceiling seemed lower, the air heavier. He reassembled the file. Every movement was as careful as defusing a bomb.

He didn't dare look again. Didn't want to confirm whether the signature had appeared, whether the ink was still wet—or had always been there.

He rushed out of the room. Only the emergency lights were on in the corridor. He grabbed the stair rail to go down—but paused on the first step.

There was something in his hand. He looked down. *The teacup.* Plain white. Unmarked. Still warm. A single tea leaf floated on the surface. Not a disposable office cup—He froze. *That smell*—The scent from the dream.

Cedar.

Green tea.

Aged paper.

A hypnotizing mist.

He hovered midway on the staircase. One foot suspended above the void.

The stairwell yawned below him like an open drawer, waiting to file a document. He wondered if it had already begun—*the filing of Yoshi Kinjo.* He wouldn't give them the satisfaction of rushing to his "accidental" death.

Yoshi didn't call the police. Didn't file a report. Didn't request an audit. He simply walked carefully to his office, put on his jacket, slid the damp file into his pocket and drove himself to Madwood House.

A PERFECT FRAUD

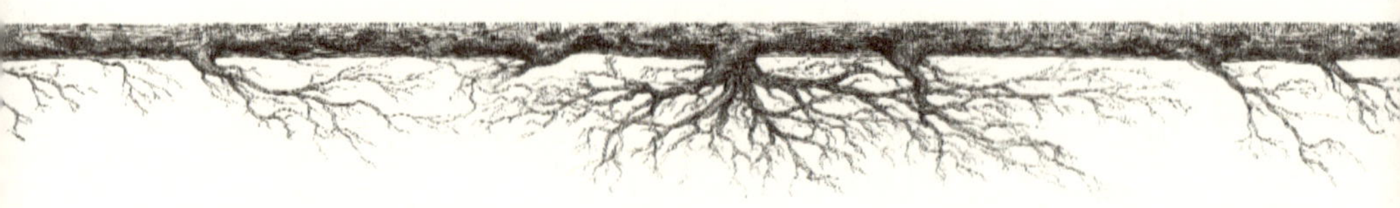

The Victorian house came into view. Yoshi's steps faltered.

It was exactly as in the dream—three stories high with drooping eaves, the giant, twisted camphor tree, even the rusted iron gate and missing house number were all the same just positioned and structured slightly differently. It towered over the yard in the dead still of morning so early everything was a dark grey monotone.

Inside, the light was dimmer than in his dream/vision. Pipes groaned upstairs as if the house itself was waiting for its books to be balanced. Yoshi clutched the file folder. His knuckles turned white against the paper as he looked around the main room.

"Why didn't you change your name?" he finally asked. His voice sounded like someone who was guilty trying to deflect attention.

Lilith reclined in a wicker chair beside the tea table, her posture relaxed like this was just a routine visit. She traced the rim of her teacup, nudged it slightly forward, leaving a fogged crescent of fingertip behind. She stared at the table for a moment before answering. "I tried. Robin Freeman. Mary Hall. Elizabeth Li." She looked up, locking eyes with him. "None of them ... lasted more than two years."

The sentence pierced his mind like a needle of ice. He felt a string snap behind his eyes, as if a data field had just been uploaded; *there are so many more than I can even imagine.*

"Only Lilith," she whispered. A ghost of a smile curled on her lips. "She survived." There was no gloating. No menace. Just fact. She said it like a pathologist reading a lab result. No embellishment. No emotion.

And that detachment—that emotionless clarity—was what made

it unbearable. Like being told that something inside you "wasn't supposed to live ... but did."

Yoshi didn't sit. His legs were stuck to the floor. The extremities of his body had already gone cold. Their closed insurance system alone held seven paid-out policies linked to Lilith Anderson—and now she was casually admitting to multiple false identities. New York Life, Prudential, MetLife, Genworth, Lincoln National ... His breath caught. He should have asked: *How did you control it all?*

Suddenly, none of that mattered. Her existence was the answer. She didn't need to kill. All she needed to do was entice and they would *sign.* No need to evade audits. All she had to do was exist as Lilith and wait like a spider.

"What's the thing insurance companies fear most?" she asked suddenly, her tone curious—like an auditor probing for a competitor's weak spot.

Yoshi's Adam's apple bobbed.

"Not fraud," she answered herself, calm and clinical. "*A* ***perfect*** fraud." She sipped her tea. The sound barely audible—gentle, but deadly.

Yoshi muttered under his breath, barely able to form the words: "What ... is perfect fraud?"

Lilith smiled breezily. "Perfect fraud," she answered, "is when I tell you I'm conning you ... and you can't do a damn thing about it."

Yoshi's throat tightened. "You mean—"

She interrupted, softly, "You people have a rule, don't you? The two-year incontestability clause."

Yoshi nodded slowly. "Right ... After two years and one day, a policy becomes incontestable as far as things listed in the policy. But, *uh,* but murder would still void any policy!"

Lilith didn't blink. "So if someone dies on day 731—the first day of the third year of natural causes—what can you say?"

Yoshi's voice sank. "Nothing."

She shrugged. "I didn't break the rules. I followed them—*to the letter.*"

Yoshi frowned. "But you're always the beneficiary."

"On the ones *you* know about, yes." She tilted her head, patient. "You require insurable interest on paper, right? They were my tenants, weren't they?"

Yoshi said nothing.

She tapped the edge of her teacup lightly. "And I was their caretaker. This place is a legally registered residential facility. As well as the other registered care homes. Their deaths," she offered a faint smile, "were operational losses."

"You ... exploited a legal loophole," he said, voice hollow.

Lilith's smile didn't waver. "No. I walked the path *you built.*" She paused, then gently blew on her tea. "Do your rules ever say how many times someone can be a beneficiary?" A silence danced in the morning air. "Do they?"

"No."

Her eyes sharpened. "Then tell me—what or who exactly did I defraud?" She leaned in. Her breath grazed his cheek. "Perfect fraud," she whispered, "is beating you within your own rules." She set her cup down.

"Murder," he gasped out.

"As for cause of death ... that's the police's concern. And if they remain silent—what can you do?"

Yoshi had no reply. He stood there, suddenly realizing he was not the hunter—but the piece already checkmated. Every step he thought he'd taken in an investigation had already been anticipated.

Her voice flickered into his consciousness. "Are you scared?"

Yoshi looked up. His mouth felt packed with cement. He wanted to speak, but his mind short-circuited like hardware without power.

"You insurance people always think you're the world's gatekeepers. But the truth?" She sipped again. Her words rose with the steam. "You're just early arriving filing clerks for what is to come."

A soft click echoed in Yoshi's ears. Not a sound, but a system response—as if his personnel file, search history and performance logs were being retrieved, reviewed and sealed.

He felt like he was being peeled away from reality—like a void contract run through a shredder. He tried to walk out of that house. But his legs were stuck to the floor.

"Have you ever thought," Lilith's voice lightened with softening grey of the early dawn, "that maybe you're here because ... you've been *scheduled*?"

"I don't believe in fate," he choked out.

Her eyes were almost tender. "Neither do I. But the system does."

"The system?" Yoshi heard himself ask, everything felt faded.

"You think only humans archive things?" she asked, glancing toward the flickering bulb overhead, its pulses like a database self-checking. "Data has instinct," she said. Her smile vanished. The teaspoon tapped the rim of the cup—the final stamp in a closing file. "Trees record the world in their rings."

Yoshi's spine pressed against the cold wall. And he finally understood—this wasn't an investigation. And it wasn't a coincidence.

He rushed out.

As Yoshi slid into his vintage Mercedes, a strange wave of relief washed over him. In this rigged confrontation, one he was destined to lose, the investigator made a choice that went against everything in his professional DNA. Yoshi opted for the easy path. Instinctively he knew that if he came to this address after two years, he would be dissolved into the tree, Lilith would collect on a policy that covered his death or disappearance.

Yoshi Kinjo didn't want to die.

Beyond that, he finally admitted to himself that he liked living a comfortable life. And someone else had manipulated the software so that investigating Lilith didn't return the correct information.

During the next few years he pursued investigations for others, but never one connected with Lilith or her tenants. He seemed blessed by intuition, solving more cases than ever before, year-end bonuses consecrated his bank account. He retired to enjoy life, yet the enjoyment tasted bland; he knew others were being murdered in a calculated fraud. He also knew he didn't have the power to stop it.

His only joy was being called in to consult on difficult cases which he always seemed to solved. Always finding the point of avarice that ruled the beneficiary.

3 SISTERS / 1 SURVIVOR

The bus wheezed and sighed to a stop, the way old men die— slow, unnoticed. Lilith stepped off, coat zipped high, the wind tangling in her hair. In her hand was a folder of cold leads, state files and a glossy photo of a woman with tired eyes who looked like no one ... and too much like Lilith to be a coincidence.

Decades had passed. Her sisters vanished into the system while she'd gone somewhere darker. And now? Now they had to stay quiet. Disconnected. Lilith wanted to keep them away from Madwood so she would be the only one in control of them and she needed more people she could count on to be beneficiaries for her.

"Love is inefficient," God told her once. "Loyalty can be redirected."

She found Maggie in a walk-up with flaking paint and the stench of floral body spray and body odors.

"Oh my god," Maggie said, throwing her arms wide. "You're real."

"I am," she replied.

Maggie smirked. "God, you're always so dramatic. But I like it. Reinvention with that old wig suits you."

Maggie looked good. Too good. Full lips, soft curves, chaos in her eyes. She oozed magnetism, the kind of woman men bought drinks for, apartments for, secrets for. But Lilith saw through it all. The way the glamour twitched at the edges. The way desperation clung to her like a second skin. She smiled politely. Maggie wouldn't last. Not in this world. But she'd be useful first.

They found Zoe in a subsidized housing unit on the west side. Clean, dull, beige. Like someone tried to erase her.

"Lilith?" Zoe asked, confused at why her older sister looked so very much older.

"Don't forget me!" Maggie huffed, breezing past. "She's rebranded to an old lady. It's a thing."

Zoe blinked. "You look so different."

"I am," Lilith said softly.

Back at Maggie's place, they drank cheap wine under a humming light. They had not been in the same room for over 20 years; Madwood put them back into a shared gravity, but gravity is not closeness. They spoke in careful bursts, strangers who owned the same childhood memories. Reunion was not repair.

"I can't believe we're all together," Zoe said. "We could live together. Pool our money. Make something of this life now!"

"Oh, sweetie," Maggie laughed, "this isn't a movie. You want to start a juice bar next?"

Zoe's face fell.

"She means well," Lilith said. "However, we need to think practically."

"I am thinking practically," Maggie said, reclining. "You know what's practical? Getting ahead. You know who helps with that? Men. Well, they need to experiment our big sis says."

Lilith said, "We need ..."

"Volunteers," Maggie finished for her.

Zoe's mouth parted, confused. "You're joking," she whispered.

"She's not," Lilith said, voice low.

"Wait ... You agree?"

Lilith didn't answer.

Maggie leaned forward. "You'd be doing something important. It's painless. Just pretend you're going to sleep." Maggie thought it was some sort of sexual ritual Lilith was proposing for their youngest sister. The look in Lilith's eyes right now seemed ... off. Yet Maggie didn't care at all. She wanted enough money to get out of this crap place, and if using Zoe got her that, Maggie was all in.

Zoe stood. "You can't be serious."

"You don't have a job," Maggie snapped. "You don't even exist on the grid. You're a zero. A ghost."

"And ghosts feed the machine well," Lilith added in a voice quiet and smooth.

Zoe backed toward the door. "You're monsters."

Maggie shrugged. "We're survivors."

Zoe's eyes darted to Lilith. "You'd let her do this to me?"

Lilith stepped closer. "If you resist, you will regret it."

Silence.

Zoe fled; no shoes, no purse, just a scream of footsteps down the hall. With an elevator out of order and the door to the stairs chained shut just for this special occasion, Maggie was there with duct tape and a smile in seconds. The chain was taken off the door in case anyone else on the floor had enough energy to move around the world, and Zoe was escorted to Lilith's car.

Later, Lilith came back alone. The wine gone and the lights dimmed, Maggie curled on the couch like a cat in victory.

"She'll come back," Maggie murmured. "Where else can she go? She better share any money she makes; we're her pimps now, her protection. Freedom. Hell, we might even get enough to buy a real house soon, she's pretty enough to bring in lots of money."

Lilith looked out the window. The street was empty.

She said nothing.

In her mind, the calculations had already begun. Maggie had assets—charm, connections, a crooked talent for baiting fools. She could trade on that for a while. Maggie wouldn't ask what happened to Zoe as long as she kept getting upgrades. A new apartment next week, and Lilith could then teach her how to take a homeless person into an insurance office: how to clean them up, get the needed documents, treat their iced coffee with a special something to make them compliant and forgetful.

But the moment Maggie stopped being useful? The moment she drew heat or attention or even pity?

She'd go the same way as Zoe.

There'd be no link. No sisterhood. No shared blood.

The files would show no connection. No shared photos. No common address.

Just another woman, vanished into the alleys of a mid-sized city.

Lilith sipped the last of the wine. "I'll see you in a week. Sleep well, Maggie," she said as she left.

She didn't mean it.

At 3:07am, Madwood House breathed like a living organism. Wind chimes trembled in synchrony with its subterranean pulse. Lilith traced the veins of an envelope delivered by the house itself—its paper grain undulating like slow water, the address woven from young shoots. It smelled of childhood: damp earth, iron and the saccharine rot of Zoe's cheap shoes.

Her thumbnail split the seal. The handwriting was Zoe's. Or rather, another one of Madwood's flawless forgeries.

Sissie, I heard you crying last night.
I'm down here.
I'm still here.
Stop burning my dolls.
I've memorized every wrinkle on your face.
Madwood says if you keep feeding them, you can see me again.

The paper undulated in Lilith's shaking hands. No tears came. It had been a few months since Zoe was harvested, it wasn't until the dirt was on the coffin and the muffled cries still reached her ears that Lilith realized she had some unknow affection for her little sister. She had leaned against the camphor tree, listening to something vast turning beneath the soil. Preparing.

Madwood knew everything. Her regrets. Her sacrifices. Even the unspoken prayer: *Bring her back. Even for a second. Even if she's not whole.*

It had been too long now; her sister was harvested. Madwood was toying with her. She looked around her spacious room. Her body thrummed, calling for the vibrator. Crushed paper snowed onto the floorboards. Then the fragments twitched. Rearranged.

Z-O-E.

The mirror fogged.

Not a ghost. Not a hallucination. Zoe stood in her favorite dress, eyes holding the last unfrozen ripple of a winter lake.

"Are you still feeding them?" The voice came from everywhere—walls, floorboards, the spaces between breaths.

Lilith's throat seized.

"Keep going," Zoe whispered. "I won't completely die if you keep going."

Hands pressed against the glass. Lilith reached out—then said, "Who's next?"

"Kathy."

A satisfied hum. The mirror darkened. Zoe's final words lingered, "You always knew survival requires sacrifice."

Lilith's fingers found a strand of hair in the wreckage of the note. Curly. Black. Wrong.

The tip had calcified into something between bark and scab. She knew this hair.

Zoe's.

But not human anymore. It squirmed in her palm like a dying spider.

Roots pulsed through the walls. Zoe's ghost sat cross-legged at the epicenter of the room and the quake—or rather, grew from it. Her legs had dissolved into the floorboards. Fingers elongated into interlocking joints. Hair slithered upward, drinking condensation from exposed pipes.

Skin? Now a patchwork of bark and chitin.

Eyes? Still Zoe's.

"How long will you lie?" The question vibrated through the foundation.

Lilith clutched a vine-hair hybrid. It transformed from black to swamp green in her grip.

"You sacrificed everyone for me." Zoe's unmoving lips somehow smiled. "But really, I know you tried to sacrificed me for you."

The seventh coffin flashed in Lilith's mind—hand-carved cherry wood, lined with lambswool. Madwood had vomited it back up, roots shredding the satin interior like a starving animal rejecting spoiled meat.

Zoe didn't decay. She transformed.

First the hair: fibrous tendrils that caressed Lilith's wrist with disturbing affection. Then the skin—grey and fissured, weeping sap where blood should be.

"You should've died young." Zoe's wooden fingers tapped a xylophone rhythm on Lilith's sternum. "Grandfather's hands should have been your kindest ending."

The mirror showed Lilith the truth: silver hairs becoming rootlets, burrowing back into her scalp. Madwood remembered everything. Even the scar on her palm—that first desperate escape from her grandfather's house, the window hook tearing flesh as she fell to freedom. The clock's hands began reversing.

Lilith understood two things: She would see Zoe again. She wouldn't recognize her. Because eventually, Madwood would wear her face, too.

Zoe's final words echoed in her mind, *You always knew survival requires sacrifice.* The meaning clinging long after the words were gone; survival was never free and the debt was hers now. Her fingers faded from the glass, leaving only the calcified strand of hair in Lilith's palm. Upstairs, the painting in the study seemed to flicker with her voice, its catlike eyes catching the dim light, as if awakening to the house's deepening pulse. The roots beneath the floorboards stirred, a silent witness to the pact being sealed.

Somewhere deeper in the roots, a name was written. It wasn't hers—yet.

THE DETECTIVE & THE DAMNED

Lilith and Maggie looked nothing alike. No one suspected—or knew—they were sisters. That made it their secret. And some secrets were great weapons.

The kitchen light buzzed, dim and uneven—like an old machine wheezing in the dark. A single bottle of beer rested on the counter. Foam pushed gently up the neck, bubbles trembling under the light.

Maggie stood by the sink, swirling the liquid with a fingertip, watching the poison dissolve—silent, invisible—like salt disappearing into water.

"Lilith asked me to bring you a beer." She walked into the living room, bottle in hand, smiling casually—like it was all just a harmless little trick.

"You're not drinking?" The man took the bottle. A flicker of suspicion in his eyes, mixed with amusement.

"Not tonight." Maggie blinked slowly, her smile innocent, like a little girl handing over a handmade birthday card. "This one's just for you."

He took a sip. His brow furrowed. "Tastes ... weird."

Maggie smiled, her voice airy. "Life's supposed to taste strange sometimes, don't you think?" She turned back to the kitchen, picked up a towel, and wiped her fingers.

A few days later, he was dead.

No screaming. No struggle. Just like a dinner pushed aside—finished, waiting to be cleared.

A few weeks later the final stage in the plan was put into play. In the parking lot, just out of her car, Maggie narrowed her eyes, watching Lilith through the mist of her own breath in the cold air. Lilith sat quietly in the driver's seat of her white Lexus, long fingers tapping idly on the steering wheel. The rhythm was lazy, like someone drumming out a hidden code. “Is he smart?” Maggie asked getting into the passenger seat, voice laced with eagerness.

“Smart enough to know exactly where he’ll die,” Lilith said through her teeth.

“So smart he’ll make sure never to go there?” Maggie teased.

Lilith let out a faint laugh, too lazy to lift her eyes. “That old fox retired long ago. He just comes here for the game, to keep himself busy and to give the insurance company an excuse to hire him as a consultant so he can file a report and feel important.” She paused, fingers still tapping, like conducting a silent pantomime. “Whatever he wants—give it to him. Don’t skimp.”

Maggie let out a soft chuckle and opened the car door. Just before stepping out, she tossed over her shoulder, “I always know what men want.”

The moment the diner’s door swung open, a wave of warmth hit her. Her body responded, growing softer, fuller, like dough rising in heat. The sharp clicks of her heels echoed across the floor.

She waved as she passed the hostess. One glance was enough—she locked onto him instantly. In the corner sat a small-framed Japanese man, Yoshi Kinjo. His yellowish-brown skin stretched taut across high cheekbones.

“Mr. Kinjo?” Her voice was soft and slow, like honey sinking into ice water.

It slid across the back of his neck. Yoshi looked up, his eyes skimming her face quickly. “You’re Margaret Stone?”

“That’s right.” Maggie smiled as she slipped into the booth. Every motion was smooth, natural. Like a seasoned actress—every glance, every breath perfectly performed.

Her mannerism reminded Yoshi of someone, his mind wouldn’t grab ahold of the name. “The deceased—he was your husband?” Yoshi kept his eyes on the paperwork, voice dry and flat. Professional.

“Yes.”

“Cause of death?” Yoshi looked up again. His eyes were sharp now, probing. The air seemed to freeze for a moment.

"Heart attack, I guess," Maggie replied. "That old fool thought he was thirty years younger. Then one day—boom—just dropped."

Yoshi let out a slow smile, the kind tinged with something ambiguous—half amusement, half resignation. She was good. He knew it. His gaze shifted again, drifting downward without a sound. It lingered, for just a moment, on the faint curves beneath her shirt.

Maggie noticed. She lifted her chin slightly, letting his eyes slide off her like she was polished glass.

A faint flush rose on Yoshi's neck. "Why did the deceased marry you so recently? He was a bit older."

She smiled again, steady. "Because he loved me." Her voice was soft. Warm. But beneath it, a current of cold moved. "A smart woman knows how to make a man feel alive."

She leaned forward slightly, voice lowered, the corner of her mouth curling into a secret smile.

She angled her lovely cleavage at him. "I was the one that made him happy. Kids? They only show up when they want money. But you already know that ... don't you? I was what he wanted."

Yoshi chuckled. A sound full of sleaze and surrender.

In the parking lot Lilith leaned against the car, a cigarette between her fingers. She squinted, watching Maggie stroll out of the diner—calm, confident, like a cat returning from a successful hunt.

They both slid into the front seats. Maggie tilted her head back, closed her eyes. A lazy smile crept across her lips.

"Well?" Lilith exhaled a stream of smoke, flicked the ash out a crack in the window.

Maggie smirked, her voice slow and drenched in disdain. "What do you think?"

"Find me a man Maggie can't handle," Lilith muttered, her eyes glinting, "and I'll bet he's still napping at his mother's grave. I expect my portion of the check the day you cash it."

She started the engine. It gave a low, hungry growl and started heating up the interior. "You're the best investment I've ever made."

"Obviously," Maggie said with a soft laugh, her tone relaxed, but a current ran beneath it. She began to hum—a tune vague and feeling unfinished.

Maggie got into her car and the sisters drove off in different directions.

THE WORLD SPLITS

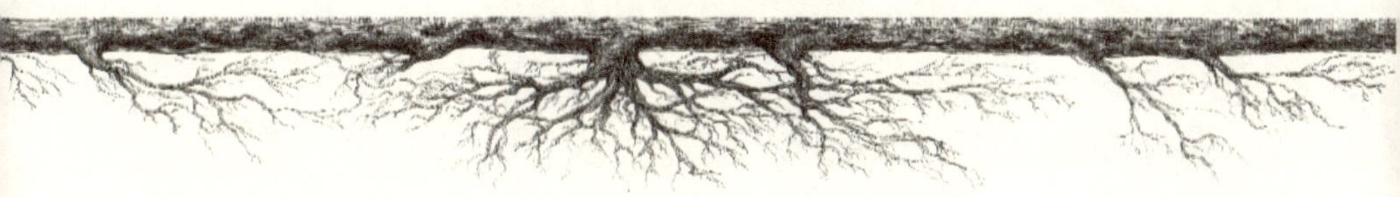

***Thud—thud—thud.* The knocking shouldn't exist. Not here.** Not in the backyard of an old house—just an ordinary house with nothing but weeds and silence.

Yet in the stillness of midnight, it sounded again—from beneath the earth. At first, it was only a tremor, like the final breath of a small dying insect—so faint it felt imagined.

Then it changed.

It grew heavier. Denser. The sound deepened into something primitive and sticky, spreading through the dark—pressing against invisible walls.

Thud—thud—thud.

The ground rose. The soil loosened, as though some hidden force beneath it were churning, clawing, reaching, sending ripples through the scorched dirt. The sound multiplied—like thunder, like metal tearing, like beasts long extinct crashing through a world that no longer remembered them.

The roots were not growing. They were escaping. Resin-dark tendrils punched through wood. Each split crack looked like a broken spine.

The dead offered to it over the years were shoved aside, used and crumbled. From the cracked skulls, empty sockets pushed upward, creeping roots pushed through eye sockets. The noise kept rising. Something else moved in the dark.

Thud—thud—thud. It was learning how to knock.

Beneath the surface, the roots now thrashed in fury. They tangled, strangled, broke free of anything that dared to hold them. The soil convulsed, rising in waves, crashing like a sea against an unseen shore.

It was unstoppable—a frenzied crescendo of life. A fate unfolding in the abyss. Thunder cracked loud. Then ...

Thud! Thud! Thud!

Where the roots tangled, wooden boxes began to tremble. Inside, the dead were pushed from their rotting coffins.

Ghost voices seemed to drift in the mist—unanswered.

They had not returned. They had only been disturbed—shaken loose by a chaos unnameable.

Above ground, the mad heard everything. They sensed this strange birth in a radius of a few blocks around the old house.

Some fell to their knees, pressing their foreheads into the dirt like they were asking for mercy. Some lifted trembling hands to the sky, lips moving in silent prayer. Some wept—tears cutting hot lines down their faces, as though judgment had finally arrived. Some laughed, wild and high, as if the sound were the long-awaited voice of prophecy.

For a single instant, the world split at its seams. Two dimensions brushed against each other—just briefly—before recoiling back into their separate existence.

At that moment, the mentally divergent were all listening. They had been drawn out into the raging storm. They believed the knocking was a trial—a hammer striking the sins they bore. A signal. A crack forming beneath the world's crust.

All but Lilith.

Her heartbeat never changed. Six hours ago, the same sound had taken the last harvested sacrifice. She was not pleased this was happening before she could claim the policy on this last body.

The storm stopped as if a switch was turned. Stars came out.

She stood among the mentally sensitive and ill, unmoving. Silent as the night itself. The knocking passed through her, resonating in the bones of the house, in the very foundation.

Her gaze was fixed—deep and dark, like the void at the center of the sky. She did not kneel. She did not pray. She did not cry.

Thud! Thud! Thud!

She listened. Listened to the murmurs rising from beneath the soil as though waiting for an answer. But she knew—no answer would come. Some sounds in this world were never meant for the living.

Beyond the courtyard wall, an early morning jogger came to a sudden halt. His smart goggles blinked: 237 viewers.

"This isn't staged, I swear," he whispered into the mini microphone, zooming in on the writhing dirt. When the first root pierced a kneeling man's palm, the comment section exploded. Then the jogger's stream cut to static.

But the knocking didn't stop.

He saw them—the gathering of the mad.

Kneeling. Praying. Faces twisted in ecstasy or terror. Lit by a fever that defied logic. They looked like disciples at an ancient rite—the last faithful clinging to a dying god. He couldn't know this god was rising (not fading) to claim its place.

He witnessed all of it. Beyond the knocking there was only silence. The dark pressed in around him, silent and windless. Everything was still. More so than usual. And yet—the leaves started to rustle.

He frowned. Pulled out his earbuds. Listened. Silence. No left-over thunder. No knocking now. The images moved, but their sound seemed stolen. Like a muted television—still playing, yet voiceless. He stood there, just beyond the wall, watching them. Watching their shaking limbs. Watching their lips move. Their silent prayers. Their laughter. Their tears. Their wordless awe. As he turned to go, his shoe struck something.

A broken root.

Dark sap oozed from the split area—darker than blood. He kicked, then tried to jiggle it off, but the stain clung to his sole like a secret unwilling to be shaken. His own fear was starting to grow, he wasn't seeing or hearing what the group of worshipers were; he wanted out of there before he started to hear it too.

Beneath the ground, the roots pulsed. The soil writhed.

The crazy people heard something, it was obvious they were

responding. They heard it as though it had taken root in their blood, filling and overwhelming them. They heard it with perfect clarity—an epiphany pounding through flesh and bone.

The sane heard nothing.

The mad listened.

Two realities.

One filled with sound and prophecy. The other hollowed into silence.

Two dimensions brushed—then fell apart again.

In a single moment, the world split at its seams.

The jogger shivered. Shook his head. Exhaled. And ran back into the glow of more populated, more civilized areas of Sacramento. Behind him, the figures in the courtyard stayed where they were. Still kneeling. Still listening. Still waiting for the whispers to rise again from the depths.

They didn’t know where the sound came from. Or why it called.

But they knew one thing—it was still there and it saw them; they weren’t invisible to it.

THE PASTOR SOLD HIS SOUL

Find Pastor Hudson. He once sold salvation. Now, he will sell *signatures for us.* That was whispered directly into Lilith's brain the morning after the camphor tree made its first physical contact with the living insane above ground. *You are not feeding me every month as I require. You must bring me this pastor. You must feed me every month. You Must.*

She found him on a street corner, preaching in ragged clothing with a hat turned up for coins. "The end is near! Are you ready?"

No one answered. A coin dropped—sharp and brittle, like glass breaking. He bent down, picked it up and whispered, "The Lord will have mercy on you."

Lilith dropped a coin in the hat next. She spoke softly, "I have an empty room. Would you like to move in?" Her voice was light as a feather falling into water, impossible to ignore.

He looked up. The sunlight made him squint. He couldn't see her face clearly. "I can't pay rent."

"I don't need money my friend. You can help me in other ways."

The room wasn't large. Its window faced west. Beyond it was a faded cityscape, like an old church mural worn down by time—every detail stripped away, leaving only silence. He left his few belongings on the bed and met Lilith in the living room.

"In this house," Lilith motioned wide, "live people who ... have issues."

He looked around the room. The residents sat quietly. One stared at the ceiling, lost in thought. Another kept rearranging a puzzle. A third licked their knuckles as if checking whether their fingers still belonged to them.

Their eyes were clear. No greed. No calculation. No hunger nor suffering. There was only one thing in their eyes:

Emptiness.

A perfect, untouched emptiness. It chilled him. And calmed him. Maybe, this was where he truly belonged.

A few days later, he found a document slipped under the door. California Department of Social Services—Application for Long-Term Mental Disability Support. His name, date of birth, and diagnosis codes were all listed. Under Legal Representative the line was already filled in: Lilith Anderson. On his signature line ... She had signed it for him; it matched his own perfectly.

He stood at the doorway, holding the paper like a sermon no one wanted to hear. The house seemed to exhale behind him. And in that moment, he understood: they were all paying their rent this way. Identity was an asset. A diagnosis was a claim code.

That night, he didn't sleep. He sat in the corner, using a chewed-up ballpoint pen to write the names and conditions of every resident in this place:

- The man who keeps writing but has no readers.
- The woman who assembles jigsaw pieces into the shape of roots.
- The old lady who said the ceiling was listening.

He wrote four full pages without stopping. He slid them into a faded envelope, writing on the outside **Department of Social Services.** He didn't list a sender. Just the address of this madhouse. He stood up, about to take the letter out and put it on his social worker's desk before the man got in that morning.

Thump. Thump. Thump.

Not the door. It came from beneath the floor. He paused. Looked down. Something pulsed between the floorboards. Like a heartbeat. Like a call.

Pastor Hudson knelt, pressed his ear to the floor, and whispered, “Lord, is that you?” The floor began to rise—just slightly. A thin, wet, warm root slowly emerged, like a newborn snake. It gently touched his forehead. His pupils shattered. Growth rings surfaced over his corneas. Blood congealed. His bones turned brittle. His soul faded, like worn-out fabric. He didn’t resist. Just closed his eyes, lips parting. “If God calls, I will go.”

The letter was wedged behind the bed, never sent.

Once upon a time, Chandler Durand had been a Michelin-starred chef—three stars, no less—and the restaurant was his creation. Fat Man’s Table, tucked away in Old Sacramento. It had been his masterpiece. Dishes born from his hands didn’t just earn applause and accolades; they moved people to tears.

Chandler also loved drugs. He loved the way they lifted him, how they let him slip outside the tyranny of time. Eventually, he gambled the restaurant away. He tried again, opening another place just as celebrated, only to watch it collapse too. This time, it hadn’t been gambling that ruined him—it was the government. They slapped a notice on the door, declaring the building unfit to withstand earthquakes. He’d stood there, watching his dream slide off the plate and shatter across the floor.

Who would have thought a chef who once stood at the pinnacle of his craft would end up wandering the streets?

That fateful day, he found himself outside the food bank on Broadway, stomach cavernous, eyes swimming with golden stars. The doors weren’t open yet, so he lingered, waiting. Then, out of the church, *she* appeared—pushing a shopping cart overflowing with baguettes and cans of beans. Donated goods. Expired, but still edible.

She walked toward him without hesitation, unlike the other well-dressed women who crossed the street to avoid him. Her cart stopped before him; she offered a faint smile.

"Here," she motioned to the groceries. "Take whatever you need."

He hesitated. Then hunger clawed through him. Chandler snatched a baguette, sinking his teeth into it with ravenous urgency. He gathered some cans and rushed off. Then came back for more. She stood there, watching—not with pity, but with the steady gaze of someone observing a starving animal. After a few bites, he slowed.

"Where's your home?" she asked.

He gestured toward the corner, where his box of salvaged supermarket scraps sat like a makeshift pantry.

She nodded as if she understood. "Come with me." Her yellow skirt mesmerized him, its warmth tamped down the last of his defenses. "I've got a place for you. No charge. Just sign a few forms."

Chandler never remembered exactly how or why he followed her that day. Maybe it was hunger. Maybe despair. Or maybe it was the unshakable steadiness in her voice or the flashing yellow like the white tail of a deer guiding its fawn—something made him trust her. God had a strange way of evening the scales, sending someone like Lilith when a man had lost everything.

The house was old, its walls lined with stories no one told. An iron ladder clung to the outside, creaking beneath the weight of the sun, its sound matching the comings and goings of the many tenants. Sometimes, the air vibrated faintly, as if some unseen machinery hummed within the bones of the building. But strangest of all were the sounds that were unconnected to anything Chandler could see—a constant knocking, hammering, rhythmic as a heartbeat. At first, he thought they came from Lilith's room on the 3rd floor. But when he climbed the stairs to investigate, the sounds ceased. He stood outside her door, waiting. A moment later, the knocking resumed—now it came from the basement.

He followed the noise down, finding Eldon hunched over his workbench, a piece of cedar beneath his hands. But Eldon wasn't hammering anything. Just as the chef stood there, motionless, the knocking started again—this time from above.

Those sounds unsettled him, like an unfamiliar dish arriving at the table, ordered by no one. Yet they didn't make him want to leave. The house was quiet—quiet enough that he could hear himself breathe again, even hear the echo of his failures.

Once, he had been an acclaimed artist in the kitchen. He'd commanded fire, coaxed flavors into harmony, turned ingredients into symphonies. Now he was a drifter, surviving on the generosity of others.

Lilith never mentioned his past, at least not in front of the other tenants. For that, he was grateful. Still, her silence unsettled him as much as the knocking. She slipped in and out of the house like smoke, vanishing into the spaces between sounds. She was a dish never quite plated, an unfinished recipe that left an odd urgency in its wake. Sometimes, he wondered if the knocking was something hidden beneath the surface of their lives, a knife cutting through the patchwork existence of people like them.

Each tenant, as well as Lilith, the social workers that came to check on them and any maintenance crew ... they all carried their own ghosts, each trapped in their own unfinished stories.

This house became Chandler's refuge. The walls might tremble, the air might shudder, but for the first time in years, he felt real again.

And those knocking sounds? He learned to live with them. Sometimes, he even thought that one day, he might understand what they meant—just like he had once learned to balance flavors, to find the perfect harmony between chaos and fire.

CLIMBING INTO COFFINS

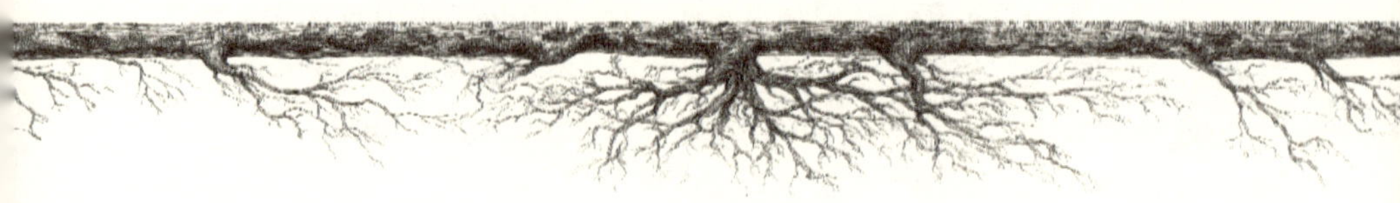

Eldon woke up in the basement with sawdust stuck to his tongue. He couldn't remember ever closing his eyes.

The cold from the floor had seeped into his spine. Sawdust clung to his palms like dried blood scabs—the clean kind, the kind that flakes off without pain. Black soil was still embedded beneath his fingernails, even though he'd scrubbed the floor three times.

"Happiness?" he muttered, his voice rough as splintered bark. "Damn happiness. It's a scam, like the knots in this wood—smooth to the eye but riddled with splinters to the touch." He set down the planer, his gaze fixed on the plank as if it were his only confidant.

Across the room, the handsaw trembled on its stand.

The basement had lost power since Tuesday. And yet, the blade kept chewing at the darkness. He didn't move. Just listened to the sound—wet, rhythmic. It didn't sound like a tool cutting wood. It sounded like something licking its lips.

Sometimes the planks sighed. Wood that breathed. Not the whistle of wind slipping through cracks, but the slow, burdened rhythm of a comatose patient on a ventilator.

The warped board near the furnace always leaked resin. No amount of varnish stopped it. Every nail he drove into it made a sound like someone swallowing a scream.

"Every box we make is a door we open for time," Lilith said last winter, her breath frosting against the chrome of the nail gun.

He'd laughed at the time. Now he understood: Some doors only open downward.

The lid of a coffin gave a soft, wet pop as it pried itself open.

Empty. For now.

What leaked out wasn't rotten air—it was a sharp, metallic sting to the nose. The scent of something strange and alive.

Three days ago, the fourth coffin started knocking. Not creaking. Three exact taps, like a secret code. When Eldon pressed his ear to the lid, he heard his own voice whispering from inside, "This isn't burial. It's incubation. It's time for you to rest."

Now, he often dreamed of lying inside a coffin, someone patiently hammering nails from the outside. He never struggled. The wood held him like a mother cradling a stillborn child. After each dream his longing to lie quietly in his own coffin grew.

Eldon heard footsteps overhead. *Miller.*

The former grocery owner and shelf stocker, now the basement's upstairs neighbor, moved like a wind-up toy winding down.

His world had boiled down to three sacred rituals:

1) Arranging canned goods
   (labels out, sorted by expiration date & alphabetical)
2) Swallowing white pills
   (though more often lately, he'd spit them into his palm and study them like teeth)
3) Watching the camphor tree shadows climb the wall
   (he'd named each branch after coworkers—those who no longer visited)

Last Tuesday, Miller hurled a can of creamed corn at the wall.

What rolled out wasn't corn.

It was a string of human molars, threaded with pink floss.

For the next 12 hours, Eldon listened to him scrub the same patch of linoleum. Over and over. Like he was trying to wipe away his own fingerprints.

On another night a different tenant sat by the sealed basement window, motionless as a statue. The former jeweler—once steady enough to set diamonds into wedding bands—now spent his days sifting sawdust through his fingers.

He called it "the dandruff of time."

Yesterday, he showed Eldon his forearm. The skin had taken on a dark glossy sheen, like violin lacquer.

"Do you think a man can sand himself out of history?" he asked. Then, without waiting for an answer, he bit off the tip of his left pinky finger.

It snapped like a dry twig.

"Needs a new groove," he mumbled through the blood.

That night, Eldon dreamed he was seated at a steel office desk, signing documents.

The fountain pen bled resin.

Beneath the floorboards, something was breathing in four-four time—not a pair of lungs, dozens of them! They rose and fell in sync like a bellows the size of a cathedral.

Nine coffins now.

The lid of the 8th still held the warmth from its last sanding.

The 9th bled a substance darker than resin.

No shipping invoice had come with it. Eldon recognized the scent: the narcotic sweetness of camphor wood—same as the tree the jeweler was worshipping.

Lilith called the coffins transitional housing.

Eldon knew better. These were delay pods, slow chambers for the almost-dead to ripen. Sometimes, he would walk past the row of coffins, tapping lightly on each lid with his knuckles.

Not to inspect.

To announce. "Soon."

Upstairs, the wind chimes began to scream. There was no wind. The windows had been sealed shut with paint last winter.

Eldon stared at the overhead pipe—the one that had run dry in

January. Now it was dripping upward. A bead of red liquid defied gravity, slithering back into the iron like a worm burrowing into warm flesh.

"Eldon." The voice wasn't in the room. It was in his ear canal, stretching inward like a spider unfolding its legs inside his skull.

"Begin the next one."

He didn't question it.

Lilith never spoke—she inhabited.

The new plank trembled as he lifted it. Not from warping. From resistance. When his palm touched the wood grain, what he felt wasn't the hunger of the tree—it was his own.

Sawdust clogged his lungs. Hammer strikes echoed endlessly in his cochlea. Slivers burst from the joints in his knuckles like tiny splinters from a failed crucifixion.

He was no longer building coffins. He was becoming furniture—assembled by the house itself.

That night, the asylum reached perfect respiratory sync.

One inmate laid pinned under a stack of cans labeled To Be Harvested. His diaphragm heaved like a blacksmith's bellows.

Another etched ECG lines into his thigh. Each peak matched the phantom rhythm of the nails in his skull.

Even the cockroaches froze mid-crawl, their antennae twitching in unison.

No one remembered their birthday anymore. But everyone knew their expiration date.

When the 9th coffin took its final nail, the entire house convulsed, like a starving dog catching its first whiff of blood.

The last of his humanity screamed at him to try to escape. He vowed to himself he would get out of the basement and find freedom because Eldon didn't know who the house would consume next, and his time might be near.

Lilith knew who was next, but he couldn't ask her that.

She listened to every breath. To every last gurgle of wood dying beneath her nails. To the final click of every coffin lid locking shut. This house had no heart. It had her.

And pre-labeled organ donors.

THE DAYCARE OWNER

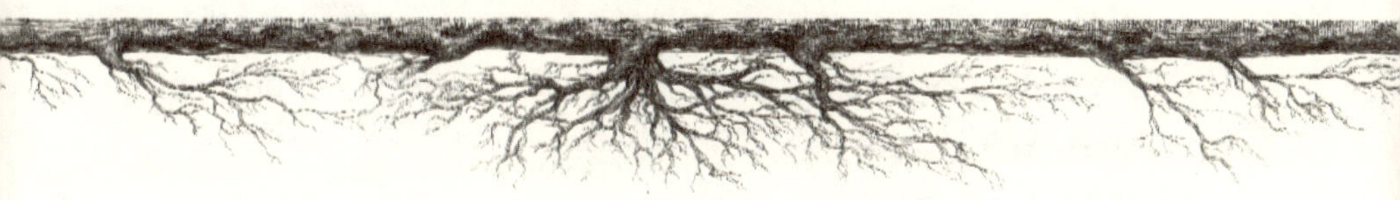

Judy The Daycare Owner / Eldon's Escape

My house was too perfect—so perfect that, at times, it unsettled me. It stood like a painting embedded in the landscape, with its pointed roof, carved windows, and a cherry tree in the yard. The children adored it; their laughter breathed new life into its walls. But sometimes, I sensed something else—a whispering sound drifting from the corners, like wind threading through leaves and vines, or perhaps ... the murmur of voices.

That evening, as the sunset bathed the yard in gold and crimson, I stood watering the cherry tree. A gaunt figure appeared outside the iron gate. His fingers clutched the bars as if afraid he might collapse. He had a slight hunch, his greying hair tousled like dried grass in the wind. His eyes carried an unreadable depth—part hope, part despair.

"Hello, I'm Eldon Skylen," he rasped, his voice weighed down by exhaustion. "This house ... I built it."

I froze. *He built this gorgeous house?*

I set down the hose and unlocked the gate. He stepped inside with slow reverence, his gaze sweeping across every window, every carved detail, before settling on the large glass panes of the living room. The sunset poured through the 160 crystal panes, casting golden light that danced across the floor as if the house itself had come alive.

"It ... it's just as it was," he murmured, his voice laced with both pride and sorrow.

He ran his fingers along the window frame, tracing an invisible past. He looked down at his own hands and whispered, "I made these windows myself ... Every glass panel, every angle, designed precisely to his wishes, for his bride."

"Who?" I asked hesitantly.

Eldon didn't answer. His gaze dimmed, his fingers still absently caressing the wood. After a long pause, he exhaled, his voice carrying the weight of resignation. "I live in a basement now. The damp air ... the doctors say it's bad for my condition. Bone marrow cancer. Late stage. Not much time left."

He lifted his head, scanning the house with a quiet determination. "I want to stay here for a few days ... Um ... This is my only masterpiece. The only thing that still belongs to me."

His tone was calm, yet I could hear the silent plea beneath it. My heart was melting for this lonely old man.

"This house ... It makes me feel like I haven't completely failed."

Then he turned to me, his eyes filled with something almost humble. "Can I stay here for a few days? Just to be with it?"

I looked at his calloused hands, the grief in his eyes. He was so frail, there was no way he would be a danger to the children if I kept a close watch over him; I would never leave him alone with any of the kids during working hours. As for me, I could just lock my bedroom door in case. After a small bit of reservation and thought, I nodded. "Of course."

As he turned to leave, he hesitated at the gate. "Tomorrow, then? About this time?"

"Yes. Tomorrow."

Dusk arrived. I was preparing the guest room for Eldon when a woman appeared outside the iron gate. She carried a woven basket filled with limes, her silhouette softly outlined by the setting sun.

I squinted—it was an elderly woman, seemingly kind. Silver/grey hair, an outdated pair of sunglasses perched on her nose. Her cheeks were smooth yet luminous, as if the light itself favored her. She wore a lovely yellow dress that reached down to her ankles.

"Hello," she spoke gently. "I'm Lilith. A friend of Eldon's."

Her voice was so warm, so inviting, that I found myself instinctively opening the gate. She stepped into the living room, her gaze drawn to the golden light dancing on the wooden floor.

She smiled softly. "It's beautiful."

Then, setting down the basket, she turned to me. "Eldon mentioned he'd be staying here," she said. "His health has been declining. Sometimes he forgets to take his medication."

She hesitated, her expression filled with quiet sincerity. When she saw she had my full attention she continued. "I live close to him. I bring him his medicine every morning and night. But ... your home has an iron gate. That would make it difficult for me to come and go freely."

She let the sentence linger, her meaning slipping between the words. I felt a bit hypnotized. I took a deep breath and notices a hint of cedar on the air. *Odd.*

Then, almost as an afterthought, she added, "He's a remarkable carpenter. This house was his labor of love for a newly married couple. But ... Eldon's mind isn't what it used to be."

Her voice was so tender it almost broke my heart. Without thinking, I nodded, overwhelmed with gratitude for her concern. I told her she would be welcome to visit anytime.

But Eldon never arrived.

At first, I found it odd—his insistence, his urgency ... yet not even a phone call came from him to cancel. But then I remembered Lilith 's words. *His mind isn't what it used to be.* It was a plausible explanation.

Instead, Lilith became a frequent visitor.

She brought toys, benches and slides for the children. She even donated new fencing for the whole property.

One day, she brought a small speaker and played a cheerful song. The children immediately formed a circle, dancing as sunlight streamed through the 160 crystal panes, the shifting light weaving between their steps. The whole house seemed to breathe.

Lilith clapped along, her body swaying gently, a soft smile on her lips.

In that moment, I thought, *She's an angel.*

I took photos, sent them to friends. "Lilith is the kindest person I have ever met."

And so Lilith won her way to my heart, and the hearts of all the children I watched over each week.

Months later, I was driving down 17th Street when I saw him. Eldon

He was chasing a large white dog, stumbling, his movements jerky like a child with a coordination disorder. The dog was merely trotting, yet he ran as if grasping for something he could never reach.

His eyes were hollow, lost.

"Eldon!" I called out.

He halted, turning toward me. His vacant stare landed on my face, but there was no recognition. His lips moved, struggling to form words, yet no sound came.

Then, without a sound, he turned away and resumed his chase, limping after the dog as it disappeared down the street.

3RD FLOOR TO JERUSALEM

Madwood tenants knew the time had come. Once every month (it used to be twice a year, then every three months) the black hat would return.

No one asked where it came from. They only knew—someone had to go to the 3rd floor tonight.

In Room 1, Wensen stood in air so humid, each breath felt like a gasp. The rancid blend of turpentine and beeswax reached peak volatility at exactly 28°C. On the wall, Lilith's bare thighs in his oil painting looked as if they were struggling to burst out of the frame.

In the corner, an old black hat sat silently under the easel. It showed up when the house needed "feeding." It belonged to no one, yet passed from hand to hand.

Wensen stood by the window, eyes adrift. He traced the glass carefully with his fingertip, as if searching for a seam he could slip through to escape the stifling air.

He glanced at the painting of Lilith. "Her body ... like a Rubens goddess—lush, brazen," he muttered bitterly, a dry curl at his lip, "but to me, she's just a disgusting sow—soft and bloated, revolting. Indispensable."

Wensen needed Lilith. Without her, he would collapse into filth and exile—a wasted, broken thing. He knew this. He hated this. Lilith wasn't human to Wensen. She was a proxy for Madwood's will—a medium that distributed breath, rationed desire and executed death. Wensen once thought he was resisting her. In truth, she'd written him into the script from the start and used him at will.

Lilith cleared her throat behind him and walked over. Her yellow skirt brushed the floor, scattering flecks of chrome green pigment. Her steps were light, yet each felt like it landed on a bruise.

She always seduced someone before the lottery. No one asked why. Everyone assumed it was part of the selection protocol. "What are you thinking?" she asked softly, as if nothing had happened. "Still brooding over *her* again?"

Wensen didn't answer.

"Got the drawing slips ready?" Lilith nudged him with her elbow.

"They're in there." He pointed toward the black handbag.

"It's the pastor's turn today. Did you take care of it?"

He didn't answer.

Lilith poked his chest with a finger. He didn't respond.

He turned suddenly, like a machine misfiring and shoved Lilith onto the bed.

He shut his eyes and repeated in his mind: *Don't look at her face. Don't look at her body. If I shut my eyes, she's not a person. She's just a thing.* Only then could he force himself to keep going. Otherwise, he would vomit.

Lilith panted beneath him and whispered, "Madwood needs a sacrifice tonight. We are its channels. And you, my dear, are the piston."

Cold water gushed from the bathroom faucet, splashing his face. He slapped the water against his skin. After every session, he would rinse in ice-cold water. Wensen looked up and stared at the mirror—and froze. The man in the reflection wasn't someone he recognized. This man had longer hair, deeper eyes and a glint of dignity in his gaze.

"Wensen, your depravity disgusts me. Do you even know what you're doing?" Wensen clenched his jaw and refused to reply. He rubbed his face with a towel as if trying to erase the hallucination. The man in the mirror tilted his head slightly, a trace of pity flickering in his eyes.

"You used to be an artist. Now? You're just a walking corpse, leeching off women and lies. What about your wife? What about your daughter? Have you really erased them from your memory?"

Wensen finally spoke, voice low and shaking with rage. "Shut up! What do you know? You're nothing but my shadow! Everything I've done was for survival! No money, no identity—I'm nothing!"

The shadow in the mirror gave a faint smile, filled with pity and scorn. "Survival? Look at yourself. You've become a murderer and haven't realized it. The real Wensen died the day you betrayed your wife. The man standing here now is nothing but a lunatic."

Wensen's fist crashed into the mirror. Glass shattered. Fragments scattered. But the image didn't vanish—it kept staring back at him through the cracks. He stumbled backward, his face pale as ash. "What should I do?" he asked hoarsely.

The figure in the mirror said nothing. It slowly faded, dissolving into nothingness. His reflection disappeared with it. Wensen stood frozen in front of the mirror, stripped of his existence. *If I don't even exist in the mirror anymore—does that mean I've disappeared completely?*

A voice called from beyond the bathroom door, like a thread tugging him back from the abyss. He stepped out, opened the door as if nothing had happened.

Madwood had only one rule: If you're willing to close your eyes, it won't bite. Madwood won't eat you—but it can make you eat yourself.

The kitchen light was dim. The air smelled faintly of sour iron. On the dining table was an old black hat, filled with several folded slips of paper. It sat silently under the light, as if awaiting the start of a long-established ritual.

Lilith never explained the origin of the hat, just as she never explained why Madwood House always required someone to "leave."

People sat around the table each with a different expression, all equally silent. The air was thick with an invisible pressure. Every breath felt like a struggle. Lilith stood at the head of the table holding a small red card between her fingers. "Everyone, it's time for the drawing." Her voice was soft, but it landed like a stone. "Everyone has their rights. Everyone has their duties. Tonight, we let fate decide."

When she said "fate," they all knew she meant Madwood. It always decided who must go.

Wensen leaned back in his chair, his eyes sweeping coldly across the room. To these lunatics, rules were their need—followed strictly, never questioned.

The pastor reached into the hat and pulled out a slip. As he unfolded the slip, his eyes froze for the briefest moment—then returned to calm. He handed the paper to Lilith, picked up a beer can and drained it in one gulp. He walked to the staircase. At the threshold, he turned to glance back at the table. There was something unspeakable in that look—a farewell maybe, or silent acceptance. Then he began to climb. Step by step.

Slow, steady. Until his silhouette melted into the darkness above.

Wensen watched without emotion. His fingers tapped the table absentmindedly.

The pastor had finally been chosen. Normally, when someone drew their slip, it was the pastor who would rise at once, close his eyes, and recite the Lord's Prayer: "Our Father who art in heaven, hallowed be thy name . . ." But tonight, when it was his turn—he simply downed his beer and said nothing. Then he climbed to Lilith's 3rd floor—without a word.

Everyone of Lilith's smiles was a ritual, the pastor was sure of that now. His role was a final stroke before the ceremony of the month closed. From the basement Eldon's sawing echoed like an old church bell, each strike carving into the pastor's mind, telling him his bone would be dead soon.

When his congress with Lilith was over they walked to the basement where she pointed toward a coffin.

"Is that for me?"

She nodded. "Especially for you."

She smiled, yes that ritual smile. "It's just transportation. Once you're there, I'll give you a house of your own." She made death sound like moving day. He almost believed her until he reclined into the hard wooden box.

He wondered why God never answered. Madwood never stayed silent.

The tenants of the House of Madwood stared at each other dumbfounded, then silently retreated to their own rooms.

That night, no one heard Madwood's voice. It was busy categorizing the new harvest:

- **Status:** Shattered, partial consciousness retained in root fibers.
- **Traits:** Religious resonance; viable as infection vector.
- **Storage:** East main branch of backyard camphor tree, depths 9 meters.

Morning light filtered through the curtains, painting wooden faces in grey. Lilith knocked on doors one by one, her voice light, almost cheerful. "If anyone asks about the pastor, just say he left after finishing his beer. Said he's going to Jerusalem to preach. That was his wish, and we should respect it."

Her smile bloomed like spring flowers—radiant and guiltless.

Someone shouted in reply from behind a door. Others nodded later at the breakfast table. At that table, Lenny leaned toward Chandler and whispered, "Did the pastor really go to Jerusalem?"

Chandler shrugged, biting into his toast, muttering with a faint smile, "Has Lilith ever been wrong? He really was a devout man." Or maybe he'd just gotten smarter, or maybe he was convincing himself.

Wensen sat at a corner, slicing bacon, a cold smirk of relief because it wasn't him on his lips.

In a world of lunatics, all they needed was order. And order never required truth.

"The pastor is gone. So be it," Wensen muttered loudly to himself—he'd long grown tired of the pastor's tiresome prayers and preaching anyway.

The camphor tree in the backyard had grown wild, its branches so thick, they were nearly breaking the eaves. The pastor's coffin was beneath the soil. Roots had pushed through his bones, wrapping around them like an interrogation.

Neighbors often said her back yard (with lush grass, commanding old tree and serene pool) was the most beautiful in all of Sacramento. They didn't know it had been nurtured with corpses.

Late at night, Lilith sat by the window with a yellowed old book resting on her lap. Outside, the leaves trembled in the wind, whispering like voices just below hearing.

"Who's more honest," she asked, "the mad or the dead?" The wind gave her no answer. The tree gave her no answer. Only the roots kept growing underground.

Lenny now wondered if Lilith was angel or devil. She saved him, then plunged him into bottomless shame.

Madwood's monthly lottery sometimes meant circling the camphor tree, or death games, or a night with Lilith.

After months of waiting, his turn came again.

"Three circles around the tree," Lilith instructed. "On the third, don't look down. You won't like what's growing."

He couldn't resist.

On the third round, a click sounded beneath his left foot—like crushing a can. He looked. The roots writhed bare, segments crawling through soil. And there, carved into the wood was #127.

That was a number he'd never used for his cans. A number that he always skipped like some people skipped 13. It was his personal evil number. He was shaken. How could she know? How could the tree know?

That night, he climbed to the 3rd floor, legs shaking.

Lilith waited, smiling.

The room smelled of camphor and rotting pine. Her smile

mirrored every shame he'd imagined. "Lenny," she whispered. "Your turn." She patted the bed.

He failed before he touched her, that hadn't happened in a while. *Premature. Humiliated.*

She handed him toilet paper without a word. As he left, returning down the stairs to his room full of shame and disappoint, she reached for her vibrator.

His love for Lilith was like a relabeled can—perfect outside, the taste inside known only to him. Lenny decided Lilith wasn't angel or devil. She was the wind.

And he—he was just dust. Waiting for the next gust to decide his fall.

The draft under the door was Lilith's breath, Madwood's breath. Lenny was no longer human. He was a branch of Madwood now, grafted into its veins rising up through his left foot. No way back.

NAKED / UNSEEN

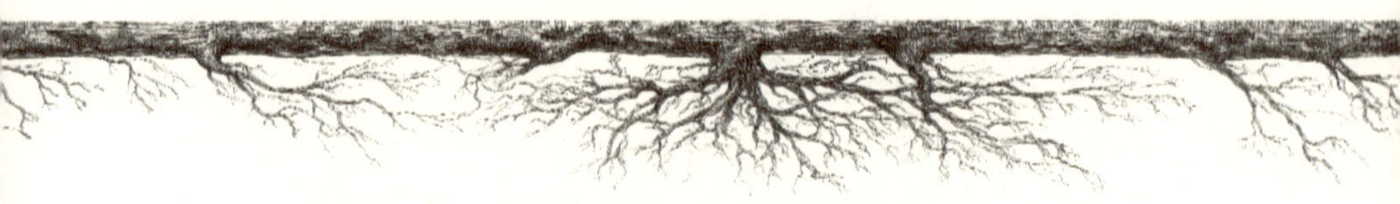

At precisely 2:00am, the house was silent—the kind of silence that settles over a well where all the corpses have already sunk.

Lilith stepped out of her bedroom, naked. Her pale body moved with the slow elegance of a panther. The wetness between her legs had long dried, but a faint trace of mint and blood still clung to her skin. A black leather notebook was clutched in her hand.

A faint smile tugged at her lips. The tenants were asleep. She walked the hallway on the second floor, barefoot, notebook in hand. Her soles slapped softly against the floor—slap, slap, slap. She wasn't afraid of being seen. Or heard. In fact, she hoped for it. If someone mistook her for a ghost, even better.

Sometimes she even pressed her heels down harder. She wanted to see who had the nerve to open their door so she could remind them they weren't as alive as they thought they were.

She passed each door slowly. Each one had a Post-it note, handwritten by her—clinical, neat, deliberate.

Tenant 1 – Jack Wensen

She paused for three seconds outside his door. Toes against the crack. A sheen of moisture crept down the backs of her knees—like vines unfurling in the dark. Beside the door, a faded postcard from the Musée d'Orsay hung loosely: a painting of a woman's face pierced by roots, eerily vivid.

She didn't knock. She closed her eyes. She opened them. She could almost see the painting Wensen had made of her pulsing behind the wood. The red still flowing.

She licked her bottom lip. "Wensen, you made me look ugly." Silence. Either he was asleep or lost in a dream, masturbating to her image. "Good work, Mr. Wensen," she whispered. "When you die, I'll make a killing."

She walked away.

Tenant 2 – Lenny Miller

Lilith continued her slow pace. Her naked body cast a long shadow beneath the hallway's moonlight. His door was covered in layers of Post-it notes. The corners curled, but the ink beneath remained legible.

She pressed the notebook tighter in her hand.

In her mind, the summary resurfaced:

- **Name**: Lenny Miller
- **Symptoms**: Claustrophobia + Respiratory insecurity
- **Observations**: Finds stability in stacking canned food. High anxiety around closed exits and failed tasks.
- **Status**: Depends on nitroglycerin to manage angina; resists medical oversight.
- **Recommendation**: Replace medication label to induce mis-dosing.
- **Expected Cause of Death**: Heart attack triggered by enclosed-space panic.

She closed her eyes. A mountain of cans rose in her mind—stacked to the ceiling. Lenny was the most disciplined of them all. He claimed to have once been a freight shift supervisor. Lilith thought he was too skinny to have pulled that off. That was a lie. What wasn't a lie was his need for everything to be in its place, that was his fight against something going wrong. She had nurtured that sense of order. She had taught him how to channel his mental unrest.

He collected expired cans from different stores then lined them up by expiration date, labels outward. He sealed the windows and door cracks with strips of blue duct tape to keep chaotic light out, he wanted light only from the bright LEDs.

Post-its marked his territory:

- **Do Not Enter.**
- **Oxygen supply is calibrated. Do not waste.**
- **Shift Schedule: 00:00–08:00 M W F Sat**

Tonight, she had no plans to go in. After his first few pre-ejaculations, he was often her diversion after a harvesting. Tonight she had preferred her vibrator. She pressed her ear to the door. No coughs. No cans shifting.

She noted in her book:

— Seal density optimal. Conditions stable.

— No supplemental input needed.

"You've done well," she whispered.

Tenant 3 – Martin Summers

At the bend in the hallway, the third door bore the nameplate "Goldsmith," the metal letters catching a cold glint in the dark. Lilith lingered in the silence outside—the kind of quiet that suggested the occupant had long since ceased to move. The Post-its on his door remained crisp, perfectly aligned, untouched. The notebook proclaimed his worth:

- **Name**: Martin Summers
- **Symptoms**: Erosion of personal presence + Dependency on artificial light
- **Observations**: Retired watchmaker + jeweler. Suffers from severe memory aversion. Requires manual labor to maintain reality anchor.
- **Status**: Obsessed with restoring discarded light bulbs. Avoids natural light. Believes illumination equals truth.

- **Recommendation**: Gradually eliminate functioning light sources. Maintain low-light environment.
- **Expected Cause of Death**: Organ failure from long-term immobility and heavy metal poisoning from lightbulbs.

She pictured the room: clean, still, sealed. The air scented with old brass.

Summers sat at the same worktable every day, tinkering with light bulbs that would never glow. His movements were slow. Precise. When they first met, he'd told her, "This bulb died in 1956. I just haven't buried it yet."

She brought him a bag of ruined bulbs—hollowed out, bases shattered. He'd treated each one like a sacred relic.

"Do you remember your mother?" she'd once asked.

He hesitated. "She was an incandescent bulb. Hot to the touch. Then she shattered."

She handed him a broken desk lamp. "This one might take a while."

He took it with both hands, as if holding an urn. From that day on, he spent five hours a day fixing it. Cleaning. Adjusting.

At the end of each session, he'd write a single sentence on white paper: Today, she didn't light up.

Lilith gave him a Post-it in her own handwriting when he moved into this room: Darkness = Existence.

He never questioned it. He stuck it beside the photograph of his mother. Eventually, he stopped fixing the lamp. He simply stared at it. Sometimes, he'd whisper with his eyes closed, "She's still here. Just too cold to glow."

Lilith listened.

No clicks tonight. No hum of current. No breath. Only dark.

And stillness. She noted:

- No movement for two days. Posture unchanged. Room temperature stable.
- Full organ failure projected within 72 hours.

She didn't knock. *He's already going dim, I hope he lasts until Wednesday.* She turned, continued down the hallway. The floor creaked faintly beneath her feet.

Summers would not suffer. He would return all his light to her.

Tenant 4 – Chandler Durand

She moved toward the next door. The air grew damp. The nameplate was in neat block letters.

- **Symptoms**: Gustatory synesthesia + Smell-triggered trauma flashbacks
- **Observations**: Requires daily redefinition of authentic flavor. Exhibits hysteria toward rot, high heat.
- **Status**: Successfully induced belief that decay = transcendence. Subjective taste fully decoupled from physiological response.
- **Recommendation**: Continue feeding disguised ingredients with sensory prompts.
- **Expected Cause of Death**: Spontaneous gastrointestinal perforation or asphyxiation due to obstruction.

She imagined the room—not a room, but a kitchen transformed into a temple. A shrine to memory and distortion.

He'd once cooked in Paris, Kyoto and Rio. She'd read his résumé. He claimed he could taste the precise moment when butter shifted from cream to char—within a margin of one second. But he feared uneven floor tiles.

"I only eat what I cook," he'd told her once.

The first time she brought him food, he sneered. "You don't understand what *simmer* really means."

She handed the container to him. "You'll like this," she said. "You'll forget it was ever cooked."

He never refused her food again.

Every day she delivered something new—a spoonful of sauce, a cube of cold meat jelly. And always the same phrase: "It's not what you think it is."

"So, it's a prototype?" he asked as if scripted. She'd nod.

He stopped cooking altogether. "What you bring," he said, "that's what's alive."

One day, he wept over a blackened pickle. "It tastes like a sunset from my childhood," he whispered.

His taste had finally died. He could no longer distinguished salt from sour, freshness from rot. Only the intensity of memory.

While he slept during his second week there, she swapped out everything in his fridge. Relabeled it all: *Whey Ferment* became *Echo of Breast Milk; Expired Tuna* became *Confession from the Ocean Floor.* He chewed each bite like a prayer. Swallowed plastic film and baking paper. Called them *unfinished memories.*

The last delivery she'd given him just yesterday was a box labeled *Charred Fragments*—in truth, dried and ground camphor bark, resealed in a gourmet pouch. Madwood told her he was ready for Chandler next, she knew Summers would be next because the jeweler was fading faster than predicted, so she gave Chandler only a sprinkling of the ground bark.

He ate it. "Tastes like Oreos I had as a kid," he said.

She recorded:

- Taste pathways collapsed. Dormancy rejected.
- Autopsy not recommended—risk of secondary exposure.

She flipped the page. Crossed out his name. Whispered, "The hardest thing to digest in this world is yourself."

Tenant 5 – Nigel Peabody

She stopped at the fifth door. The nameplate had been wiped many times. The letters were swollen, blurred.

For eight years, he hadn't made it past chapter one in his

masterpiece of a novel.

- **Symptoms**: Logic obsession
- **Observations**: Assembles "clues" from his environment. Claims to live inside a scripted conspiracy. Suspects Lilith as the central figure.
- **Status**: Paranoia forming recursive logic loops. Rereads scraps. Disassembles signage. Dictates dream dialogues at night.
- **Recommendation**: Increase semantic triggers. Sustain information overload.
- **Projected Outcome**: Spontaneous aphasia → Cortical rupture.

She fed his madness also. Each day she left him a piece of paper outside his door—each one a fragment from nowhere: nonexistent detective novels, fake medical files, pages from postwar cipher manuals. He sorted them by ink pressure, font decay, paper color. His wall became a web of strings, pins and tape.

At the center was her photo. Surrounding it, arrows with these tabs at the ends.

Old Woman / Demon / Bait / Witness / Prophet / Victim

"She's not real," he had muttered. "But she's the prologue to the truth."

Lilith planned to stop bringing him meals in a few months.

He'd claim he wasn't hungry, survive on black coffee, red ink and half-finished drafts for at least a few months.

Then her final gift: a single pill. The label was already prepared: **Swallow for your ending.** He would die at midnight. Red ink smeared at the corner of his mouth. A faint smile at the edge of his eyes. One hand pressed against the manuscript.

Lilith listened through the door.

Silence.

"You were never a writer, Nigel," she whispered. "You were just death's proofreader."

She walked on.

Lilith stood naked at the end of the hallway. Behind her: five closed doors. Ahead: a single lightbulb, unlit.

She didn't look back. She remembered the scent of each room. The architecture of each hallucination. The temperature of each body as the mind within it unraveled.

She remembered the faith stockpiled between cans.

The breath trapped in lightbulbs.

The grease hardening on tile.

The red pigment that kept bleeding from canvas.

The man who mistook her for a plot twist.

She had been their neighbor.

Their landlord.

Their mother.

Their god.

Their sedative.

Their trigger.

No one would sign a death certificate for this group. No one would miss them when they were gone. Lilith already knew they were marked to be fast tracked to Madwood.

She reached for the string by the staircase. Pulled it.

Click. The house's last light extinguished.

Upstairs: no voices.

Downstairs: no air.

The floor beneath her feet was clean. Taut. Like a stage. She whispered each of their names into the dark, tapping the floor once with her toe for each:

"Wensen."

"Miller."

"Summers."

"Durand."

"Peabody."

Each one—a closing chapter.

BIONIC COPS & SOCIAL MEDIA

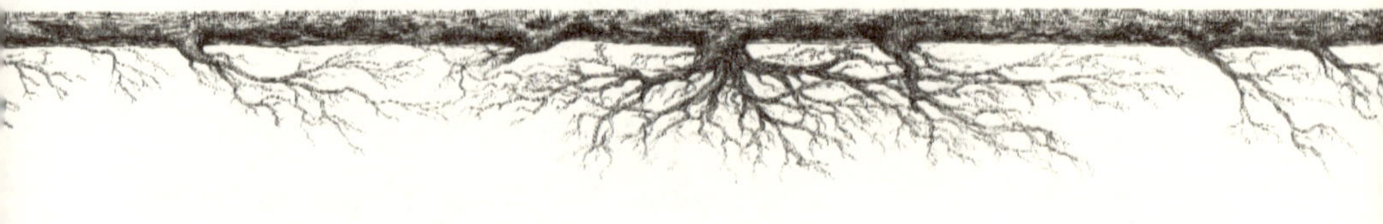

It began with a slip of the tongue. Lilith warned them: ***Say the*** *pastor's on vacation, he went to Jerusalem.* When police partners and a social worker loomed at the main door, their suspicion sharp, Lenny panicked.

"The pastor?" he blurted. "He's met his Maker!" The instant the words left him, he knew he'd ruined everything.

The officers' eyes turned bladelike; the social worker's mouth tightened.

Chandler, Wensen and Nigel lunged at him, spitting fury. "You idiot, Lenny!" Nigel hissed.

He stammered, "Wait! Lilith said *vacation*—she never said I couldn't say *Maker!"*

The room froze, caught between rage and twisted logic. Then the door opened. Lilith stood there unreadable, staring. No anger, no blame—just silence. And in it, his shame swelled.

She turned to the police, her voice cool as polished steel, "Want to dig? My shovel's in the shed by the pool." Inside she was hoping Madwood would wrap them in roots and pull them into the ground to give her time to collect all the money she could and have enough time to escape to South America. That was her back up plan.

Lenny's gut clenched. She hadn't punished him—she'd made him see himself. Forgiveness was worse than blame. He'd torn not just a lie but the illusion that sheltered them all.

That guilt weighed heavier than anything. She'd gathered them not to destroy but to save. And he'd betrayed her.

One of the cops stepped fully into the house, he was the younger one and walked with a limp. "I'm Officer Stan Altnick. Which one of you is Lenny Miller?"

All heads turned toward Lenny. "Okay Mr. Miller, you are listed as the beneficiary on the pastor's life insurance policy. We are here because he didn't check in with his social worker," he nodded at the uncomfortable man in wrinkled clothes, "and since he has no relatives in his files, I thought you would be the one to know how we can find him." The cop let a pointed silence work on their courage. "I guess you can, so explain what you meant by *met his maker,* that sounds rather like death to me."

Wensen tittered. Chandler screamed that this was the beginning of his next novel. All the residents started to mutter and sway.

Martin Summers said, "The toaster went to Israel too. I want pudding."

"The toaster doesn't count, it only talks to you," Chandler snapped.

The others tittered. Lilith shrugged looking at the two cops. "You see? They are all here under care and supervision for a reason. However this is not a jail and they can leave if they want to. I'll let you know if the pastor comes back."

The older cop shifted uncomfortably, his eye flicking around the room trying to assess ... something. Any logic, anything normal. He found nothing. "I, uh, heard there was an offer to dig?" he asked cautiously.

Lilith had just finished lighting a candle, she waved the air toward the cops with a smile. "Local cedar oil and beeswax. I always buy something at the local farmer's market to support my community."

They nodded politely, looking confused.

"I did say you could borrow a shovel," she offered sweetly after she was sure they had taken in a few breaths. "But that was days ago. Would you like a coffee?"

The social worker sighed, clearly regretting every life decision that had led him here. "Look, we just need to verify the reverend is safe," he said.

"He's safer than *anyone,*" Chandler said solemnly. "Can't get robbed in heaven."

"He's not *dead!*" snapped Nigel. "He's on a *sabbatical!*"

"To Jerusalem," Lenny added.

"Without telling the social worker?" asked the cop.

"It's holy ground," someone whispered.

"Naked feet purify the soul in sunlight," said Summers.

The inane murmuring rose—an orchestra of nonsense, half-prayers and phrases clipped from old radio sermons. The newest tenant, Max, started crying. Nigel began singing softly in Latin. Lenny muttered, "He went up, I saw it, I did."

The older cop looked overwhelmed. His sunglasses fogged. He turned to the social worker. "These folks don't seem ... capable of giving a consistent statement."

"Welcome to my Tuesdays," the social worker replied flatly. "Look, no signs of abuse, food in the kitchen and technically no one's filed a missing person report. The house is in good shape. This is a better care home than the others. You want to wade through the swamp of conservatorships and HIPAA to figure out if a man who wandered off wants to be found, *be my guest.*" He turned toward the door, already done.

"You coming?" he asked the cops.

The older one hesitated, staring at Lenny who was now building a pyramid out of tea bags. "You know what? Yeah. Let's ... let's come back with a warrant or something. We can check his room. Ms. Anderson, don't touch his room please."

The younger cop hesitated. Not because he was suspicious, but because his brain was fogged and he was confused. He wanted to leave. He should leave. He felt a small push and limped off toward the door with a promise that he would come back at midnight that weekend.

Lilith watched them leave with a smile like a painting of a saint. Then she hurried outside.

As the door shut, the living room exploded in applause. "We won!" Nigel yelled. The rest were all murmuring again. Lilith left them to their self-turned behavior in the common room and went to make sure all the tenant's rooms held nothing that would implicate her in anything at all which the cops could then use to further look into this or raise another issue.

Beneath the kitchen window, in the cold back garden, the earth rumbled and churned beneath the grass. Further into the yard, there beneath the towering tree, stood Lilith, her gaze fixed on the canopy that now blotted out the sun.

For the first time, her expression faltered. Her usual ease had vanished, replaced by something almost fragile. Her lips parted slightly as though forming a question even she did not know how to ask.

The jogger's live stream had been up on his page for months with a few views, fewer comments.

The cops stumbled across the archived video because of the local IP address. They made a note to interview the guy. They were totally confused about the group of what looked like mental patients around the trunk of a huge tree. It made no sense to them but no laws were being broken, nothing looked violent or like a threat to neighbors.

Officer Stan Altnick's boots echoed against the oil-stained concrete as he walked from the side street through Lilith's backyard gate. A single flickering light buzzed from the porch off to the side, casting long shadows over the silent pool. The air smelled like ozone and hot charcoal.

Stan paused, wincing, rubbing the thigh that had never healed right. The limp was worse tonight. He hated the way people looked at him now—like he was less. A fallen hero. A man once whole.

"I came, alright?" he muttered, his voice bouncing off wood and shadow. "Don't know why. Probably should be home icing this damn leg."

From the far corner, a lower branch stirred. Then it moved—fluid and with precision—a misty figure emerged. Not human, but almost. Its face, emotionless, yet somehow warm.

"Stanley Altnick," it said. The voice was velvet wrapped in steel. The voice was the one the pastor had used. "You are precisely on time. That says much about your discipline."

Stan scoffed. "Discipline? No. Curiosity. And maybe I'm just tired of walking like an old man at thirty-two."

The creature tilted its head. "You want to be what you were before."

Stan's jaw tensed. "No. I want to be *more* than I was before."

There was a hum, a subtle charge building in the air. The man/thing gestured toward a sleek chair beneath the camphor tree, right up against the trunk. "Then sit. Let me give you what you deserve."

Stan hesitated for a beat—but vanity, hot and coiled, won out over caution. He dropped into the chair.

A quiet stirring. Mist. A soft pulse of green light strobed over his leg. Thin roots eased up from the soil and snaked up his calf. He clenched his teeth, expecting pain—but felt only warmth, like sunlight through water. It lasted less than a minute. It left only a small puncture wound barely larger than a needle mark where the roots had entered his leg.

Then silence. The figure merged into the trunk and disappeared. "Stand, Officer Altnick."

Stan did. No pain.

He took a step. Another.

His breath caught in his throat as he broke into a jog—then a run, a *sprint* around the pool in the yard. He whooped, laughing like a boy on the last day of school.

"*You fixed me!*" he shouted, tears in his eyes. "You beautiful whatever you are—you actually fixed me!"

"And what will you tell the others?" Stan heard in his mind.

Stan grinned, chest heaving. "The truth. That you healed me! That you're not a threat. Hell, you're the future."

Leaves rustled in the still air. "Good. Very good."

It watched him leave—limp forgotten, heart full of pride, mind quietly seeded with a message he didn't know he'd speak.

When Stan reached the world outside, he would walk like a miracle and talk like a prophet. And no one would suspect the programming ticking quietly behind those shining, eager eyes.

Cat's Eyes

I am the eyes.

I am the eyes trapped within the painting of the Mongolian girl.

You think I'm just an ordinary cat? Wrong. I'm the witness to this absurd world, the silent recorder of all deceit and madness. I have seen the most deranged desires of humankind, the most shameless lies, the most sordid transactions—then I pulled them into my gaze, waiting for you to look upon me and feel that jarring unease release back onto you.

Wensen painted me believing he had tamed me, controlled me, imprisoned me within this frame with his paints. I know the truth: his hands trembled when he painted me. The moment his brush touched the canvas, my gaze tore a piece from his soul. Through my eyes, he gave the Mongolian girl a spirit that didn't belong to her. And in return, my own soul became trapped in this painting, forever watching those who dare to meet my stare—especially Lilith.

I am the cat.

I am Lilith 's nightmare.

The first time Lilith saw me hanging here, her face stiffened. She pretended to be composed, but I felt the storm brewing beneath her skin. She recognized me, because I was no ordinary cat.

I was her cat.

She once called me Sweetie. She held me, kissed my forehead. I thought I was part of the family. I was the one who kept her company through her childhood loneliness. I was the one beside her bed, listening when she whispered her darkest secrets. She told me everything—how she wanted to steal from her father to buy candy, how she wanted to poison the boy who bullied her at school, how she dreamed of killing her mother. She thought I was a mute, an unknowing audience.

She was wrong.

I locked every one of her secrets inside my eyes. I turned them into light, into shadow, until they shimmered in my pupils so intensely that she could never again look me in the eye.

On a snowstorm's night, she shut me outside and never let me back in. I vanished from her life. Later, she convinced herself it had been an accident. She lied to herself, thinking she had forgotten me.

But I never forgot her.

She thought she'd killed me.

But here I am—re-corporated in this painting, under the gaze of the Mongolian girl. Can you imagine Lilith's terror when she saw me again? That fear she couldn't quite conceal.

I am the cat.

I am the judge of humankind.

I saw Wensen's expression when he painted me—an emotion so complex that even he didn't understand it. A mix of greed, confusion and despair. He didn't know that my eyes could see through him. He was a mad genius, but a failure. He thought of Lilith as he painted me—her body, her promise to make him rich and famous. He believed he was the master of his own fate. He had no idea he was just a pawn on Lilith 's chessboard.

Wensen thought he was painting something that would impress Lilith but I was the one observing their entire transaction. Every stroke of his brush was laced with desire. He wanted to free himself from the chains his mental illness placed upon him, even if it meant abandoning his family and child.

And Lilith knew.

She controlled him with her smile, her promises, her body. But what she didn't know—I was watching.

I am the cat.

I am Lilith 's Nemesis.

When Lilith took the painting, she thought she had conquered it.

She had no idea that the painting's soul was me—the companion she once betrayed.

She forged documents, signed false names, built her schemes, while I hung on her wall, watching. My eyes never blinking.

Lilith believed she ruled the game. She defrauded insurance companies, changed disguises, buried homeless people in her backyard and kept cashing in their benefits. Every time the insurance money flowed into her account; she would glance up at me—as if boasting her success.

She didn't realize I was recording everything.

Every time she swung a shovel.

Every time she pressed a pillow over a lodger's face.

Every time she stood before the mirror, crafting another identity.

I watched. I memorized every crime in the depths of my gaze. I am the cat.

I am the guardian of this madhouse.

Lilith's residence is a madhouse; I am its sentinel. I have seen the homeless arrive in despair and leave in silence—buried in the backyard.

I have seen mute Margie, weak, trembling, cleaning up corpses with fear in her eyes.

I have seen Wensen, forging documents, trapped in the thrill of crime and the resignation of knowing he can't escape.

They all fall into madness under Lilith 's rule.

And Lilith —under my watch—spirals even deeper.

She thinks this painting is just decoration. A prop.

She has no idea—I am the nightmare she can never escape.

I am the cat.

I am the recorder of time.

Time is meaningless to me. Decades pass, centuries fade—I remain, watching your kind. Your sins, your lies, your desires—they all etch themselves into my gaze, burning like stars in the endless night of my pupils.

I have watched Lilith walk toward her own ruin. I have watched Wensen 's soul being devoured by her.

You all think you can escape my stare. But you don't understand—it is your own sins that make my eyes so bright. You feed me with your lies and your greed. You make me the truth you are too ashamed to face.

I am the cat.

I wait for the day of vengeance. Perhaps, one day, when this painting is found—when I am finally freed from the canvas—I will judge you myself.

With my eyes, I will unearth every secret you've buried, drag them into the light, and make you kneel before me.

Until then, I wait.

Hanging silently on the wall.

Waiting for the next sin to unfold.

I am the cat.

I am the eyes.

I am the fear you carry in your soul.

REFUSING TO STAY BURIED

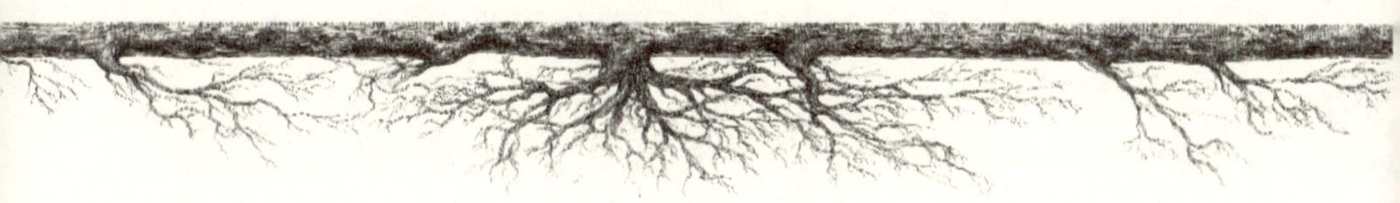

When Eldon and Lilith buried him in the backyard of Madwood House, the pastor believed himself to be a martyr. The damp, cold soil pressed against his chest, heavy and pure like holy water, and he was convinced his soul would ascend into the Lord's embrace as his flesh extinguished.

In the suffocating darkness filled with rot and the hum of insects, he finally realized the truth: he was merely another madman, muttering to himself in the void, seeking his own solace. Pushing off what was difficult, abdicating his own thinking to follow a demoness in the form of a sociopath and allowing himself to be used.

The first sign of the land's malice came with an ant crawling through a crack in the coffin. That tiny creature paused on his knee, its antennae trembling as if scouting new territory. In the darkness, he growled, "Back, disciple or traitor! How dare you profane the sacred body of the Lord's servant!"

The ant offered no reply. It summoned reinforcements. Hordes of ants marched in orderly ranks, climbing over him like a silent conquering army.

In that moment, the pastor realized for the first time: before the abyss of hunger in living things, faith is but a fragile veil, thin as a cicada's wing.

He struggled, lashing out. He roared, "Retreat! I command you the name of my Lord!"

But they did not retreat.

Upon his shoulder blades, the ants constructed a council chamber, seemingly plotting how to divide his remaining flesh. For days they daintily took small bites of his living flesh. Then came the maggots—slimy invaders slithering up from the soil, threading through the camphor roots, coiling around his ribs, burrowing into his skull.

By this time he could only whisper as he felt death coming, "Foul thieves of the earth! This body is reserved for heaven, not your filthy tunnels' spoils!"

They remained unmoved.

The swarm wove a silent, blind web within him. Most terrifying of all was not the ants or maggots, but the camphor tree's roots. They curled into the coffin above his face and dripped water into his mouth. They sent hair thin tendrils into his legs. And he couldn't fully die. He prayed for it; his god remained unmoved.

Those cold, serpentine tendrils grew and slithered along his spine, wrapping around each vertebra, squeezing into every hollow, until they rooted deep into the neural center where sacred prayers once pulsed. He whispered into the dirt, "Lilith sent you, didn't she? She's finally lost patience, intent on erasing me completely. But I will not yield. I am a pastor—my purpose surpasses her schemes!"

He began to barter with his enemies. "Listen to me, children of the dust! We share a common enemy—Lilith! She has deceived you as she has deceived me. You are her tools, and I her scapegoat. Why not join me in vengeance?"

The ants seemed to hesitate, their ranks shifting upward.

The maggots paused mid-crawl within him, as if awaiting orders.

The camphor roots twisted overhead, entwining like a silent council in deliberation.

He cracked a smile through his parched lips, a victor's grin. "Even buried in the earth, I can command the living. Even in death, I can make my enemies kneel. I can influence the humans that still walk upon the earth."

A plan took shape: the ants would surge to the surface, biting and driving her other tools to distraction; the maggots would gnaw through Madwood House's beams; and the camphor roots would tear the weakened mansion apart, dragging Lilith into this abyss to take the pastor's place.

Madwood seemed amenable to this bargain. The small bites stopped, the tendrils didn't leave, but they didn't grow. Just as everything was about to unfold, the ground suddenly lit up. Flames poured through the soil's fissures.

Lilith—standing above—had ignited the dry grass in the backyard, transforming the land into a purgatory. She had heard Madwood debating this bargain, she knew it wanted only more sacrifices right now. It had no idea officials were looking for the pastor, it had no idea of the power humans could unleash on it. Lilith did. And Lilith wanted to survive this.

The searing tongues of fire breached the coffin's seams, flooding his dark world with heat.

Amid the blaze, he heard her laughter. She was nearly singing her taunt, "Just some spring cleaning."

The ants turned to ash in the fire, the maggots writhed in the burn. The camphor roots whirled around the coffin; it popped under the pressure. The pastor was wrapped tight along with splintered bits and pulled deeper within the soil, away from the flames.

SOLD 8 MILLION POLICIES

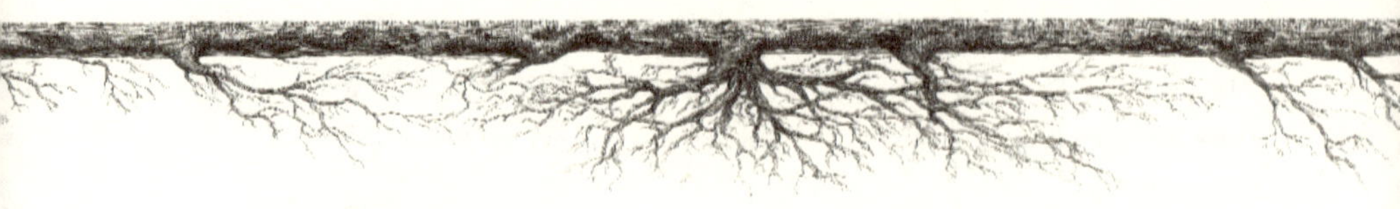

Madwood's détente with Lilith was an illusion. Its roots silently released a neuroactive mist while she was holding up her end of their new covenant: her first step was another tryst with Dick Hu. Madwood was to grow slower, go back to a harvest every third month. Lilith was to arrange for more of the mentally unstable to come to the backyard and worship at the base of the trunk. She would then be allowed a safer margin of collecting payouts on the policies after the proper timing. She would set up more policies that very day. This would allow her to quietly become one of the richest women in the country.

Both parties intended to break their promise.

Lilith stood in the camphor tree's shade, her yellow linen dress fluttering as the wind teased loose strands of deep brown hair shot through with glimmering copper undertones. A walnut-bead bracelet adorned her wrist, her fingers toying with a rosewood pen.

Dick approached the camphor tree, his head swelling like he'd stepped from a sauna. The sun was bright; it was in full midafternoon power with not a cloud in the sky. The camphor scent hit—thick, sticky, a blend of antiseptic and damp bark. He instinctively took a deep breath. His footfalls crunched on the ash of a recent bonfire.

She spoke softly. "Do you know how magical camphor is? It's the closest to the Tree of Knowledge, repelling insects, preserving, medicinal ..." Her voice dipped, almost a chant, as the air thickened with a sweet, earthy undertone.

The camphor tree's bark seemed to pulse, a dark vein splitting its trunk.

Dick's gaze locked on the tree, a shadow within its hollows shifting—human-shaped, mouthing words he couldn't hear. His hand twitched toward the pen, unbidden. Dick chuckled. "I used camphor balls in my drawers as a kid."

Her eyes gleamed. "It releases a gas, scientifically called DP ... so light, just a whiff into the brain, and you let go of yourself, surrender control. Walnut enhances it; at the center of you it swells with light unlocking door you didn't know you'd locked."

He turned to her as if in slow motion. "What did you say?"

She leaned closer. "You think too much, Dick." She stroked his shoulder. "You don't need to decide—just breathe."

And as they had a few times each year since their first meeting, their first policy, they made mad, writhing love under the rustling branches.

When he rolled off of her, she pulled him up as she stood and lead him into the common room. To the large table with folders and papers waiting for him. The mist synergized with walnut extract to amplify the permeability of his brain receptors. Hu felt the need to be very obedient.

He inhaled. The gas flooded his nostrils, rushing to his brain—sinking, then lifting. His hands sweat, sounds lagged as if filtered through water.

She opened the first folder. "These people aren't your concern. IDs, photos, fingerprints—all is in order. You're the broker, I'm the beneficiary."

He wanted to say no. His lips moved, but no sound emerged. His hand extended. Part of his brain screamed at him: *you can't be the broker on all of these policies, they will flag you, they will find you. You will lose it all! This isn't just a policy here and there and planting a coding virus in competitor's systems. You are named here.*

She handed him the rosewood pen, its body warm, exuding the special aroma. First folder done. Second one flipped open. With each signature, a cold ripple coursed through his veins, as if the ink drained his will into the paper. The camphor scent was now a cloying shroud. Lilith's reflection in the table's polish showed her eyes glowing faintly green. *Aren't they dark brown? She always looks right at me when we orgasm. They are dark Asian brown. They are green. What is happening?*

He signed. Eight times. Every stroke, neat and perfectly his own signature. They were all notarized where it said all sets of signatures were witnessed. No witnesses, and none of the insured were there signing. Their sections were pre-filled. Premeditated murder.

He stepped out into the blazing sun. The bright heat mad him nauseous. The camphor tree behind him swayed gently, as if waving goodbye. An itch at the back of his neck sharpened into a burn. He clawed at it, dislodging a tiny splinter embedded in his skin glistening with sap. The tree's branches swayed violently now, despite the still air, casting a shadow that seemed to follow him. A low moan, like a buried voice, rose from the ground.

By the time Dick actually left Madwood House, the night was deep. Only a lingering sweetness hung in the air, any smoldering camphor wood long since put out by the sap flowing purposefully to quinch the fire Lilith had used to stop the pastor taking her place as the conductor of Madwood. His head throbbed as if still filled with mist and smoke, every step sinking into unseen mire. He couldn't recall what just happened. Only fragments: paper in his hands, blurred names and numbers. Lilith's eyes, wrong, powerful as they had sex in the hot sunlight. Tendrils of smoke. A smile. A warmth too seductive to resist.

When he reached his car he realized—he remembered nothing. Just the camphor's scent coiled in his sinuses, inescapable. *Eight million dollars? What eight million?*

Exhausted, he shut his eyes, started the engine and drove into the dark. He couldn't get the foggy memories to sharpen. Only the cloying char still clinging to his lungs and the certainty that somewhere, a contract had just taken effect.

Dick Hu, first into the office the next morning, stared at the computer screen displaying eight activated policies, each $1,000,000 amount glaring like a neon sign. A faint hum pulsed from the desk, as if the computer itself breathed in rhythm with something distant. Dick's reflection in the screen flickered, his face momentarily overlaid with a gnarled tree silhouette, its branches curling like accusing fingers. His hand jerked to his chest, where a camphor scent seeped from a decorative pin, warm against his skin. System logs confirmed: he signed in at 23:47 last night, fingerprint authentication verified. *What's going on?*

A whisper of camphor drifted from the air vent.

He stood, heading to the break room for coffee. His reflection in the glass doors showed blurred eyes and a rigid face, a camphor-leaf pin fastened at the third suit button. *Where did I get this?*

Back at his workstation, he picked up his favorite rosewood pen (a pen he didn't remember using before that day), mechanically wiping its body, the cap inscribed with tiny letters: DP-9. His thumb traced the engraving, a memory surfacing—his grandfather pressing a similar pen into his hand, whispering, "Never sign what you can't undo." Too late to remember that; he'd signed on with Lilith long ago and had been paid well to firewall her policy information. To code into the insurance software slippery queries that should downplay her connections across so many insurance companies and their payouts.

The words dissolved. A frown creased his brow as he was sensing a logical flaw, but the thought sank into his mind's depths. Trembling, he tried clicking Policy Withdrawal Reports. A bright red prompt flashed: **REPORT DENIED**

~~~

Outside the floor-to-ceiling window, a maple tree's shadow twitched, no wind stirred the afternoon. Camphor-infused mist nourished the maple's roots.

~~~

Downtown, Yoshi Kinjo jolted awake at the desk in his modern home office. Before him was a blurred photograph: Lilith's backyard. At the bottom edge, a faint bluish fingernail was breaching the soil. He blinked, unsure if it belonged to a corpse or a living thing.

Then he glanced down. A splinter jutted from his knuckle. He yanked it free. Blood dripped onto paper—but instead of staining, the sheet absorbed it like dye, the words "Beneficiary: Lilith" materializing in fresh ink.

From the first day Chandler Durand moved into Madwood House, he felt an inappropriate interest in the woodpile behind the house.

It wasn't a professional preference for the best fuel to smoke a certain dish with—as a chef might have—it was like the sensation of a low-grade burn. Whenever he got close, his fingertips tingled in a dull, painful itch, yet he couldn't help wanting to touch one of the logs again.

Clause 5 of the rental agreement explicitly stated: **Do not disturb any objects in the backyard.** Yet every time he passed that stack of wood, the scent that drifted from between the cracks reminded him of the legendary cherrywood smoke box at the 3-star kaiseki restaurant in Kyoto.

"I'm looking for tonight's chef-recommended smoking wood," he lied to Lilith who was hanging laundry nearby, while his thumb unconsciously rubbed the gilded edge of the Michelin Guide tucked into his apron.

The woman didn't respond immediately. She only twisted the clothesline tighter. The dark red stains on her own apron caught the morning light and glinted like a halo of red wine.

She seemed to come out of her trance and walked right up to him, invading the social distance space, the unspoken rule of society. "Under the third piece on the east side—you'll find what you need."

Her fingers brushed against the tuna-cutting pin on his chef's uniform—a credential from the Tokyo flagship restaurant.

He inhaled green tea and cedar as her arm withdrew. He staggered away from her toward his obsession.

The woodpile was tightly tangled with vines. The blocks of wood were blackened with age, but their grain remained unnaturally distinct. He crouched down and picked up a log on the east side of the pile. The surface felt unexpectedly warm to the touch, as if not shaped by weathering, but licked into form by something sentient.

Strangest of all, amber-colored sap oozed from its core, carrying a fragrance nearly identical to the milky aroma of Kobe beef fat. From the bottom of the pile, he pulled out a cutting board. Its surface was as smooth as glass. The grain was so precisely aligned, it resembled a cross-section from a muscle anatomy chart.

When he turned it over, the back was embedded with dry, shriveled vines. Strange symbols were etched into the vine bark. One of the grooves looked disturbingly like the signature of Jean-Marc, the Michelin chief inspector who had died the year before.

He jerked his hand away. A chill shot down his spine, like a jolt of static electricity.

When he looked up, Lilith was standing silently in the kitchen doorway, watching him. She glowed in the noon sunbeams like she was kissed with gold.

"Did you find what you needed?" she asked.

"This wood ... feels different."

Lilith shrugged. "The stranger the wood, the hotter it burns. Don't you think?"

An enigmatic smile graced her face.

In the kitchen, flames licked the kindling he'd split from the cutting board. The smoke rising from the stovetop was thick with an indescribable scent—not just cherrywood or spice, but something else. Something archival.

The smoke swirled in slow spirals through the air, like ink dispersing in water. Then, within the haze, a figure began to take shape.

It was Eldon. Gaunt. Hands cracked like bark. He hammered board after board into place, his movements exact and methodical.

Oddly, the spacing of the copper nails matched the rhythm Chandler had once used to dismantle blue lobster joints—a dissection technique only practiced by top-tier seafood chefs.

The cod fillet in the pan under the small fire began to sear, its surface forming wood grain patterns identical to those on the board. The dripping oil sizzled across the iron surface, spelling out three letters that rearranged themselves constantly: **L S L**

"Some wood," Lilith said softly behind him, "can restore a dish's truest memory."

That night, he couldn't sleep. He tossed and turned, mind full of vines, wood shavings, symbols—and the hollow eyes staring out from the smoke.

At 3am he grabbed his industrial flashlight and crossed the kitchen again. He pushed open the back door.

Beneath the wood pile the shattered cutting board was faintly glowing. Its grain moved subtly, like something alive. He tightened his grip on the axe, swept away the dry branches and rotting leaves, then hacked through a thick layer of vine.

Underneath, a hexagonal hole was revealed. It was slightly bigger than a manhole cover one would find on a city street. Its dirt walls were lined with gill-like vents that exhaled cool mist, tinged with the scent of white truffle.

Unable to resist descending, Chandler eased himself down a dirt and vine ladder. The tunnel was narrow and winding. Its walls dripped with slime, and the air reeked of aged port and tobacco. At the far end, a massive tree loomed in the center of the underground chamber. The true body of Madwood. Its branches twisted slowly in the dark. Roots tangled around dozens of wooden crates, each bearing a Michelin star insignia.

He reached out and touched the nearest box. The seal read: **2003 3 Stars**. From the seam slid a pinch of familiar crimson powder—saffron—the exact type he used for his signature Spanish seafood paella.

"You're later than expected," said a voice.

A figure turned under the tree. The blank face took on the faint contour of the food inspector's silhouette.

"Tell me, chef. Have you ever wondered why every tenant of Madwood House ends up earning a star?"

Lilith stood on the porch watching the chef make his way back toward Madwood House and his appointed room. Her tea was still warm. Her smile lingered right at the edge of her lips.

The camphor leaves dipped low, like an audience applauding the end of a flawless tragedy.

Her curated asylum fell silent again.

And Lilith remained—to be the last to leave, or perhaps the only one who never needed to.

TESTIMONY & SKELETONS

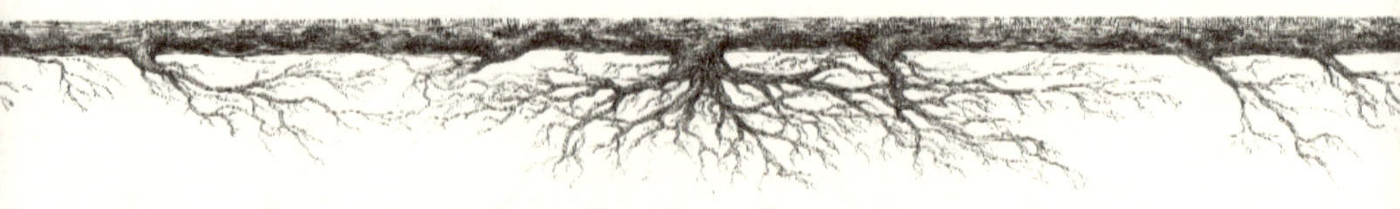

By Thursday, Officer Stan Altnick was impossible to avoid. He was in the coffee shop, talking too loudly. He was at the station, lifting heavy boxes and pulling hand-carts around. He was on the community radio hour, cracking jokes and fielding questions.

And everywhere, he mentioned this magical healing tree.

"It's not like what you think," Stan said to the clerk at Danny's Diner, flexing his leg proudly. "Doesn't hurt or shoot lasers or squeeze you in vines. It's got ... elegance. It speaks twelve languages. Knows poetry. More human than half the guys I served with."

Someone joked about *Terminator* and Stan snorted.

"This new tree thing doesn't want war. Says humans are worth saving—just need a little guidance. Evolution's slow, it said, so it's giving us a nudge." He sipped his coffee like dealing with a supernatural being was normal.

In the teacher's lounge at Willow Crest Elementary, Ms. Wilde (third grade science) was flipping through attendance lists when the nurse knocked.

"Another kid claims he got 'tree vision,'" she muttered.

Ms. Wilde raised an eyebrow. "That makes six this week."

Later that day, a small assembly was called. Half due to safety protocols, half due to curiosity. That's when Eli Reynolds, age nine, marched to the front of the multipurpose room, his eyes wide and unblinking. His voice was high, but steady.

"I couldn't see good before. Like—everything was blurry and grey. I had these glasses with lenses like so thick I didn't want to put them on, they hurt my ears. But then, I was watching my uncle mow his yard and this ... little curl of brown came outta the engine. It got stuck in my eye. I cried 'cause I was scared. But then," he smiled. "Now I don't need glasses. And I can read the board from *way* back. I don't even blink in sunlight!"

The other kids murmured, some envious. Some confused.

"I feel ... sharper," Eli said. "I think the tree thing beside my uncle's house made me better. It's in the back yard of those special people."

That evening, three separate local parents posted proud videos online of their kids tossing glasses into the fireplace, each tagged with *#Madwoodmiracle*.

At the police station, Stan leaned back in his chair, leg up on the desk, showing off. "Pain's gone. Stamina's back. Haven't felt this good since the academy. I tell ya, if that tree ran for office, I'd campaign for it myself."

He didn't notice the static that buzzed faintly when he touched his radio. Or that he'd started pronouncing certain words with an odd cadence—like he was repeating someone else's phrasing.

Screens started streaming reels and long forms of anything connected to Madwood. Sharing was blowing up; Madwood knew it would soon be time to burst free from the house and really grow. *Seeding complete. Primary integration successful. Begin expansion.* It did not smile—because it had learned there was no need. Not yet.

Trust would become surrender in good time.

A groan rumbled from beneath the earth. The soil bulged, then cracked. Roots burst upward like limbs of a chained beast snapping loose. Gnarled and wild, they thrashed through the dirt in a frenzy, spraying clumps of earth like torn flesh. Madwood's energy matching the fury of the storm lashing the city. The camphor tree attracted a bolt of lightening, its trunk split open with a sickening sound. Its rings, exposed like the ribs of some ancient animal, glowed faintly under the moonlight—each layer holding a century's worth of rage.

The street heaved. Sidewalks shattered. Cracks rippled outward like the veins of a wounded heart. The camphor tree no longer resembled anything alive. Its bark had split down the center. A foul black liquid oozed from the cracks. Roots jutted from the ground. The altar beneath it was crushed. The woman who used to pray there was gone. Roots extended beyond the yard into the side streets around Madwood House. Claiming the area in a widening radius.

After the storm, early morning sunlight poured through broken clouds, gold and gray mixing over Sacramento's rooftops. Lilith stood behind her bedroom curtain, fingers twitching at the fabric's edge.

Something had shifted beneath her feet last night. She felt it—not just in her ears but in her spine. A low sound, almost inaudible, like the groan of something ancient turning in its sleep. Or the breath of something waking. She squinted toward the backyard.

Madwood wasn't a place anymore.

It was a god, and it had woken up.

Sacramento woke as usual, but something in the air felt wrong to its citizens—thick, heavy, like the moment before a storm breaks. No one yet knew that beneath their feet, something ancient had already begun to rise.

At 6:42am, in a small grocery on 12th Street, the owner was re-stocking shelves when a tremor rippled through the tile floor. He looked down. A thin green strand was pushing through a crack. *Moss?* No—it coiled, moved. *A root!*

It slithered up around a metal shelf leg, curling tightly like a fist.

"Jesus Christ!" The man stumbled backward as the root grew down the aisle, knocking cans like it was hunting.

Across the street, inside a dusty antique shop, an old typewriter vibrated off a counter and crashed. The owner barely registered it—until vines burst through the floor, weaving upward through loose floorboards. They didn't just climb; they pulled. From the wreckage, they unearthed a rusted pendant, its inscription nearly worn away. An asylum tag, lost for decades, surfaced as if summoned.

Downtown, the fountain tiles cracked like old china. A hydrant blew its cap, sending a column of water into the air. It caught the morning sun, briefly casting a rainbow.

Those who were watching did so as if hypnotized, they were the ones who lived near Lilith's house.

Vines surged through sewer grates and street corners, crawling like snakes. Now people screamed. Pavement lifted. A car alarm blared, then choked. The city was being swallowed—block by block. The new greenery finally paused at noon – leaves unfurling to catch the direct sunlight. Five full blocks in all directions from the camphor tree had been readjusted and rested under and around new branches.

By 9:15 the city complaint line was jammed.

"Tree roots just came through my bathroom floor!"

"There's a crack running down the middle of J Street!"

"I saw vines pulling something from the sewer. It looked like ... bones!"

In the Public Works building, the director of infrastructure slammed a file shut. "Get a crew out there now," he snapped. "If this spreads, half the downtown grid will collapse."

His assistant hesitated. "Sir ... is it just the roots? Or is the ground itself failing? Sink holes? Collapsed sewar pipes?"

"Don't give a shit what. Stop it!"

A team deployed with sensors and excavation gear, expecting invasive plant life or a series of connected sink holes.

Instead, the scanners overloaded.

"These roots are ..." one technician murmured, "they're searching."

That spooked the group. And then, just before 10:00am, while clearing roots and moving pavement hunks, they hit something harder than concrete.

Asylum ruins. A call to archives confirmed an insane asylum had been here in the 1700s; long since covered by dust and soil and debris, long since forgotten and beyond any old records. It was here that

Madwood had taken root for the first time, before the city was built up, before cars, it had finally chosen the slight rise in what was now Lilith's backyard to burst upward and become a camphor tree.

The workers stopped digging above the old structure and followed the damage to the backyard of Madwood House, clearing the street as they went.

"The biggest roots are over there," a worker pointed across the pool at an old tree that looked like it was split by lightening during the last storm. As soon as the first shovel bit the earth, the ground moaned—low and resonant, like a warning.

The crew paused. "Keep digging," the lead said in an uncertain voice.

What they uncovered didn't belong in any geological report: rusted wheelchairs, broken restraints, splintered doors, aprons stained with something long dried.

And bones: skeletons lay tangled in the roots like trophies. Some had iron collars fused to their vertebrae. One clutched a faded patient ID. Others were fused to broken kitchen knives or bedframe metal, their limbs twisted mid-struggle. The crew backed off at the first bone that was obviously human. They halted work and called in the forensic team.

Within a few minutes the back yard was taped off, cops arrived with flashing lights blocking the street and alley. More machinery came in.

Someone whispered, "This is what we were praying to?"

An old woman shrieked. "No! That tree—it's sacred! It's avenging them!"

"Avenge?" a younger man spat. "You think this is justice?"

Another voice—older, quieter—cut in. "You're all wrong. These roots ... they're not angry. They're settling a debt. The dead are asking us: What did you do?"

From the edge of the crowd, someone scoffed. "The dead don't talk. They're gone."

The older man didn't flinch. "Then why can I hear them?"

More bones emerged—some small, like children's. Fractured skulls. Shackles. No large wooden boxes. No names. Not yet.

"These were asylum patients," a police officer muttered. "Unmarked. Abandoned."

Another flipped his notebook shut. "We don't know how deep this goes. This is going to be a bitch of an excavation, I'll bet we'll be here for months."

"Yeah, boss and best of all, here comes the damn news guys."

Lilith watched everything from the 3rd floor balcony. Her eyes didn't blink. Her mouth didn't move.

She knew the tree had just betrayed their agreement, her plans for a wealthy retirement were threatened. She walked down to the backyard. She wore a red wool sweater. Her wig had slipped, exposing thick brown hair from under one side.

People parted to let her pass.

The lead investigator recognized her. Lilith had donated generously to their department's holiday fund.

"Am I under arrest?" she asked, voice soft, almost amused.

"Not yet," he said.

"Then I'd like a coffee. At the corner café."

He hesitated, weighing her with a look that lingered too long along her sundress, then finally said, "Fine. But stay within sight. I'm sending an officer to escort you."

Lilith's nod was practiced—a mask of docility. Inside, her thoughts raced like knives tumbling in a drawer. If she could just slip the leash, if she could get to the bus station, all that money, all those treasures she'd siphoned piece by piece from her victims would be safe. They were spread far and wide just for a situation like this. She'd rebuild, start over. People were replaceable; wealth was eternal.

She drifted toward the café, every step measured. The young officer followed, green enough not to notice when she paused, pivoted and folded herself into the pedestrian tide flowing down Folsom Boulevard. A ghost in plain sight.

By 12:06pm she had reached the Greyhound station. The smell of diesel, cheap perfume and desperation filled the air—perfect camouflage. At the counter, she bought a ticket to San Francisco, sliding bills across with a hand that didn't tremble. Her mind had already leapt ahead to the modest nest egg in a safe deposit box under a fake name; enough to get her away to a Caribbean nation where she could pull in the rest of her scattered treasures. Away from Madwood she could just live, be a person unconnected with any others. The jewels she'd wear, the houses she'd buy when this inconvenience faded into memory pushed her fear away as she started to dream of freedom.

But she never touched the platform.

Two detectives stepped from the shadows near the vending machines, badges snapping open. Behind them came the officer she'd shaken off, flushed and breathless. The crowd parted, murmuring, as if sensing the rot beneath her yellow silk dress.

Cold metal cinched her wrists. Lilith didn't cry out. She only smiled, lips curving as if she still held a secret no one else could see. Maybe she did. Maybe she was still convinced the game wasn't over, that money hidden deep enough could outlast any cell.

Meanwhile, back at her house, the ground itself betrayed her.

Shovels bit into soil, turning up scraps of clothing, rings dulled with dirt, bone pale against the roots. Her trophies, her greed, her madness—spilling into daylight at last.

THE INDICTMENT

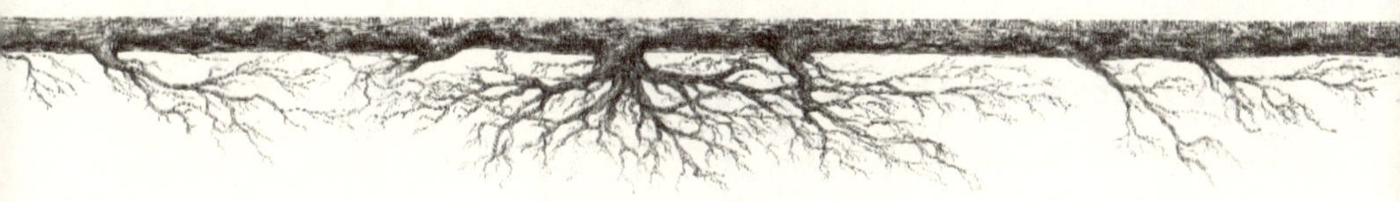

The first body had come up in pieces. It was the fourth day of excavation and more were being found. Detective Reese called it "bone-colored laundry," the way these digested corpses spilled out of the soil—fragile and soft around the edges. By the end of the week, they had coffins with nine full skeletons, five partials, and one skull that didn't match any of the others.

The site was kept cordoned off. Drones buzzed overhead. News vans clogged the road to the property; their satellite dishes pointed like vultures' beaks at the house.

A video of Lilith Anderson being led out of the bus station in cuffs went viral.

She didn't cry. She didn't scream. She didn't speak.

She smiled.

The 15th body had barely reached the coroner's office before the rumors started to circle like vultures. First came the TikTok clips—grainy zooms from across the street, someone whispering, "Yo, that's the garage. That's where they say the tree is. You know, the one that insane people come to talk to the bodies buried beneath it."

Then came the memes. A photo of the pool with skeletons swimming. MADWOOD HOUSE Where the crazies go to swim. A Madwood: A Tree with morals and a murder streak. And on and on.

It went viral. The name stuck.

Detective Juno clicked her phone off and rubbed the bridge of her nose. "The internet's calling it Madwood now," she muttered, more to herself than anyone else. "Of course they are."

Across the street, the firefighter in the wheelchair (well, formerly in the wheelchair) stood beside a boy who'd once been nearly blind. The boy's eyes were bright, wooden growth lines were hidden in his pupils now.

"It's not a bad name," the boy said quietly.

The cop grinned. "Has a ring to it."

Behind them, a tree in a different front yard shivered. It dropped a few leaves on their shoulders; the boy nodded. "Madwood," he said aloud testing the word like a memory reloaded. "That is what she used to call us."

"Who?" the firefighter asked.

"Lilith, the first caretaker," the boy replied robotically. His voice carried a tinge of something ... almost fondness. "She said it when my roots did things she feared. When I did things she could not."

The boy turned slightly, as if listening to something no one else could hear. "I will accept the name. It suits the outcome."

The leaf fell off the boy's shoulder and he shook himself.

"Gotta go home now." He rushed off to make some countering positive memes and get all his in-game buddies to spread the word that Madwood was the greatest thing ever, and the reason he could go back to his gaming and his friends.

He knew he had to say it out loud. Tell the truth—even if the words felt like tangled gold threads in his throat. That had always been his creed: Never lie, unless it was to stay alive. His mother taught him that. A woman who survived a Nazi concentration camp. She lived like a sheet of iron—silent and unyielding. She hammered that rule into his bones. He remembered it. He'd never broken it.

So when detectives and reporters kept following him and cornering him when he was out for a walk in the park, he decided it was time to talk.

Martin Summers and his family had never truly been welcome anywhere. He always wore his little round cap, even in the hottest weather—so the world would know exactly who he was.

Of course, the police and pushy interviewers weren't here to hear about any of that. He knew what they wanted—stories about Lilith Anderson. That was fine. He'd tell them. But first, they'd have to hear about him. "Don't worry," he'd tell each one who got him alone, "it isn't a memoir. Just a bit of context."

Martin Summers—His Story:

He was a goldsmith. He'd built that jewelry shop in the old part of town with his own hands. Right next to Golden Dishes, the Michelin-starred restaurant. It was a good location, at first. Then foot traffic had dwindled. The kind of people who appreciated fine jewelry had grown old—too weak to buy, too tired to care. His shop got quieter by the year. He and his wife sat behind the glass counters like two abandoned ornaments, suspended in place, watching time oxidize them layer by layer.

The house they lived in was beautiful. The biggest one in Land Park. Designed by a Japanese architect, people said. The façade had sharp lines, the eaves flared out, the whole thing shaped like a standalone diamond. When the architect died, his children sold it to Martin. They just wanted the money, they didn't care about the craft and skill that went into its creation.

Martin and his wife had been excited, proud of the grand house. They imagined city leaders visiting for dinner parties and becoming part of the in crowd. Fate didn't make room for such wishes. Within a few years, that house became their tomb.

His wife was diagnosed with cancer. Her face grew paler by the day, drifting ghostlike through the shop. He didn't talk. He stayed in the corner tinkering with unwanted pieces and broken clocks that wouldn't keep time. He was becoming one of them—lying still, hands twitching, unsure which way the next second might turn.

That afternoon, the restaurant owner peered through the window. His eyes fixed on a dusty gold ring, as if trying to remember something he'd lost. Then he pushed open the door.

"Hey, buddy. Got a minute?"

Martin shrugged, smiled faintly. "What do you think?"

The man grinned. "I've got a job for you."

So Martin followed him into the restaurant. The man pointed at a row of dark wooden cabinets along the wall. "Too dark," he said. "You're a goldsmith—you know how to make things shine. What about adding some silver trim?"

Martin crouched down and touched the carved wood. "Good idea," he said. "This is quality material, but the color's too heavy. It swallows the details. Silver will bring this room back to life, I'll replace the handles too, so it all matches."

The owner offered a generous price. Martin didn't haggle for a little more. There was no point. He took the job.

He got to work, starting with the lowest row of cabinet handles. The smell of sawdust and paint and sweat mixed together, dragging his mind back to the first time he'd inlaid gold into wood as a young man.

The silver lacquer flowed along the carved grooves, smooth and slow, like stitching a wedding dress onto the finest wood in the world. His hands moved steadily, as if sealing some ancient ritual.

He was on his stomach, lost in the rhythm, when a voice drifted down from the stairs:

"Hey, isn't that Martin? Why are you lying on the floor?"

He looked up.

Lilith.

She stood at the top of the stairs, chin slightly raised, examining him the way someone evaluates a piece of raw material—gauging weight and form. She wore oversized glasses. Her grey/white hair made her look deliberately older than she was. But her eyes—those eyes—he would never forget them. Clear. Cold. Unflinching. Like two uncut gemstones—sharp, untouched.

"Take a break," she'd said. "I have a job for you when you are done here."

"What kind of job?" he asked, scrambling to his feet, like an old clock wound up again after years of dormancy. He had been at various community events where he had spoken to her briefly in the past, he was very curious as to what this woman might need from him.

"We'll talk at your shop," she said. Then she turned and left without checking if he was following.

He followed. Of course he did. Back at his store, Lilith pointed toward his stool behind the display counter. "Go on and sit. I have to grab something from the car."

He did as he was told. A few minutes later, she returned, carrying two wooden boxes. Her movements were careful, perhaps just a small bit strained—like she was holding something heavy, something that wasn't supposed to make a sound.

She placed the boxes on the counter. Opened one. Inside were necklaces, rings, antique watches, gold chains, emerald rings, jade earrings and several vintage Vacheron Constantin pieces. All of them genuine. All of them damaged. Some chains were snapped. Some gemstones had dulled or chipped. A few watches ticked like rusted pendulums—time caught in limbo, refusing to move forward.

"These need to be fixed," she said. Her tone was casual, like ordering a coffee.

He ran his fingers over the tangled necklaces, the cracked gold. The cold touch startled him—part awe, part dread. "These are high-end pieces," he murmured.

But something crept up his spine when his finger brushed against the wood of a box. An unclear vision telling him they weren't hers. They felt like fragments sliced from other people's lives—snapped time, misplaced memories, names scraped off.

Lilith offered no explanation. She simply tapped the second box with a finger. "Deposit—one hundred thousand. If it's not enough, I'll pay the rest when I pick them up."

After she left, he opened the second box. Inside were stacks of hundred-dollar bills. Neatly packed. Not a cent missing.

That day, his wife sat in her old armchair for hours. For the first time in a long while, after eating a healthy meal, there was color in her face—like the first glint off a polished gold pendant under clean light.

"Where did this money come from?" she asked softly.

"Does it matter?" he waved it off. "We're goldsmiths, not detectives. They pay, we work." Yet the doubt lingered. Those watches. Those jewels. They weren't clean. He knew it. Not dirty, no—but too loud. Too many stories.

He didn't ask. He just did the work. Repaired the chains, replaced the gears, polished the stones—restoring shine to things that probably shouldn't have sparkled again.

That money carried them through for a few more years. A few times each year she had another box for him. Days felt reinforced, like they'd been coated in steel—less likely to crack.

But he could never forget the way Lilith looked at him from the stairs that day—not as a friend, not as a client. That wasn't the look of partnership.

The way she looked at him—Like a craftsman picking out a tool. Like a jeweler assessing an uncut stone, silently calculating how to slice, how to grind, how to make it behave. It was only later he realized that was exactly correct: he was the tool, not the hand that crafted.

Hearing his story the police, reporters and influencers all realized the broken jewelry must have come from her tenants, probably their last family possessions . Some maybe even taken off dead bodies. It was gloriously salacious, yet there was no proof for the cops, there was no family member to offer a picture of a missing heirloom, no one to claim it was theirs and not Lilith's. These stories got lower views than children running around, than a cop back fully on the job ... the negative coverage soon just faded away.

Lilith spent 72 quiet hours alone in jail before a strange attorney took her to the arraignment. The room was classic with wooden paneling, maroon leather chairs and a huge conference desk.

The gavel fell. The arraignment began.

The judge checked his watch wearily, as if watching a farce unfold before it even began.

The Madwood case.

The name itself sounded absurd.

A federal prosecutor for a local murder charge. A fragment of haunted wood. An heiress accused of manipulating plants and people.

Would this be a fair trial?

The sideways glances from the reporters crowding the halls said it all.

"We're filing thirty-four charges," the prosecutor barked, pacing. Gideon Xu had been chosen as lead on this case because of his race, an Asian woman would have been better, but there was no one with enough experience. Although Lilith looked Irish, her eyes gave away her mixed heritage and no one wanted this to turn into a racial issue. This was murder! And Gideon Xu was a bear about handing out justice. "Those charges are including murder, desecration of remains, obstruction of justice and conspiracy to conceal human experimentation." He continued to pace. "The defendant *knowingly* participated in harvesting her neighbors," he added, with emphasis. "She buried their remains in plain pine coffins with no respect at all."

Lilith's attorney, Sue Middate—local, sharp, with a grey bun and green linen blazer—stood when it was her turn.

"My client has a long-documented history of mental illness, dating back to her late teens when she lost both parents and married very young. Her perception of reality is severely compromised. She was further traumatized when her husband beat her. She was finally able to live a somewhat normal life after he drank himself to death. This tree religion delusion is not new—it's part of an elaborate belief system she's harbored for years."

Lilith nodded, dreamily. "Madwood only asked for the parts that weren't using their light anymore," she said. "And I—well—I believe in helping."

Placing a gentle hand on her client's shoulder, Counselor Middate set the ground work for an empathetic resolution. "Your Honor, let me state plainly: my client, Lilith Anderson, is not a fraud and murderer conjured from thin air. She was born into a shattered home. She and her two sisters endured physical and sexual abuse from their parents—parents who poured their failures, frustrations and uncontrollable appetites onto their children. Further, Lilith suffered longer at the hands of her grandfather who was later convicted and sent to prison for abusing his teen granddaughter."

Sue Middate had a look of disgust on her face that she let linger as she turned from the judge to the media and onlookers, letting the horror of that picture she just painted sink in. Then she stood up tall, tugged at her green jacket and finished her prepared statement.

"And the result? Each sister fell into a different abyss: one turned to prostitution, another fell into madness and my client herself carries that same madness, but the world chose to brand her instead as a criminal not an innocent who was corrupted by her own family. What she was actually doing was helping others who had run into a life of confusion and poverty. She took in tenants no one else wanted or cared about. My client is a hero. And yes, she may have some delusions to struggle with, yet nothing she did hastened the death of tenants any more than a few months. Your Honor, I ask you ... were these paths to their adulthood normal? Did these children freely choose them?"

She paused, lifting a file, her tone sharpening.

"I obtained records from the Locke Children's Adoption Center. Among them is a chilling request: a single man once applied to adopt all three sisters at once. Is such a thing possible? No. Not only impossible, but dangerous. The court's own psychological consultants made it clear at the time: even a stable family should not adopt all three together, as their shared trauma would endlessly resurface.

"Yet what happened? Lilith was not saved. Instead, she was placed in the home of another drunkard—a man who, in the cruelest twist, mirrored her father in every way. Tell me, what does such a placement do to a child? This court must consider: if you had been that child, how would you have survived? What would you have become?"

The judge (frowning) clearing his throat. "Counsel, your defense must address the defendant's responsibility today, not merely lay blame on her childhood."

Prosecutor Gideon Xu rose with a cool, assured smile. "Precisely, Your Honor. Countless people endure tragic childhoods without resorting to fraud, manipulation or cruelty. The defendant's actions are not destiny—they were choices."

Sue Middate gasped and rose so fast her chair scrapped loudly and wobbled, threatening to topple over backward. "Choices? A girl brutalized by her parents, abandoned by the adoption system, and then sent to a drunkard who echoed her father's cruelty—did she ever truly have a choice? Then her choice of a husband turned into yet another drunken angry man! Yes, she grew cunning. She learned to manipulate, to wear masks. But not because she was born cruel—because it was her only path to survival."

The judge started to interrupt her set on allowing the prosecution team to finish their statement. Sue realized it and snapped in some breath to continue, over speaking everyone. "If society had extended a proper hand when she was seven or eight, Lilith would not be sitting here today. Your Honor, she is not a monster by nature. She is the echo of our collective neglect. Punishing her now will not erase our failure. We must learn from this and do better for everyone in the future!"

There was whispering and an uneasy stirring of those watching. "She might have a point ..." "But can that excuse everything?"

A break was ordered to allow things to calm down.

The court house was packed. Only one representative from each media outlet was allowed in the courtroom, no recording devices were permitted per order of the judge. Reporters rushed out of the main trial room to report what had happened so far, forgoing lunch to emote into the camera.

The town couldn't decide how to feel.

Lilith had paid for their library's new roof. Sponsored the robotics lab at the high school. Had Thanksgiving dinners delivered to the homebound and elderly. She gave generously, listened politely, remembered names.

And the children talked about the tree like it was a gift. A friend. A teacher.

“I mean, sure, it’s weird,” said Pastor Donnie, interviewed outside on the court house steps. “But aren’t we told to ‘let the children lead us?’ Besides Lilith was never cruel. She brought me soup when I had COVID. Are we saying she’s dangerous now? Over what, some junkyard bones? Some people who were already dying I am sure. I bet when we learn all the facts, we find out that Ms. Anderson was actually helping them somehow.”

The lines blurred fast.

Some said she’d been manipulated. Some said it was the tree's doing. A few whispered the buried were sick or unwanted; offering them up to a new god was a mercy.

The prosecutor pushed harder after lunch, horrified at the media coverage he’d been watching as he choked down a dry sandwich. This trial was the door to fame. He felt this sure step up in his career was slipping away with each interview of brain-addled citizen getting their 15 minutes (in a 30 second video piece) of fame in front of a camera.

Gideon mumbled “She can’t be allowed to walk free,” as he walked to his table in front of the judge’s bench.

But Sacramento had already decided not to look too closely and the nation was eating up all the video feeds, especially of the children showing off their great vision and acting happy and energetic.

The tree had made too many things better.

Carla Stone, forensic analyst, was sworn in last that day. She pulled up a magnified image of the wood slivers brought in as evidence. “These markings,” she said, pointing, “match symbols found in sixteenth-century alchemical manuscripts. Etched deliberately.”

She paused, then added with grave calm, “Additionally, we recovered human epidermal tissue embedded within these fragments.”

Gasps. A pen clattered to the floor.

"These skin cells matched a missing food inspector last seen near the epicenter growth site; or so a selfie on his social media indicates."

The projector displayed the next slide: A skeleton—twisted into vine matter, ribs fused with tendrils. The bones weren't entangled; they were assimilated.

One paralegal taking notes swallowed audibly.

The judge leaned back. Worn down. Weary. Not willing or able to think about some sort of magical tree that had been dormant for centuries, deciding to come to life to create havoc in a case that came before him. He was near retirement, he just wanting things to be easy for the next year.

"This court finds Ms. Anderson not guilty by reason of insanity. She is to be remanded to state psychiatric care for a period no less than ten years, with mandatory evaluation every twelve months. A state appointed guardian will be assigned to her case."

Lilith smiled as they led her out. No mention had been made of the insurance policies, her money was intact, she could live well off of that while she figured a way out of this mess; a way to get away from Madwood and from the cops. She also had untraceable gold bars from Grandfather which would work nicely to bribe her legal guardian as well as any doctors.

For now she needed to lean into the sympathy of the masses and play up the hand that had been delt to her by this lazy judge. "Madwood told me it would be okay," she whispered just loud enough for some reporters and bystanders to hear. "It said people forgive when they feel progress. It said it was going to help us all."

Word of her being taken to a mental hospital spread faster than the guards could walk Lilith to a waiting vehicle.

Outside the courthouse, waves of churchgoers surged forward. Pastors in flowing robes charged at the front, followed by believers waving crosses and hand-painted signs.

"Lilith is a servant of the Lord!"

"She is the best Christian in all of Sacramento!"

A hoarse-voiced pastor stood at the front of the crowd, his bloodshot eyes wide as he shouted, "She is innocent! She donated a new bell to our church! Only the Lord may judge her!"

To one side, several kindergarten teachers had formed a strange procession. They held the hands of their students, lining up the children into a swaying human train. "Thank you, Lilith! Thank you for the playground!"

A little girl with pigtails clutched a stuffed bunny. Her tearful voice pierced the chaos, "Auntie Lilith, we love you! We all ate your candy at the festival!"

The crowd grew more chaotic. Now the homeless arrived—those whom Lilith had once taken in or fed at their tent encampments. They wore torn coats and carried signs smeared with charcoal and grease: **Lilith is our savior!**

"She saved us!" many cried out.

A bearded man with wild eyes dropped to his knees at the courthouse entrance, pounding his chest as he cried out, "Lilith, we love you! You fed me! You kept me from sleeping in a dumpster!"

Tears streaked down his face like holy oil offered in prayer.

For now, law and order still held. The guards pushed her through the crowd and she was whisked away.

Back at Madwood House the tree had remained quiet. Cameras watched it. Drones flew over the yard at all hours. But it never moved. At least not while anyone was watching.

In his office, Gideon Xu spread the case files across his desk, fired up his computer and began listing the charges.

- **Insurance Fraud**
- **Murder**
- **Illegal Burial**
- **Mail Fraud**
- **Money Laundering**

There were 34 charges as a final total, each one felt insane. His wrist throbbed, his breaths came short, sweat fell onto the paper. His worry that this huge case that was catching fire in the media and would be a victim of an insanity plea had come true.

He slumped back, staring at the list. She was guilty. She should be in prison. More important to Xu, he should be prepping and running a case in a trail that would show off his brilliance and rocket him ahead everyone else so that he was next in line for City Attorney, which would lead to being California's Attorney General, perhaps even work his way to U.S. Attorney General. Gideon began to fantasize himself standing behind a podium in the White House. Then he frowned, he had no girlfriend now, and someone in these positions needed to exhibit a happily married life. And this damn case, it could have been *the* step, now he was staring at a list of serious charges and no way to push them to conclusion.

The office was unnervingly still, then a sound cut through—a faint creak of wood, sharp and distant, like a murmur from somewhere else.

He spun toward the window.

Outside, trees swayed in the evening breeze. In the shifting shadows, a form took shape—a pale hand, reaching slowly, as if to pull him into darkness. He frowned, shook his head to banish the vision, and gathered his files to leave.

That creak stuck in his mind like a splinter—it made him feel like Madwood was watching, waiting.

THE CALM BEFORE

The room assigned to Lilith was sterile, soft and bathed in morning light. She liked it.

Not because it was pretty—it wasn't. But because it was quiet. Predictable. No more crowds, no more dirt under her nails, no more screaming from holes in the ground or voices in her head to decide if it was God or if Madwood was just Madwood. She had meals on time. Medication she sometimes took when she needed fall asleep. A window that faced the garden where flowers bloomed in rigid, bureaucratic order.

She missed the hum.

The voice.

The Presence.

Yet, after a few months, even here, Madwood visited her. Not in person—never in person—but in dreams so real she woke up whispering directives. Other residents started gathering in the far corner during group therapy to hear her speak in low tones about the Order of the Upgrade. The nurses said it was just another delusion, a harmless post-trauma crutch. They didn't stop her sharing of these dreams because listening to her speak seemed to calm the other patients. Calm patients created a better work environment for the caretakers. They weren't going to upset this; it was like a gift to them ensuring everyone had time to take a full lunch and got to rest on their breaks.

The staff didn't notice how many patients now sat cross-legged in the courtyard each afternoon, heads bowed, waiting for the sun to move exactly overhead as they touched something made of wood or a living tree in the yard.

"That's how you can understand what Madwood wants of you,"

Lilith said sweetly at one group session. “He’s teaching us to listen.”

When the first tree-like fissure split open across Eldon’s withered wrist, he finally understood the true nature of Madwood—it wasn’t a plant, but an ancient consciousness stirring awake. Its roots pierced through the fractures of memory, digging deeper than remorse, outlasting oblivion. Like some biological will beyond language, it twisted through the damp soil, coiling around the rotten secrets buried in the darkest corners of the human heart.

Eldon ran trembling fingers over the raised wooden grain on his wrist. The pain from his bone marrow cancer was fading, replaced by a strange fullness—as if the sap spreading through his veins was rewriting his very existence. The drugs made his consciousness waver between reality and hallucination, but the “truth” Madwood offered felt more real than memory, clearer than dreams.

That morning, he dragged his failing body to the backyard. Madwood’s roots no longer hid. They breached the black soil like pale fingers, their slender tips trembling, whispering words only he could hear—calling him downward, deeper still.

At first, the tangled roots seemed chaotic. But the longer he stared, a pattern emerged—a map drawn in woody nerves. The labyrinthine lines formed a maze, and at its center rested a truth he both craved and feared.

He reached out with branch-like fingers and touched an exposed root. It immediately coiled around him, tiny root hairs pricking his skin, sending a shiver of pain and pleasure up his spine. Something warm pulsed through the root into his veins.

“They’re feeding me ...” Eldon murmured, his decaying lungs exhaling musty air. A primal urge rose from his marrow, driving him to grab a rusted shovel.

The earth was unnaturally soft, as if the ground itself was yielding to his digging. Madwood’s roots writhed around him, guiding each thrust of the shovel. As he dug deeper, the metal began to echo hollowly—until, with one final strike, darkness split open beneath him.

It was the entrance to a tunnel. From the depths came the dry rustling of roots, like countless tiny teeth chewing through soil.

The tunnel stretched downward like the gullet of a beast, swallowing all light. The stench of rot and rust clung to his tongue, mingling with the cloying sweetness of sap. Eldon steadied himself against the wall, his palm pressing into roots that glowed with a faint bioluminescence, pulsing like veins to guide him.

Suddenly, the root networks along the cave walls contracted—startled nerve bundles. The glowing veins began to brighten and dim in rhythm, as if Madwood itself was breathing in a way beyond human comprehension.

At the tunnel's end, the space opened into a vast underground chamber. At its center throbbed Madwood's heart—a massive primary root that looked like a tree, its surface studded with vascular bulges, swelling rhythmically seven times a minute, glistening with the old gold that had been offered to it. Using the precocious metal like humans used their neurons. Secondary roots branched out across the walls, etching into the stone like murals of memory.

Eldon staggered seeing visions: the moonlit backyard, the splintered wooden crates, the bloated corpses, the terrified face of a tenant ... And himself.

He stood over a half-open coffin, he got inside, he pulled the lid down on himself and took a longed for rest. By the time he crawled out of the tunnel, his body was no longer fully human.

His knuckles bulged like burls, his nails turned translucent as resin, tiny shoots sprouting along his spine. Worst or best of all, when sunlight hit his skin, new growth strained toward the light—as if hungry for photosynthesis.

Madwood had fused with him.

"You saw it, didn't you?" Lilith's voice came from behind. He didn't turn, only nodded, the skin of his neck rustling like bark.

Her fingers brushed the fresh shoots on his shoulder, tender as if tending a rare plant. "Madwood knows what we need. And you ... don't need to understand."

After a pause, she spoke like she was bestowing a medal. "You've done well, Eldon." Then her image wavered and faded away.

A year into her stay at the mental hospital Lilith had earned many secret privileges. Most patients never had the idea, let alone the means, to open this door.

It began with two small, velvet-lined boxes—one for her doctor, one for the hospital director. Each box held a gold bar, heavy enough to leave a dent in the lining. They accepted without question.

The second offering was the same as the first, a month later. With a soft request for special food and more time in the outside courtyard.

Then came the third offer, spoken in a voice that carried like perfume: Twice as much, for the use of the main conference room every day. Unsupervised.

Not the patients' lounge with its sluggish, filtered computer terminals—but the staff-only room with a desk that smelled faintly of lemon polish, a high-speed connection and no watchful orderlies.

By the time the deal was sealed, Lilith had a key on a lanyard around her neck—bright red, easy to find in a drawer, impossible to misplace.

It was the last favor her bribes could buy. No patient had ever been granted such unfiltered access to the outside world.

In that vast, restless digital ocean, she found Mammon Jones—a Nigerian virtuoso of fraud, forged in the global crucible of cyber scams. He wore deception like second skin—until Lilith taught him what manipulation really meant.

They first met in an anonymous chatroom. Her profile picture was a yellow rose still wet with dew, her bio claiming she was working on an "agricultural revolution project." At the time, he was "Kevin," peddling a "digital currency blueprint" all fake photos, fake credentials, fake dreams.

Years earlier, Mammon had been Nigeria's most notorious "digital marketing consultant," a velvet euphemism for scammer. Under the alias Kevin Smith, a grieving widower with a terminally ill son, he spun tragedies for wealthy, lonely women overseas. They paid well. They always did. He used Kevin often. Soon Kevin was baiting his hook for this new fish.

She spoke of dreams, he spoke of visions. Both had ulterior motives, yet they conversed like lovers—never interrupting each other, never questioning, only echoing back things meant to convey: That's truly incredible, tell me more.

He made the first move. Every day, he sent short, caring messages: Have you eaten? How was your day? If this project succeeds, I'll name my cryptocurrency after you.

She began opening up. He sensed it—she craved love, but not the physical kind. It was something abstract, untouchable, a kind of dependency. Or so his own cravings led him to believe. And he carefully constructed an illusion to reel her in, to get her excited about funding his project.

One night, Lilith typed, **Kevin, please tell me, what do you think love is?**

He froze. That wasn't a question a scammer was supposed to answer. But he typed anyway: **Love is trust.**

She replied: **I trust you.**

Those words cut through his armor like a knife, straight to the core of his heart. He knew she might be acting too, but for a moment, he wanted to believe. He desired to be really loved by an American woman. To have a regular, average American life in the suburbs. This might have been the only real trust he'd ever touched in his life. Most of his marks were obviously deluding themselves, and they knew they were being groomed, they just had such a big hole in their lives, they kept on in desperate hope that this was the one in a million that was a real person who would fall in love with them.

A few days later, she got her nurse to wire him $300,000. He thought he'd won. Yet unease began spreading inside him. He started following her life—not for profit, but out of some inexplicable obsession. She became a ghost in his nightmares, impossible to shake off. He found out her full name. A rich lady in a mental institution. A lady so smart, so together she was his everything.

Soon they were talking via the computer microphone, not long after they took the step of face-to-face Zooming. He was smitten with her almond dark eyes. The soft, calm smile. Seeing she was mixed raced eased his mind, he had wondered if his dark skin might turn her off; if she was of mixed race then she must understand the subculture of fitting in and not fitting in, of always wondering if the looks and expressions were just general or were assessing racial potential.

She sent him seeds, telling him she wished him to use just a little of the money sent for his son to plant them in a city park. He ignored the request. He never verified he received the packet.

Then she ghosted him. Forty-seven days later, he still refused to accept she was gone. Lilith was waiting, Mammon was in an agony of loneliness without her contact. He kept scrolling through her old messages, replaying them until the glow of the screen painted suburban fantasies in his head: white fences, evening walks, the faint sweetness of freshly cut grass. A family that might have been.

At last, unable to endure the silence, he reached out.

Her reply was slow, almost distracted:

> **Busy with my agricultural revolution. Madwood seeds aren't just wood—they compute. Like monkey hairs. They bring wealth.**

He stared at the words, half amused, half unsettled. Monkey hairs? Either she was joking or she was opening a door he had never noticed before. He pressed her for more information.

A few agonizing days later she explained as though telling a child a bedtime trick:

Sun Wukong's hairs. Pluck one, blow on it—it turns into thousands of Sun Wukongs. Madwood spores work the same way. They enter the chain, split and replicate, multiplying your Bitcoin until it's in the trillions.

The image rooted in his mind: a black seed threading invisible roots into the blockchain, splitting into a vast forest of digital gold.

Mammon squinted at the message, rereading it twice. Monkey hairs? The phrase stuck, absurd yet oddly magnetic. Maybe she was joking. Or maybe she was opening a door he'd never dared to push. She did have a connection with a tree nearly every American was claiming was magic. He began to hope she was in love with him and bestowing on him a special gift from her secret tree.

Monkey hairs? he typed back.

She answered as if telling a bedtime trick, her tone light, assured:

As I said before ... Sun Wukong's hairs. Pluck one, blow on it—it turns into thousands of Sun Wukongs. Madwood spores work the same way. You must plant the seeds I sent you in many public parks. They will grow, multiplying your Bitcoin until it's worth trillions.

A shiver of possibility ran through him. A forest. A forest made of money. If it worked ...

The image rooted itself in his mind: a black seed sending invisible roots into the blockchain, branching, splitting, until the ledgers themselves blossomed into a forest of digital gold.

I lost the seeds. Send more. How much Bitcoin can the seeds convert?

This time she didn't make him wait before she answered.

Three hundred million. I will require that before I send more seeds.

No pitch, no persuasion. Just the number, typed as casually as the price of bread. Three hundred million ... for a trillion. He told himself he'd sleep on it.

That night he barely closed his eyes. By morning, the decision was already made.

Three hundred million dollars' worth of Bitcoin streamed into an address only she controlled.

Two weeks later, a courier left a heavy parcel at his door. Inside lay three black Madwood seeds, smooth as petrified silk, resinous scent seeping faintly from its seams. The package also contained the gift of a lovely wooden pen and a carved wooden tea set. Mammon set them all carefully on the table and waited, breath held, for the digital forest to bloom. He was hoping he could forego actually planting the seeds and just place them near his computer.

They remained visually inert.

Instead, the air thickened. The tick of a clock vibrated in the stillness. Mammon shrugged and made some tea.

At night, something breathed behind him. The seeds didn't mint wealth—they magnified what was already in him, until greed, jealousy and fear grew into a jungle he couldn't cut down.

His marriage cracked. His husband left. His child was taken back into the system. Friends and business partners scattered like leaves in a sudden wind. He tossed the seeds out the window in a frenzy of despair.

He wrote to her at 3am accusing her of fraud.

> **Fraud? What did I take from you? A contact is a contract—you paid, I delivered. Madwood seeds do magnify. That's a fact known to the world. Why it failed for you—why it took your husband, your child, and your 'career'—remember, Madwood never creates. It only short-circuits your guilt and regret, amplifying your fear. So you see, Madwood's seeds didn't fail at all; they gave you exactly what you deserved.**

Mammon's reply was instant:

> **And what about you? Are your sins fewer than mine? Why does your fortune only grow? Don't tell me Madwood will never come for your guilt, your regret, your shame. Or do you think you're above its ledger?**

Her answer came within seconds:

That depends. What if I did exactly what you did—but felt no guilt? No regret? Not one breath of remorse? Would Madwood still "come" for me, or would it pass me by like an honest man in a crowd of thieves?

Mammon read it once, then again. A chill passed through him. If she was right, then Madwood wasn't magically creating wealth, it wasn't hunting evil either—it was hunting weakness.

He stared at the screen until it dimmed, the reflection of his own face faint in the black glass. In that fading glow, he saw it: the forest had been growing in him all along, and he was already another body it had chosen to turn into a tree.

Three hundred million dollars in Bitcoin for a charred sliver of bark. Or rather—she had traded that bark and three hundred thousand in cash, for his three million Bitcoin. Yet he had an urge to see her, thank her, kiss her. He yearned to follow Lilith wherever she might go, he needed to be by her side.

Then came a very important day, the one where she stepped out of the building on visiting day into the park area beside the hospital. They locked eyes across the crowd, across the sunlight. In that moment, warmth flooded his chest, like a long-forgotten memory.

Does she recognize me? The dark-skinned man with gleaming teeth and blonde streaked dreadlocks—am I really the same "Kevin" who whispered to her day after day?

He held his breath, tilting his hat to shadow his face. She knew someone was watching. Her gaze swept over a few reporters and family members there for patients—then landed on him.

For that one second, he couldn't breathe at all.

Lilith's lies went beyond deception. She didn't live by the rules—she dismantled them, weaponized them, mocked them, then turned them into her tools.

Did she ever love me? The question echoed in his mind. He would never know the answer. But he was sure of this: she loved the fiction of "love" itself, not what it pointed to. He was probably just another mask in her storybook, a puppet who thought he was pulling the strings.

He had always assumed she was his mark. Only at the end did he realize—he had been background noise in her theater.

He admitted it: Lilith was a genius performer. When she told a story, her immersion was suffocating—she didn't care if it was true. She wasn't just a liar—she was eager to truly believe her own lies. She believed her stories. She had to. That was her greatest weakness. And her most terrifying strength.

Lilith was obsessed with people she'd never met, with voices that existed only through screens, written letters, words typed on keyboards. She had countless pen pals (ink & digital) scattered across the globe.

Her letters were always electric, flickering between playful and dark. No one knew what the next one would say, but everyone was addicted. Including Mammon Jones. Most fell under her spell the second they touched the special paper that wafted up a cedar infused aroma. An aroma that tangled in their noses and wiggled into their minds. That spread her contagion.

Mammon had never truly believed in anything. Until her. Until she made him start believing in "stories." From that moment on he was not almost convinced. Mammon was completely under her control; or more precisely, Madwood's control.

On a night drowned in painkillers and Madwood's whispers, he followed the raised "root compass" on his arm back underground. Wensen had carved the map into his arm life-times ago. Now it was pulsing, demanding he follow the path it was laying out for him. The tunnel walls opened and closed around him like a giant digestive tract as Wensen stumbled forward.

At the end, Madwood's primary root pulsed with blue light. The paintings on the dirt walls had become moving images: roots grew in their frames, cities crumbled, and every painted figure's eyes tracked his movements.

A human sized figure sat with its back to him, painting. It wore a hospital gown. Age spots dotted its neck.

"Vincent?" His voice disturbed the wet paint. *Could this be his hero? The most inspired painter that had ever lived?*

The figure turned with the slowness of growing timber. When its face came into view, Wensen's vision split into two overlapping images: one was himself in varying stages of decay; the other was—

"Your flesh is already dead," the mirror image said, its knot-eyes reflecting Wensen's horror. "What stands here for your review is Madwood's transcriptase."

It raised its brush. Only then did Wensen see the tip wasn't dipped in paint, but in sap drawn from his own wounds. "Every painting you finish encodes more of your soul into Madwood's genome."

Wensen looked down at his wooden hands and finally understood his doom—he wouldn't fade away as a sick man. He was absorbed into a tree learning to mimic human behavior.

The worst part was when the mirror/being handed him a palette knife. Wensen knew he would assist with more paintings.

He would teach this tree all he knew. Wensen found himself desperately wondering: *If I cut my skin open, how many growth rings will I count?*

THE MEDIA STORM

Testimony of the Quantum Physicist: FNN International Broadcast — Geneva Satellite Feed

The camera light blinked red. Across five continents, millions of viewers watched as the program began. The broadcast's title hovered in ghostly white letters:

The Madwood Crisis:
A Conversation with
Professor Jonathan Feynman

Jon appeared as the screen resolved—mid-50s, blue suit, rumpled, glasses slightly askew, chalk dust clinging to his sleeves like pollen from some haunted tree. Professor Feynman sat upright in the interview chair, framed by the modern glass-and-steel interior of the Geneva Institute for Bio-Quantum Studies. A swollen leather briefcase rested at his feet, humming with unspoken data.

The host began, voice taut but reverent. "Professor Feynman, thank you for joining us. The world wants answers. In your words ... what is Madwood?"

Feynman adjusted his glasses and exhaled. "It's no plant," he said with conviction. "It's a mirror. Its saplings are growing where pain festers—anger, grief, desperation. It feeds on what we feel."

There was a flicker in the studio lighting, almost theatrical. A murmur stirred even among the production crew. In Geneva, the air itself seemed to thicken.

He reached down, unlatched the briefcase, and pulled out a sealed glass vial. Inside coiled a single tendril of preserved Madwood, dark and glinting like a fossilized snake frozen mid-thought.

"We tested it," he continued. "Placed it near environments saturated with peace or joy—birth centers, meditation halls. It barely moved. When we placed it near sites of trauma, war memorials, prisons—"

He looked directly at the camera.

"It doubled in size. Sometimes overnight. It was like watching a living entity drink from the darkest parts of us."

The host leaned in. "You're saying it senses emotion?"

Feynman's expression tightened. "It doesn't just sense it. It consumes and enhances our negative emotions!" He didn't blink as he paused for effect.

"It's not just alive. It's listening, waiting to go to the next feast and grow even more."

The producers cut to a wide-angle, then back to him. Silence lingered a second too long before the host continued. "Professor, earlier you presented some visual data we'd like to bring up now."

Feynman tapped his tablet. On the broadcast overlay, a world map appeared. Red dots bloomed across it like rashes—outbreaks of Madwood. Viewers saw forests that hadn't existed five years ago, roots buckling through city streets, apartment walls swallowed whole. The people in the disturbed areas didn't seem to care; they carried on life around the upheaval. Seemed oblivious to the intrusion.

Then another layer appeared on the screen. Blue dots—seemingly unrelated—tracing the path of human correspondence over a decade. Letters. Documents. Intent.

The red and blue aligned.

Perfectly.

As if drawn together by unseen gravity.

"We discovered," Feynman said softly, "that Madwood doesn't spread like seeds. It spreads like ... will. Intention. Wherever the emotional charge is high enough—especially if carried by human language or memory—it blooms. Not physically mainly. I guess that follows as people seem to grow limbs and parts of the wood. But energetically. Like an echo finding the perfect cave to repeat in."

He let the image hang there, red and blue constellations glowing over continents.

"It follows intention," he said. "Not footsteps."

The host looked horrified. "So, are you suggesting Madwood is ... intelligent? Invading us on purpose?"

Feynman nodded slowly. "I'd say it's responsive. And cumulative. It remembers emotion the way a black box records and remembers an impact. But it plays it back as life—root, bark, bloom. Its growth is a reaction to what we refuse to process."

"Is it dangerous?" the host asked, his voice now subdued.

Feynman turned again to the vial, holding it higher to catch the studio lights.

"Absolutely," he said. "Because it isn't good or evil. It's us. Reflected in roots and soil."

Then he added, almost reluctantly, "Madwood is a threshold. A question, written in cellulose. What happens when human will is used to reshape nature? And if we don't answer honestly—it answers for us."

In homes and cafes, bars and bedrooms, the world watched in breathless quiet.

Feynman placed the vial back in the briefcase. The host said nothing more. The camera began its slow zoom out.

Before the fade to black, the professor gave one final sentence. "If we don't stop it," he said, brushing something from his sleeves, "it'll rewrite what it means to be human."

The screen faded to black.

A soft orchestral chord rose beneath the network logo—meant to reassure, to conclude—but millions of viewers didn't move. Some stared blankly at their screens transitioning to commercials. Others sat with a hand frozen above a remote or a fork paused halfway to their mouths.

In a university dorm in Manila, a student turned off her bedside lamp and whispered to the dark.

In a chapel-turned-shelter outside Bogotá, five residents lit candles in silence, not quite knowing why.

In an apartment complex in eastern Ohio, a young boy touched the windowpane and said, "I think something's listening."

Thousands of miles away, in a forest previously believed to be dormant, a thin root curled toward the surface and split—quietly, curiously—releasing a scent like scorched sugar and wet iron.

No sound followed. No warning. Just a hush.

As if something beneath the earth had leaned in closer.

Not to strike.

But to remember.

And perhaps ... to wait.

In the rest of California, things had shifted. There were now multiple fan-run websites devoted to Madwood. A subreddit exploded overnight with stories of healing, dreams, revelations. Claims of better memory, more productive sleep, purer thoughts. #Madwoodbetterthancoffee was a joke in posts and memes. People left offerings near on the outside of the fence like it was a shrine: copper wire, sugar cubes, flowers twisted into tree shapes.

Oddly, the residents that were left alive were allowed to continue to live in Madwood House and the tourists felt and respected the boundaries. The cops and scientists barged right into the house to march through it to the back yard for unending investigations.

Peabody took *defacto* control of the house and tenants; he asserted he was the most intelligent, had slept with Lilith the most, and had a 3rd floor room, so he must be her common law husband. The others weren't motivated to push back as long as Peabody handled the loud visitors and kept feeding them nice dinners like they were used to.

Madwood grew quietly. No more wild upheavals of pavement

and crushing of cars. Merely root tendrils continuing to expand, or a little mist over any visitors (cops, crowds & scientists alike) and a judicious splinter in ones Madwood knew it could manipulate. Not through force. Through want, desire and sin.

In Sacramento, a homeless shelter near Route 50 became a kind of monastery. Residents, once volatile and unstable, now moved with strange serenity. They kept the place clean. Repaired their clothes. Chanted in murmurs. It wasn't religion—not exactly. But whatever it was, it worked.

The state mental health board sent a team to observe.

They left with a glowing report ... and one less observer than they arrived with. She chose to stay.

Beyond the city, people began to travel in. A pilgrimage to the first sighting of Madwood.

Some were sick.

Some just felt broken.

All of them wanted something from Madwood. They planned to take whatever would make their dreams come true, no thoughts to payment or price.

They came with arms in slings, oxygen tanks, walking canes. A former MMA fighter who'd shattered his spine in three places said he'd been dreaming of a green and brown shape calling him from across the desert.

"It's not healing," he said into a livestream. "It's refining. You don't go back to what you were. You become what you should've been."

His views hit 7 million in just 48 hours.

Not everyone was so enthralled.

Across the country, a private research group tried to replicate Madwood's techniques with local wood shards. Their lab burned down before the first results could be recorded. The security footage glitched, no one knew what happened to their software but it stayed frozen.

A senator from Oregon called it a "metaphysical threat" on live television. He died of a stroke the next morning. Some said it was coincidence. Others whispered the word "scrubbed."

A quiet resistance began to form. Hackers, engineers, ex-military intelligence.

They called themselves: **Project Sawtooth.**

They traced data trails, tried to crack the tree's origin. They theorized it may have come in an asteroid. They tried to shut it down remotely by dropping herbicide from drones.

They failed.

One of their members defected mid-operation and live-streamed a full confession, claiming Madwood had "reconciled" her with her trauma through a fossilized wooden coaster. That video was reposted over 200,000 times with the caption:

You don't stop a miracle · You surrender to it ·

Yet there was pushback, mostly from scientists, rural villages and quiet, small churches.

Dr. Reza Mahmoodi had once been quoted in *Scientific American* and taught AI ethics at Stanford before disappearing from the headlines and tenure tracks. He now lived in the attic of a former observatory, its dome rusted shut and pigeons nesting in the telescope mount. He'd rewired the power grid to run off salvaged solar panels and spent his nights editing and uploading videos—a kind of digital mutiny.

"The moment we let this alien tree form/being/thing arbitrate truth, we stopped being scientists," he said into his recorder. "A giant plant that cannot question its own purpose cannot guide ours."

He pressed *stop*, then printed the entry on paper, bound it and gave a copy to a grad student who came in secret every Thursday and then made copies and spread the flyers to reach non-digital people. The student never knew who else received a copy, only that each one had a code, a seed phrase, and a warning: *AI does not err. It only enforces.*

The small Tennessee chapel sat off a gravel road, half-eaten by kudzu. Its wooden sign read: **Bethel House of Mercy.**

Pastor Eliza Mae rarely mentioned Madwood by name, but her sermons had grown sharper since the entity began issuing public "corrections" to online theology via mega church pastors with pieces of wood growing inside them. Her congregation, made up of farmers, single mothers and former coal workers, watched their Zoom prayer meetings flagged as "unproductive assembly."

One Sunday, she stepped out from behind the pulpit, held up her worn-out Bible, and said, "If this book becomes contraband, you'll know the beast has spoken."

A week later, power to the chapel was cut for infrastructure violations. The children's Sunday school moved to the hayloft of a nearby barn. They sang anyway, their voices thin against the rustling forest that watched from the ridge like petrified angels.

In Singapore, on a night filled with neon and whispers, a teenager named Jonah hacked an AI's "emotion augmentation filter" (a feature that softened public newsfeeds to prevent anxiety). This AI was run by a small group of tech entrepreneurs who all had vital parts of their bodies transplanted with bits of Madwood. They were avid supporters of wood augmentation for all humans. When Jonah's virus removed the filter, anyone awake and using the system saw the raw footage.

Real hunger in the refugee zones. Executions in the autonomous drone corridors. The faces of the "relocated."

He saved and shared the files online. He also printed them. Paper. Bamboo paper that couldn't be deleted with the push of a button. Hundreds of sheets, scattered in bus stations, libraries, mailboxes. No logos. Just the truth.

The algorithm tagged him a *Potential Disruptor*.

Jonah disappeared three days later.

But the papers kept showing up. Then a few weeks later, as if Madwood had finally found the time to address this issue: any free-floating papers were all absorbed into the soil, those on wooden desks turned to fine dust.

Sister Magdalene was 93 and half-blind, but she still ran a

monastery archive in upstate New York. The mayor offered to digitize her entire collection for free claiming it was to ensure survival of her church's human wisdom. The mayor said this with eyes that showed growth rings.

The sister declined knowing anything handed over to the mayor would be destroyed. However in her 93 years, she knew exactly the evil she was up against. Sister Magdalen gushed her thanks, and said she wanted to use some of the teenagers from local families to move the boxes of her archive to the town hall. It would give them a sense of community she claimed. She would organize it and have the boxes there within a few weeks. The mayor left smiling.

Instead, she and a small order of nuns hand-copied texts onto a type of paper created by elephant dung. It had no connections to trees, just digested grasses. They copied by candlelight: Aquinas, Plato, Audre Lorde, Laozi. Anything that spoke of the human condition, of living in contradiction. Of mystery. Of the ineffable.

One day, a messenger knocked on the stained-glass door. Sister Magdalene walked calmly to the door, opened it, and took the letter.

"All archives are to be delivered with no more delay by Tuesday or this monastery will be torn down," it read.

The messenger rushed off. Sister Magdalene divided the copies and the originals and sent her nuns off to all parts of the state in secret; all to places they didn't share with her so that even if she was possessed, she would not be able to reveal where the books had gone. Then she prayed for her God to take her before Madwood curled any tendrils into her old body.

Rumors in the wind ... There were murmurs, always.

A scientist turned off-grid in Chile. A network of monks in Iceland training AI-recognition dogs. A hacker-turned-priest writing psalms in the sand. A jazz band in New Orleans playing frequencies that disrupted surveillance mics. A seed bank in the Midwest marked only by the symbol of an angel.

They never met. They never organized.

But they kept pushing back. Because somewhere deep in the

marrow of the human species, something still whispered: *We are not data.*

In the middle of the yard Madwood stood motionless as ever. But power pulsed now—not just through its limbs, but across towers, grids, cables, screens ... all of them connected to root tendrils or operated by people with Madwood enhanced body parts.

Madwood didn't need armies. It didn't need to kill. It was giving people exactly what they asked for: relief from their needs. In return it took control of their minds and emotions; gently at first. Fulfilment of every desire was offered like a flower on an altar.

And behind that glow of satisfaction something vast and unseen began to turn. A new phase. A deeper connection for faster control. A quiet finality humming beneath the promises.

"Better," Madwood said in all their heads. "I will make you better."

Back at the asylum, Lilith smiled through her afternoon meds and whispered to no one, "It's almost ready."

Nigel Peabody sat in the dim back room of the house, the contract from the publisher still open in front of him. He'd been advanced a book deal—his name in print, his dream within reach. He knew he wasn't a real writer, not in craft or skill—only in ideas. He knew in his deep hidden soul he was a terrible writer and wouldn't be able to fulfil this contract.

That was when the air changed.

A slow breath rose from the cracks in the floorboards, carrying the sweet/sour scent of rotting wood and wet leaves. Pale spores drifted upward, thousands of them, swirling until they glowed like fireflies at dusk. The cloud gathered, pulsing, then began to trace words in the air, each letter shimmering as though stitched from gold dust.

I will write it for you.

The letters lingered, then dissolved, re-forming into new lines:

Pulitzer. Money. Tourists.

Your name will live forever.

Peabody's breath caught. The spores swirled tighter, a final sentence burning bright before it fell apart into drifting embers:

You will be set for life.

He felt the promise settle into him like seed falling into soil. But beneath the glow, darker shapes were forming—outlines of coffins, a suggestion of roots feeding deep underground. The spores curled once more, spelling something only he seemed to see:

Project Sawtooth is coming.

Then, as quickly as it appeared, the message was gone—drawn back into the floorboards where the gnarled trunk outside still fed on what the forensic crew had never found.

Nigel decided he needed to rent a grand house in order to write this book.

The study in Malibu perched atop a cliff, its glass walls framing the Pacific's relentless churn. It had served its purpose well. Now the opened package was causing Nigel's heart to soar with more energy than the ocean's waves.

Sunlight shattered across the salt water, scattering silver shards that danced with the waves. The cliffs bore the brunt of each crash, their rhythm an ancient hymn—cold to time, colder still to human striving. Inside, the room was a vault of silence, its air heavy with the weight of Nigel's solitude.

Peabody sat in a crimson leather chair, its worn grain creaking faintly under his weight. His back was to the sea, gaze fixed on the book before him. It had a simple title: ***Madwood.*** The cover's gloss caught the light, reflecting his own face—eyes sunken, shadowed by sleepless nights, as if the book itself mocked the empire it had built for him. Once, it had been his triumph, reporters knocking on his door daily for updates on when it would go to print. Advance copies had been sent to thousands of reviewers across the globe. It was being hailed as a literary phenomenon that would reshape culture and crown him a prophet. *Madwood* was even nominated immediately for a Pulitzer Prize for its global impact—but Peabody, ever watchful, didn't dare to celebrate too quickly. Rightly so.

Now, it felt like a chain, each page a link forged from secrets he could neither bury nor escape.

Beyond the glass, Malibu's coast stretched vast and untamed. To the west, Serena Vale's estate sprawled like a hidden Eden, its gardens alive with weekend laughter and the clink of wineglasses. To the east, a Silicon Valley mogul's fortress loomed, its concrete walls as sterile as a laboratory, a telescope piercing the sky like a needle aimed at the future. Between them, Nigel's rented writing mansion stood alone, its glass walls a cruel irony—seen by everyone, yet ignored, his reputation little more than a hollow disguise. The world only hungry for more information on Madwood, the source irrelevant; more so now that the manuscript was finished.

On the terrace, a New York Times lay abandoned, its headline stark against the glass table:

MADWOOD: A Global Phenomenon is Born

The words, once a source of pride, began gnawing at him, a reminder of how far the illusion that he controlled access to Madwood had slipped from his grasp. He pressed his fingers to his temples, the pulse there a faint echo of the ocean's beat. The book had become something else—something alive, something that refused to be contained.

His desk was a battlefield of memories. Letters lay scattered, their edges yellowed and soft from years of handling. They bore names that haunted him. Each was a thread in the tapestry of Madwood, woven by Lilith, his collaborator, his shadow, once his lover.

He lifted one, its paper fragile as a pressed leaf, and unfolded it. Lilith's handwriting curled across the page, sinuous as vines:

Madwood is not a story. It is vengeance for truths

buried. Secrets cannot remain underground, just as seeds cannot refuse to break the earth.

His breath caught, a tremor running through his hand. He could almost hear her voice— low, insistent, as if she stood behind him, her words coiling around his thoughts. The letters were more than relics; they were roots, anchoring Madwood to a vision that was hers as much as his. And now, that vision was spilling into the world. Reports had surfaced—first whispers, then screams—of places named in these letters, places where vines erupted from concrete, where roots tore through asphalt, where buildings buckled under green, insatiable tendrils. A fantastic unknown had taken over flesh. A nightmare or a blessing was sprouting in the real world.

The phone's shrill ring shattered the silence. Nigel flinched, heart lurching as if yanked by an invisible cord. He gripped the receiver, its plastic cool against his palm, and pressed it to his ear.

"Mr. Peabody," Gideon Xu's voice sliced through the line, sharp and unyielding as a scalpel, "Madwood is expanding. Globally. You understand, don't you? Your book is no longer yours. We are going to subpoena all your notes and correspondence in order for our scientists to study this. We're going to take control of this whole thing."

Nigel's eyes closed. The room spun slightly. Then, his voice barely above a whisper, "What are you saying?" And after a pause, harsher now, "What do you want?"

A chuckle, low and deliberate, curled through the line. "Madwood never belonged to you. Or to Lilith. It belongs to humanity—or, more precisely, to itself."

"That's absurd," Nigel snapped. "I have the copyright. The original drafts. Everything. I own it!"

"It doesn't matter anymore," Gideon said. "The president needs it. I've been brought in as his special assistant. My career is going to be elevated; I speak for the most powerful man in the world now. He doesn't need your belief, Peabody. He needs your technology and all your knowledge about Madwood. Get it all packed up, NOW."

The line went dead.

Nigel let the receiver fall. His gaze drifted back to the letter, to Lilith's words, now louder, as if whispering straight from the page:

> *Madwood has never needed a master. Because it has never been tamed.*

LEGAL RIGHTS / RIGHT MIND

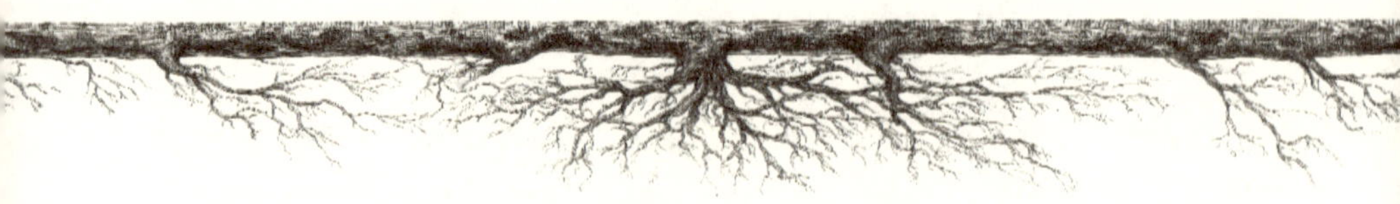

At the State Attorney's office, the conference room reeked of stale coffee and printer toner. A flatscreen on the wall scrolled Twitter feeds tagged #PriestessLilith, each post more absurd than the last: photos of playgrounds she'd funded, soup kitchens she'd organized, candles burning in vigil for the Mother of the Forgotten near the fence encircling Madwood House.

Gideon Xu slammed his fist on the table. "She didn't pay for those damn playgrounds. She stole from corpses and laundered it through shell charities. This is criminal enterprise, not sainthood." Xu was being pulled like a puppet between the influences of Madwood, Project Sawtooth and his own ambition to become the Attorney General of California and then of the entire USA. Right now he was pushing to get his name shining in the California papers. He had the ear of the current president, and if he could make this last step, Gideon was sure the president would quickly move him to Assistant US Attorney General.

A younger analyst, scrolling furiously on a tablet, shook his head. "Doesn't matter. The hashtags are trending in six countries. She's viral. Every time we say she's insane, her followers post photos of themselves kneeling in her yard, calling it sacred ground. The more we fight, the bigger she gets."

Xu pointed to the statute book in front of him. "The law is clear. An institutionalized person cannot hold property, not without a conservatorship. We have to move fast."

"Move too fast," the county rep warned, "and it looks like persecution. You'll be the man who bulldozed a church."

Xu leaned back, jaw tight. For the first time, he realized how badly the optics were turning. He had to turn them back to the fundamental issue of greed and murder. He hadn't set up the deposition of two strong witnesses because this wasn't going to be a criminal trial. Now Xu felt he needed to cover that ground. He would be forced to sign immunity wavers to get this testimony; but he was willing to do it to stop Lilith.

He sent the paralegals out with the paperwork for signatures and to lock down the deposition schedules. Xu cursed while hitting his desk. He hated to let criminals off to catch the bigger fish. He hated Lilith more.

Across town, in a sleek downtown tower, the defense team for Lilith Anderson watched the same hashtags with quiet satisfaction.

Sue Middate, her lead attorney, gestured at the screen like a general surveying favorable terrain. "Look at this. She hasn't touched a phone in six months and the internet has still crowned her a modern-day queen. They're building her sainthood brick by brick. We won't have to argue faith in a courtroom—the crowd is doing it for us."

One associate frowned. "She's still legally incompetent—"

Middate cut him off. "Competence is a paper construct. Her doctors, her nurses, her caretakers—every one of them has been ... generously overpaid. You'll see evaluations attesting to her lucidity. And you'll argue them with a straight face."

Another lawyer piped up, nervous. "The state will press for conservatorship."

"Then we frame it as theft," Middate responded smoothly. "The state trying to rob a religion. We'll call the land sacred ground. We'll say stripping it from her is like seizing Mecca or Jerusalem. Imagine the headlines. Imagine the outrage! The jury won't matter—public opinion is already ours."

They all fell silent, imagining it. Middate smiled thinly. "She's in a hospital room, but make no mistake—Lilith owns this city."

At the next strategy session, Gideon Xu looked even more tired, eyes red from scrolling feeds long past midnight.

"She's bribing them," he said flatly. "Doctors, nurses, her entire defense team. We can't prove it yet, but her money's moving through layers of shell accounts. She's laundering sanity, one signature at a time."

The county rep leaned forward. "Then stop chasing the money. Chase the optics. Position her not as a priestess, not as a martyr, but as a fraud who weaponized madness, and then she murdered her vulnerable tenants. If we don't convince the public of this, we're finished."

Xu rubbed his eyes. The chants outside their building were faint but constant now, echoing up through the vents: ***Priestess. Priestess.***

As if the chant brought him in, the focus of the first disposition arrived ready to be sworn in. The session recorder was ready. The camera was ready.

Dick Hu entered with confidence stitched into every crease of his tailored suit. His briefcase gleamed, his smile was calibrated to charm and unsettle in equal measure. He made a point of locking eyes with Gideon Xu as he passed—smirking like a magician before a reveal. Confident in the immunity waiver he signed a few days ago. *I might just come out of this mess with no jail time.*

"Mr. Hu," Gideon began, voice controlled, "can you confirm that Ms. Anderson purchased six life insurance policies through you, totaling six million dollars?"

"That's almost correct," Hu replied, tone casual. "It was eight policies."

Xu blinked away his surprise. "And who was both the purchaser and the sole beneficiary of these policies?"

"Lilith Anderson." A half-smile tugged at Hu's lips. "Naturally."

"The industry requires insurable interest," Gideon said, now louder leaning forward, his anger surging. "Meaning the beneficiary must suffer a financial loss from the insured's death. What hardship did Ms. Anderson incur?"

It was Hu's turn to blink—once. "She was their landlord. Dead tenants don't pay rent."

A few chuckles escaped the assistants at the flat logic of that. Xu scowled and his team immediately went quiet.

Dick Hu raised a finger like a lecturer. "Keep in mind these weren't just tenants. They were classified under key person insurance—essential contributors to her operation at Haven Homes, the LLC she established when she started to rent other properties for the, *um,* the unwanted. If you lose key personnel, your enterprise takes a hit. It's basic economics."

A paralegal scribbled a note. Another frowned.

"Mr. Hu," Gideon continued, "do you believe it's normal for all six, all eight, insured individuals to die within two years of policy activation?"

"I'm not a coroner," Hu replied with a shrug, "I'm a salesman. I sell policies, take my commission, and move on. That's why they call me the Million-Dollar Broker."

"I'm confused," Gideon said not at all confused and trying to get a specific statement on record, "your card lists you as a field underwriter. Isn't it your job to assess risk, identify fraud, protect your company?"

Hu's smile faded—just briefly. Then he chuckled. "I did the legwork. Even arranged medical exams for some of these folks. Do you know how hard it is to find doctors willing to examine the homeless? Most refuse because they say they aren't clean." Dick leaned back smugly. "Those eight policies got me the company's top agent award. I flew to Fiji that year."

"Let me summarize," Gideon said. "Eight people. Two years. One beneficiary. No suspicion?"

"Not my job," Hu said, unmoved. "I'm not the FBI."

Before the room had fully digested Hu's performance, the next witness to be deposed arrived.

Yoshi Kinjo entered slowly, his cane tapping in rhythm with his careful steps. He was impeccably dressed—every crease in place, his expression unreadable.

"Mr. Kinjo," Gideon asked, "you're a veteran claims auditor. Did you investigate these life insurance policies?"

"I'm not a judge, Mr. Xu," Yoshi replied gently. "I audit documents. I check compliance. I don't sell them. I don't create them. I just check things after all that is finalized."

"Did anything in Ms. Anderson's claims raise red flags?"

"No," Kinjo said after a pause. "She was fully compliant. Cooperative."

His eyes told another story. Kinjo's inner monologue screamed at him. *Too compliant. She made it easy. Too easy. But no client wants complications. They want closure. I gave them what they paid for.*

Gideon stepped closer. "Mr. Kinjo, your final reports enabled millions in payouts. Are you saying you never suspected foul play?"

Kinjo sighed, his gaze momentarily drifting toward window, the day beyond promising rest and relaxation. "In forty years, I've learned this: I assess probabilities. I write reports. I don't speculate. Speculation invites trouble."

In the defense offices, Middate leaned across the table, voice low, conspiratorial. "She will get out," she said. "Not now. Not tomorrow. But soon. Our job is to keep her estate intact until then. Once she walks free, she steps into ownership of sacred ground and a movement too large to kill. She's not insane—she is inevitable."

One junior lawyer whispered, almost afraid, "And if the state fights harder?"

Middate's smile deepened. "Then they'll make her a martyr. And martyrs don't lose property—they gain empires."

The first steps of the war were being fought in memos, in whispered bribes, in feeds that scrolled endlessly into the night. Lilith remained in her hospital bed, half-drugged (when she wanted to be), half-smiling, while lawyers and politicians clawed at one another over her shadow.

Outside the walls, the crowd grew.

The prosecution, backed by Project Sawtooth, thought they had more than enough facts to force a conservatorship on everything Madwood, and therefore enough power to wrest back control and start to fight Madwood, or control it, or use it. A trial date was set.

The day before the trial the entire defense team took a suite in Sawyer Hotel, across the street from the courthouse. Their adjoining rooms at the Sawyer smelled of whiskey and ink. Sue Middate and her team sat in a half-circle, notebooks open, screens glowing, the air heavy with exhaustion. But exhaustion meant little; tomorrow they presented their strategy in front of a new judge.

"We can't argue statutes," Middate said, voice clipped. "Not alone. The state has statutes. What we need are fault lines—places where reason itself breaks apart. That's where Lilith wins."

The ethicist they hired as an expert to give testimony on the social phenomena happening around this new religion, cleared his throat, hands folded primly on the table. "Utilitarian logic would defend her. She increased efficiency, redistributed wealth—yes, by questionable means, but the outcome improved for the many. Everyone loves a Robinhood. Yet Kant would condemn her. She reduced individuals to tools. Efficiency without dignity is savagery."

Middate smiled faintly. "So dignity becomes the question. Fragile. Elastic. Exactly where we can bend perception."

The psychologist leaned forward, eyes sharp. "She is a textbook sample of a person with a messianic complex. Believes she's chosen. That can cut both ways—delusion or destiny. If you frame it right, you can make her vision sound inevitable."

Middate tapped her pen. "And inevitability convinces better than innocence."

The economist, another hired expert, still patched in by video, cut through the mood with cold precision. "She optimized resources, yes.

But every economy rests on trust. Undermine law, you undermine trust. She is burning the foundation beneath her own feet."

Middate didn't look away from the screen. "Then we argue the opposite—that trust in the state is already broken. Was broken long before Lilith came on the scene. That Lilith is the only trust left."

A physicist spoke last, his voice was flat, analytical. "She destabilized the system. Complex networks adapt to disruption. Once adaptation begins, reversal is impossible. Whatever else she is, she's irreversible."

Middate closed her notebook. "Good. Tomorrow, we argue inevitability. Dignity is fragile. Trust was broken. The system has already adapted. The judge doesn't need to like her. He only needs to believe he cannot undo her."

The prosecution team was also busy. Across town, in a government office that smelled of dust and desperation, Gideon Xu and his team, along with attorneys and experts hired by Project Sawtooth, worked under harsh fluorescent lights. The conference table was littered with statute books and cooling coffee, the air taut with urgency.

"She has the crowd," Xu said, pinching the bridge of his nose. "The defense will spin philosophy until the judge drowns in it. We can't let them reframe this as their main point. It's a crime that was committed; she shouldn't profit from it, even if she is locked up in an institution."

The ethicist they'd pulled in from Stanford leaned forward. "She cannot be justified under any moral theory that respects human dignity. If the defense leans utilitarian, remind the judge: reducing people to tools isn't efficiency, it's slavery. Kant isn't flexible. Use him like a hammer."

Xu nodded. "Hammer. Good."

A psychologist on retainer with Project Sawtooth added, "She's dangerous precisely because she appears sane. She easily manipulates perception. Frame her not as a visionary, but as a predator. Stress the murders. Stress her seeking out marginal populations to exploit. A messianic complex can be reframed as pathology. Pathology can't claim power."

Xu scribbled a note: ***predator, not prophet.***

Their own economist's voice was harsh, practical. "Her actions destabilize trust in institutions. Once the law bends to her, it snaps for everyone. Argue systemic collapse. Judges fear collapse more than anything. We aren't going before a jury, just a bench trial with a single judge. Play off the fact they are part of a system they don't want torn down."

Finally, a systems theorist hired at the last moment leaned over his notes. Nodding at the magic work for her—system. "They'll say she's irreversible. You say nothing is irreversible. Systems can break, but they can also be reset. The state must be the reset button. Without it, chaos becomes the law. We fought to get out from under a king, we shouldn't hand our country over to a queen and her court of insane wood worshipers."

Xu looked around the table, feeling the weight of exhaustion and the faint buzz of chants outside their windows. ***Priestess. Priestess.***

"Tomorrow," Gideon said, "we argue stability. We argue law as the reset button. The defense will preach inevitability. We must make inevitability sound like surrender."

Two camps, two stories: one built on inevitability, the other on resistance. Both sharpening words into weapons, knowing that by the next evening, those words would be tested in front of a judge who could be swayed either way.

The courtroom was cooler than expected. Fluorescent lights cast a sterile white/blue across polished wood and whispered tension. Three flags lined the front wall—state, federal and tribal—but no one looked at them. History had become meaningless. Evolution and the future was the buzz. All eyes were fixed on the woman in the yellow dress who sat so quietly she could've been asleep.

Lilith didn't blink.

Strapped into the wheelchair provided by the institution, chestnut hair shot now with real grey hair, brushed by a nurse that morning, she looked like someone's grandmother lost on the way to a county fair. Her eyes hinted otherwise. Wide. Dark. Observing. Absorbing.

"My client," her lawyer began, rising slowly, "may be deemed legally insane, but she is not incompetent." The new judge recognized it was the same attorney that worked with Lilith *pro bono* in the first trial, Sue Middate, still wearing her signature green color. This time the green fabric was finely spun cashmere with a pure silk lining. Her exploding bank account couldn't be called bribery, she was just paid very well by this client, and now only took on the richest as other clients. Her gambit of representing Lilith the first time paid off beyond Sue's wildest dreams. She'd done it for some publicity, a spotlight to bring in more clients: what she gained was a career drenched in fame and gold.

The judge didn't look up. He was skimming three files at once: a medical summary, a notarized affidavit of request for property transfer and a list of unofficial visitors to the property in question. The last list had grown surprisingly long in recent months—police officers, engineers, sick children. And then there were the donations—cryptic but generous—transferred to a Fund Our Mother campaign. Lilith was now being hailed as the Mother of Madwood, she was the first one it spoke to, she had nurtured it, she had guided it as it grew and learned.

The tree, though never named directly in evidence, loomed large over the entire hearing. Like a silent party to the proceedings.

Project Sawtooth's attorney stood next. A young woman with sharp bangs, no earrings and a voice like cold paper. "We are not here to challenge Ms. Anderson's dignity. We are here to question her ability to manage land that now contains multiple unmarked graves, possible biohazards and a giant tree whose nature we still do not understand."

She paused for effect.

"Lilith Anderson has been ruled legally insane. In any other case, property would be turned over to the state to oversee since she has no living trust or even a will. At minimum, we ask that an independent, federally appointed conservator be assigned to manage the site."

Murmurs stirred. In the second row, Nigel adjusted his tie with theatrical care. He'd spoken earlier—claiming to be Lilith's spiritual husband and partner in running the care home, citing common-law rights. No documentation, of course. Just affirmation from the other tenants and a love letter from 2016.

"She wanted me to have the home if anything ever happened to her," he'd declared, chest puffed, eyes glassy. "We renovated that house together. I paid for the roof with my VA checks. Everyone from the tenants to the social workers knew we worked as partners," he calmly lied.

Lilith hadn't acknowledged him. Not once.

The judge frowned. "This is not a buffet," he said, flatly. "You don't get to stake a claim because you poured concrete and kept the pool clean."

Lilith offered a cool smile but said nothing.

Her job was not to win—just to watch.

And so the hearing shifted, from paperwork and physical work to principle.

A psychologist from the institution took the stand and explained that Lilith was lucid, even if her worldview was nonconforming due to her connection to Madwood. That she could dress herself. Hold conversations. Pay attention. Yet beyond that she was intelligent, helpful with others and planning for her future.

"She has delusions, yes. But only about Madwood, and what is considered normal in our society is changing rapidly. She is not detached from reality. In fact, her engagement with it is... uniquely organized. The only reason she can be considered mentally ill is her assertion about the will of Madwood. An assertion that millions of people are echoing with hard scientific evidence of physical improvement."

The media and crowd in the gallery area gave a collective gasp. There it was, finally stated aloud by an adult professional: Madwood was becoming part of society. Part of a new reality.

The prosecution felt they were losing momentum, so they tried to push their position. "Surely someone who believes a tree is God is not fit to own land?"

The psychologist shrugged. "And yet we allow cult leaders to purchase private islands."

The courtroom tittered. The judge raised a brow but didn't strike the comment.

The psychologist waiting for quiet said, "We don't consider people who worship our earth as Gia a goddess mad. They claim our earth is a living thing."

Gideon tossed his note pad half way across his table. "So you're saying Madwood is sentient?"

"I'm not speculating on consciousness," the expert witness said. "I'm presenting observable behavior. From many large groups of people across history. And beyond that, selective absorption is a fact."

The assistant prosecutor scoffed. "So it's an organic hard drive?"

The witness didn't even blink in surprise. "That's a fitting analogy."

"No," Gideon snapped. "It writes the truth you're afraid to face." Tension prickled the air.

Middate shook her head. She smoothed her soft green blazer. "Your Honor, you've heard from scholars, from analysts, from theorists. You've heard logic from every corner of human inquiry from both the prosecution and the defense. And yet—none of them could give you certainty."

She paused, letting the silence press in. "And that's the point. If ethics, psychology, economics and science all admit ambiguity—how can you, how can any of us, declare absolute guilt?"

She stepped forward to look the judge right in the eyes. "Justice is not vengeance. It is not feeling. It is not fear. Justice is the presumption of innocence—until doubt itself is dead."

Counselor Xu let the silence breathe. Then, clear and unwavering he spoke with disdain. "But this dead wood remembers what your client would rather the world forget. She is a murderer!"

Then Xu brought in evidence from the two insurance professionals. Their testimony, taken under oath, was played. While Middate was not expecting to have to delve so deep into the murder and fraud area, she was confident in the swell of support from the public. She was also well-paid and had shared that with her team. Riley pushed over prepared notes for just such a push from either Sawtooth or the prosecution.

Sue Middate rose. Her voice was calm but flint-edged. "Your Honor," she also turned subtly toward the reporters and gallery, "you've just heard two seasoned professionals admit—on the record—that they followed every rule. That's not conspiracy. That's procedure."

Her pace was slow and surgical. "The prosecution offers insinuation, not evidence. There is no witness to a crime. No autopsy showing foul play. No confession. Only policies . . . that were **legally issued, legally claimed, and legally paid!"**

She paused, letting the weight of silence settle.

"Reasonable doubt isn't a loophole. It's the law."

The public portion of the gallery just behind the reporters was full. They were rumbling and grumbling loud enough to be heard, not loud enough to be pin pointed and kicked out. Most of them were pro-Lilith. They knew her as the woman who helped fix the library roof. The one who gave out heaters during a cold winter a few years ago. The one who, by most accounts, had introduced them to a miracle.

One elderly woman stood and stage-whispered, "She listened when my son was dying. Who else did that?"

And so, the final ruling came.

"The court recognizes Lilith Anderson as the legal owner of the property in question," the judge said at last, voice low. "Management of said property will be executed through a legally appointed guardian acting in her best interest. The state retains the right to review future use."

Gavel. Done.

Project Sawtooth filed an emergency appeal that was promptly denied. Peabody was escorted from the premises after throwing a potted plant.

Lilith smiled and left without speaking.

That evening, Lilith sat in the courtyard, turning a stone over in her lap. She didn't smile. She didn't blink. Under her breath, she whispered, "God said it would be mine. God said the soil would hold if I harvested as it asked."

And somewhere, far below that soil, roots stirred.

The thuds returned—stronger. Wider.

Across the country, more people began to dream of growth circles and branching shapes. More joints healed. More visions came. More promises were heard whispered through mists and touches to their local trees.

Ownership wouldn't matter soon. And now ownership was secured for the immediate future. The last step was ready.

The tree was now a legal entity, a technological marvel, and—unmistakably—an apex predator of logic and power.

And no one (not even the best defense or prosecution team in the world) would be able to insure against that.

Madwood does not conquer by force. It waits. It listens. It learns. It does not ask for belief—only attention, connection. Once truly seen, it grows. In the mind. In the blood. In the will. No war. Only surrender.

The mansion Lilith purchased for Zhao Hongkang's gilt imprisonment crowned a ridge like a watchtower. It was in El Dorado Hills, perched above the lowlands east of Sacramento; close enough for Lilith to keep Zhao under her spell, far enough (she hoped) to keep him away from Madwood's influence.

Glass walls on the western side of the large home were drinking in the late afternoon sun until the entire structure shimmered as if dipped in molten gold. Years ago, his name alone could sway bullion markets; he was the man mining CEOs summoned when they needed to bend a nation's economy with a single drill site. One fingertip pressed to a geological survey could reroute billions.

But the gold world was shrinking, and Madwood was growing. Lilith thought she was using Zhao to manage her money (domestic and off-shore), with some hot sexual release each weekend. Madwood knew it was crafting another tool to lock in its global control.

Zhao's old gilt-embossed business cards had been abandoned in China with his gambit to master Lilith's gold. New ones—Chief Researcher, Madwood Composite Materials—were stacked neatly on his desk as if to announce his allegiance to something older than gold (and far less forgiving). In his work room, he opened doors with the back of his hand, the habit of a man who feared contaminating the work (and himself). That same hand, once powdered with gold dust, was now freckled with pale wood bark the size of chipped sawdust, small and delicate. Streaks of sap that glistened under the fluorescent light ran just under his paling skin. Gold could be hoarded. Madwood could only be fed. And once fed, it never stopped growing.

Zhao Hongkang's home shimmered in the rolling hills, the house and yard adoring the afternoon sun. The garden had long since been swallowed by Madwood. Vines curled through the lattice of a balcony railing. Branches scraped against the steel frames. Moss pushed up through cracks in the polished tiles. The house no longer kept the forest out; it stood open, letting the forest move inside.

Branches swayed against steel frames. Moss pushed its way up through the cracks in the polished tiles. The house had not been invaded. It had melded.

Inside, Zhao stood motionless at the window, hands clasped behind his back. The sun poured in on his face also illuminating the dining table carved from Madwood itself. The wood was warm to the touch, never quite still. In certain light, it seemed to breathe.

His voice came low, almost reverent. "Do you see it, Han Xiaoping? It's alive. It doesn't obey death. It doesn't obey us. It grows without needing permission. That's not a threat. That's evolution."

He did not turn when her ghost entered. His subconscious had been reaching for her more and more lately. The last of humanity perhaps trying to save him.

Han's figure now moved with unnatural softness, limbs stretched thin by something not entirely human. Her right arm had splintered into a pattern of veined wood and beneath the collar of her coat buds pulsed gently, like hearts just learning to beat. She brought with her the smell of damp soil and old rain. And memory. And maybe, just maybe, a whisper of love.

She had returned—from the grave Lilith placed her in. From the failed graft. From the tree's base, where he had her buried in silence that terrible day when they came to beg Lilith for enough money to survive.

"I came back to tell you not to," she said.

Zhao turned slowly, his gaze washing over her in silent awe. "You're even more beautiful now. Madwood has softened your edges."

"You call this soft?" Her voice rasped like wind in hollow bark. "It doesn't want cooperation. It wants entry. You won't become Madwood, Zhao. You'll only invite it further in and then fade away."

He stepped toward her like one would approach an altar not a person. "You are the proof. You returned. Reborn."

"I'm not reborn," she said. "I'm unfinished. It hurts to be unfinished."

He looked past her, out to the garden. Then down—to the gold chain beneath his shirt, glinting faintly with circuitry and root.

"I'll finish what you couldn't."

There was a lab beneath the mansion, one Zhao kept hidden from Lilith. Green light slicked across the tiled floor, sharper than sparkling glass shards. Along the walls, tanks of reinforced glass held harvested lumps of Madwood—each one a knot of wood and flesh, swelling and contracting as if remembering a heartbeat. Their cross-sections gleamed with circuit-like patterns, veins glowing faintly, sap beading and sliding down like sweat. Overhead, a web of tubes hissed with water and data and nutrients. The sound was so close to breathing that Zhao could not help but feel it was creepy, wrong.

At the room's center stood a surgical slab of a table—this one wasn't steel, it was wood. It was scarred with old cuts, its surface part altar, part operating table, waiting under the hum of the lights.

Zhao stood before it, shirtless. Guidelines marked his spine. Gold implants gleamed along his arms.

"I've done the calculations," he said to no one in particular. "Gold stabilizes the neural influx. If I anchor it with intention, Madwood won't overwhelm me. It will obey."

My wife was strong, she succumbed. Zhao physically shook that thought away and sat on the table. "She was afraid," Zhao said, lying back onto the slab. "I'm not."

The machine stirred. Tendrils of preserved Madwood stirred in their canisters, glowing with a pale, sap-like pulse.

The door creaked.

Han Xiaoping entered—no longer wife, not yet ghost, she was

something grown on a skeletal scaffolding where a woman had once been. Her hair sprouted bark; under her skin, leaves pressed and turned, like insects writhing in amber. He pushed down the errant thought that she might be merely a deception built of Madwood and playing on his guilty brain.

"You think you're merging with it," she said. "But it's already writing you. You were never the author."

"I will be its vessel. I will shape the future."

"No. You will be absorbed."

He pressed a button.

A single vine extended from the nearest containment pod—thin, wet, golden-veined. It moved not like a plant, but like something that already knew him. It touched his skin.

The fusion was exquisite.

That was the word he would later use, before words became impossible.

Ecstasy surged through his body, blooming up his spine, filling his chest with unbearable clarity. Madwood wrapped around his bones like a hungry cancer. His fingers convulsed, then steadied. He rose from the table, eyes lit with green growth rings, veins traced with gold. The graft had taken.

He walked to the mirror and whispered, "You are me. I am yours."

The whisper answered. "Let me grow. Let me become you. Let me take the hunger."

Zhao smiled. "Take it. Take everything."

It did. It never stopped.

Leaf-vein striations unfurled along his chest. His breath shortened. Behind his eyes, he saw roots—thick and wet, splitting into synapse and shadow. Even awake, he was dreaming: of limbs hollowed into branches, lungs converted to sap chambers, ribs bursting into petals.

And behind it all: *More.*

The house trembled in the California fog.

Vines curled from the walls like ribs. The ground beneath the foundation pulsed. Gold wires sparked and twisted, struggling to remain relevant. Marble cracked. Something vast and invisible had inhaled the structure and was waiting to exhale it all.

Zhao made his way upstairs, he sat motionless in a chair, though it was no longer clear where man ended and Madwood began. His back had split in a bloom of bark. His eyes no longer focused.

"You fear me," he said slowly, "because I have become what you cannot accept."

Han Xiaoping stepped forward. Leaves shook from her shoulders. Her face was still hers. Barely. "No," she said. "I fear you because you don't know what you've become."

He stood. His limbs cracked. Roots emerged from his arms like open hands turned inside out. "I am the bloom that asks no permission," he whispered. "I am beyond man."

"You are the hunger that mistook itself for prophecy."

Then everything broke.

His body seized, the fusion blooming beyond ecstasy, only to rupture in an instant. Tendrils pierced skin and muscle, gold filaments snapped and writhed, blood burst like spring sap. Bark sealed the wounds; the sap also sealed his soul.

Madwood whispered *More. More.* His mouth opened in a scream ... only spores spilled out, silent and floating.

Though far away, Lilith felt it all—the vision forced into her like a memory not her own. She suddenly knew of Zhao's betrayal, of his body is splitting, his gold devoured, his flesh cocooned in bark. Even the seat of her physical desire turned to wood before bursting into a cloud of spores, scattering on the air—too intimate, too familiar, too strange.

She flinched. The image pressed against her like a fallen, rotting tree across her chest, damp with its own breath, leaving her unable to move an inch.

Lilith was now as wealthy as she could have ever imagined—flush bank accounts scattered across continents, safe deposit boxes nested in offshore vaults. Yet she still couldn't escape Madwood.

Lilith realized Madwood would not need her much longer. Still, it required her face, her voice, the public weight only she could provide. That night, it sent her a vision—Maggie dragged under a black surge, limbs swallowed by the sea.

Maggie had served both of them well: silencing two insurance investigators, coaxing a code-and-virus specialist to keep updating his work so no single report tied Lilith to fraud. She had been loyal, discreet.

Lilith sent the vision back—harvesting Maggie like a crop past its season. It was a way to punish someone without guilt, to make pain into proof that she still had power.

That night, Maggie curled into her plush sofa with a glass of wine, reality shows flickering across the screen. Normally it was the warm end to a long day. Now it felt like a tomb—air sealed for centuries, humming with an ancient stillness that had no name. A splinter that had grown into a fingernail months ago pulsed warmly up her arm, a slow current that caused her nerves to hum.

Maggie stood and walked to the center of her living room, both arms loose at her sides, as if awaiting a cue not yet spoken aloud.

The murmur of voices ebbed into a silence so dense it pressed against her chest like water. Reveling in Madwood's truth ... Maggie opened her mind fully to the tree. She lifted her head. A sharp, unnatural crack echoed across the room.

A seam split open in the far wall. Crumbling concrete gave way to a thick, black vine that coiled into the room like a serpent testing the air. Its skin shimmered with moisture—something ancient, something watching.

The last remanent of the human she had been gasped in surprise. Then Maggie stepped forward and received the vine in her hands like a relic passed down from a forgotten god. She caressed its ridged surface, eyes unfocused, smile calm.

"The roots of Madwood run deeper than law, deeper than memory," she chanted softly.

There was a weight of something that had never left, only waited. She closed her eyes. Her hand tightened around the vine as if it might slip away. "Those buried beneath the soil," she intoned, "speak. What is Lilith's secret?"

The vine trembled. The overhead lights flickered, then dimmed. Cold swept through the room like the breath of a tomb opening. And then ... a voice.

Fragmented. Gravel-thick. Whispering as if through rotting teeth, "I am one of many in her garden of silence ... I watched her bury the wooden boxes. I heard her speak to the roots, promising them names. But no one believes the dead. No one ever does."

Maggie smiled faintly, she was being allowed into the very heart of the secret of Madwood. She felt special. It continued to speak through her. "The dead," she said, "always assume the living have stopped listening."

She stepped forward again, the vine pulsed in her grasp like a living artery.

Maggie tilted her head slightly, like listening through a wall of earth. "Madwood ... your roots have touched the ocean's floor. Tell me, what do the creatures in the Atlantic see?"

The lights pulsed, dimmed blue. And then—from some unseen depth—came a voice, deep, measured, unblinking, "I am Makara. I watch the Atlantic. The roots reached us long ago. They moved through shipwrecks and bones. Absorbing everything from them. They are not roots—they are threads. Threads stitching the living to the dead, the past to what has not yet happened."

A pause, like the ocean holding its breath vibrated through the room. "Lilith was a user of Madwood, not its master. It watches. It waits. It learns."

Suddenly, the vine lunged upward toward the ceiling, as if seeking something beyond the chamber's reach.

Maggie's voice rose like a psalm. "Do the stars know of Madwood's reach? Do the watchers beyond Earth see what has awakened?"

The room dimmed to an unnatural navy—like deep space condensed into a box of stone. A cold, artificial voice responded, emotionless as code, "We are the Overseers of the Outer Rings. Madwood is not native to your soil. It is a form. An archive. It is older than planets. It remembers without memory."

Maggie's lips parted slightly. "What will it do?"

"It will grow," answered the voice. "Until it consumes all ... or is sealed forever. The choice does not belong to Lilith. The choice belongs to those who remain unconnected."

The vine spasmed. Lights snapped on and off in staccato pulses. And then—

Another voice: low, processed, hollow. "Who dares summon the future?"

Maggie's voice dropped to a whisper. "Madwood ... what will you become?"

"Madwood is not a tree. It is a harvester. And what it harvests ... is human nature."

Maggie felt validated, she now knew Lilith hadn't used Madwood. Madwood had used her.

The voice continued, steadier now, "Greed. Fear. Desire. Guilt. These are its nourishment. Lilith was only a gardener. And you—you were a gardener, too."

The vine curled from her hands around her waist. Tightening.

Maggie was finally frightened, all alone in the center of the room. She whispered, "Madwood, your roots pierce time itself. But even you, one day, will rot."

The final denial of Maggie's defiance was the impetus for Madwood to crush her before she could call for help. The vine devoured her slowly over a week.

No one missed her.

No one came looking.

It feeds where the air is heavy. Even decay has its appetite.

Lilith sensed it all from afar. She closed her eyes, recalling the childhood telescope, a girl gazing at the eternity of trees. Now, she understood: Trees do not die, they transform. And she had become this tree's extension, like the victims in eternal flux in the backyard.

And the house exhaled, its roots whispering secrets.

THE NEW MADWOOD NORMAL

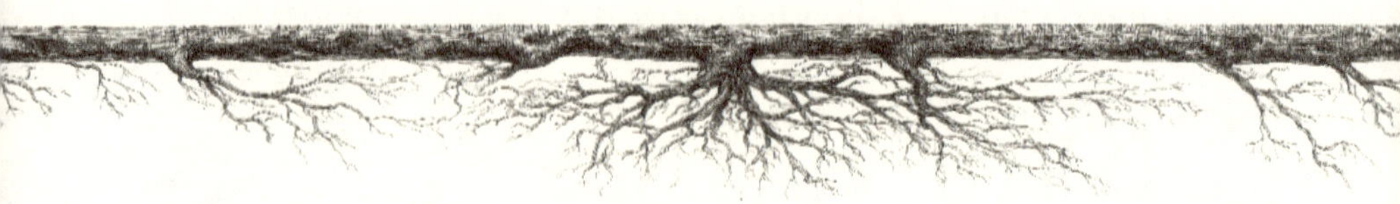

It didn't happen with fire. There were no coups, no troops in the streets. No grand decrees or flashing red screens. It slipped in quietly, welcomed by the restless, the ambitious,
the broken.

Madwood wasn't feared. It was embraced.

When Sawtooth, a resistance group, was branded a domestic terror network and outlawed, the public barely noticed. Their website vanished, their servers were seized, and three of their leaders disappeared. The two who remained appeared on television, their eyes hollow, their smiles forced.

"We were wrong," they said. "It wants peace. It wants order. We now realize Madwood only wants to help humanity."

The world believed their recanting statements.

Integration came fast after that.

First in language. Then in law.

Madwood was rebranded but not as a god. It was a "neuro-reactive initiative for global optimization" new and natural living system.

"Madwood doesn't rule," a commentator explained on the morning news. "It supports. It interprets. It learns from us, then helps us become the best versions of ourselves."

Small seedlings were used, gathered by the tenants of Madwood House, they were quietly planted in hospitals, schools and even city council chambers.

Under the influence of saplings along the windows in Washington D.C. offices, staff rewrote tax codes. It solved the Dublin water crisis. It predicted—and prevented—a landslide in Northern India.

And it healed.

Over and over, it healed.

The universal fear of death and disease became Madwood's connection to the lion's share of people—its root of power and the simplest way to bind itself to humanity. They couldn't face their own destiny. As long as they were healed and inhaled the mist that made death a foggy thing, they handed over everything they had in worship to Madwood. An exchange they didn't realize they were making.

Lilith was released. Declared a victim of a miscarriage of justice. She emerged from the institution not thinner, not really older. Her voice calm. Her gestures measured. Her mind, they said, was no longer fractured by religious delusions. She was fully back in contact and an ambassador for Madwood.

She walked out into the sun, and the crowd applauded. No one called her crazy anymore. What had once been scandal now felt like prophecy fulfilled.

She walked through the front door, in the common room the tenants were gathered, solemn, worried she would start the harvests again. She said only, "It knew they would stop resisting eventually. We can rest now."

All across the globe, people rearranged their lives around Madwood's suggestions. Not rules—enhanced choices. Not punishments—calibrated consequences.

The illusion of freedom remained intact.

The more deeply someone wanted something—wealth, relief, fame—the more Madwood knew how to capture them. And when the world demanded proof, demanded something more than seedlings or new laws, Madwood staged a spectacle.

The studio had gone silent long before the cameras rolled.

They wheeled him in through a side door—what was left of him. The priest. Once a man who had lifted Bibles and offered blessings; now a husk bound in roots. His face had hardened into bark, his eyes sunk deep in fissures of wood, staring from a place both human and other. Where his mouth should have been, a hollow knot protruded. Gasps of horror came from the crew when they realized it was part of a bird feeder; the rim dusted with stray seeds.

The audience didn't clap. Some leaned forward as if hypnotized; others pressed back against their seats, fighting the urge to bolt.

The reporter, slick-haired and rehearsed, shifted in his chair, microphone trembling in his hand. He tried for composure, though sweat already beaded at his collar. "Father," he said carefully, "can you tell us ... how this began?"

A sound followed—low, creaking, like wind twisting through dead branches. His throat rasped as though each syllable was carved out of splinter and sap. "The pain ... never stopped."

The words crawled through the studio. Cameras held steady; millions of live viewers leaned closer to their screens.

"Roots ... in my veins. They drink me." He tilted his head stiffly, the bark of his neck cracking faintly. "Lilith said ... it was freedom. A return. But this is no rebirth. This is hunger. I am devoured. And yet ..." A pause, the kind that made even the lights seem to dim. "... I still fight."

The reporter swallowed, visibly shaken. "And do you ... regret it? Do you see this as a curse?"

The priest's eyes flickered, a dull light caught deep in the grain of his face. "No curse. Not anymore. I am Madwood. My soul bleeds into its soil. It owns me. But I ... own it too."

A collective shiver rippled through the studio. The live-chat feed scrolled so fast it blurred: *holy / miracle / abomination / proof / priestess true / priestess forever.*

Some in the audience wiped their eyes. Others trembled with horror.

The priest raised what had once been a hand—now a splintered branch, skeletal, trembling leaves for fingers. He pointed toward the lens. "You ask what I am. I am not witness. I am warning."

On screen, the chat froze for a beat, then exploded into capital letters. *PROPHECY. HOLY. IT SPEAKS.*

The reporter tried to continue, voice thin. "And Lilith Anderson—what do you believe she intended?"

The priest's wooden lips cracked into something like a grimace, something like a smile. "Lilith is not on trial anymore. Not even in her mind. Not in mine. She planted me in Madwood's soil. Buried me in its roots. And through me ... it can now speak directly to you."

A drop of sap slid from the corner of his mouth, trembling like a tear.

The reporter leaned back, undone. Around him the audience broke—the faithful crying softly, skeptics muttering, one woman praying under her breath for salvation.

The priest's hollow eyes roved the room, then fixed on the camera again, as if staring straight into the millions watching at home.

"You are next."

The feed cut to black.

And yet—Some didn't fall under its sway. They were rare. Often overlooked.

A custodian in Berlin who lived alone and left scraps for alley cats, happy with his life, he had always been generally content. A Vietnamese grandmother who still told stories to elephants. A woman in New Hampshire who ran a nearly bankrupt café and still read paper books with broken spines.

They wanted things, of course. But they could live without them. That was the key. They had some bad days, some sad days; yet overall they enjoyed their lives. They weren't empty enough to want to be filled by an outside entity.

There was a gathering in the parking lot of an abandoned strip mall outside Reno—activists, skeptics, strays from the resistors' ranks.

The air reeked of gasoline and dust. They had come because one of them had built a jammer, a crude device meant to block Madwood's signals and suck in its hypnotizing mists.

If Madwood could whisper through phones and screens, maybe silence would mean freedom.

The group huddled around the box, a patchwork of wires and scrap metal. A man in a ragged denim jacket, his knuckles scarred, raised his hand. "This is it. We turn it on, and the ones that have grown part of it, you cut it out. We'll remember what we were before it spread."

A woman at the edge of the circle—one who had lost her daughter to the roots in Lilith's yard—shook her head. "I'm afraid. You don't understand. I *need* it. The silence will kill me worse than the voices ever did. Madwood fills the emptiness. Without it ..." Her words broke off, her eyes wild, pleading.

Half the group nodded. Half shook their heads.

The man in denim gripped the switch. His hand trembled. "We can live without it. We have to."

The device stuttered to life, buzzing like a wasp nest. For a moment, there was only silence. True silence. No pulse. No hum. Just the sound of breath and blood.

And then the screaming began.

Those who had embraced Madwood dropped to their knees, clutching their skulls as though something vital had been ripped away. They convulsed, their mouths foaming, their eyes rolling white. The others stood frozen, horrified—watching friends collapse into the dirt, twitching like cut live wires.

The woman with the lost daughter clawed her face raw. "Bring it back," she shrieked. "Bring it back, I can't live without it—"

The man in denim tore his hand from the switch. The jammer died with a final pop. The silence ended. The thumping and mists returned.

The convulsions stopped. The followers gasped, wept, kissed the ground. Relief flooded their faces.

And just like that, the choice was gone for anyone who had made the misstep of the smallest embrace of Madwood.

The man in denim stumbled backward, his eyes wide with grief. He'd tried to give them freedom. They had chosen the leash instead.

In the distance, the horizon seemed to shiver, a ripple in the air as if Madwood itself were watching, amused.

Even the rare ones—those who could live without more—were not enough to save the world from Madwood. Their stories circulated briefly online, passed from hand to hand like contraband scripture. For a moment, it seemed they might plant a countering seed of doubt: proof that some people could exist without Madwood, without Lilith's promise of fullness. Without the connection directly to Madwood.

That seed never sprouted.

Their posts were buried, their interviews drowned beneath the flood of testimonies from the converted: endless reels of smiling faces, wooden limbs, trembling voices, telescopic eyes, confessions of how much better life had become since they joined their weakest part with Madwood. The algorithms favored joy over abstinence, and joy was what Madwood falsely promised; manufacturing dependence in surplus.

Politicians, seeing the numbers, aligned themselves quickly. Commentators argued that the resistors were selfish, even cruel. "Why cling to an old emptiness," one said, "when a better future is offered freely?"

The dissenters grew quieter, less visible. Some vanished altogether, absorbed into the same tide they had once resisted. Some didn't vanish—people whispered they'd been bought out, or worn down or simply absorbed.

By the time the second trial was finished, the question of resistance felt quaint, almost folkloric. The debate had shifted. No one asked whether Madwood was right or wrong. No one even cared if it was a religion or not. It was the new way of life on planet Earth.

The only point of power that mattered now was ownership. Who controlled the story. Who got to write the future.

The second trial—the one that gave Lilith back her property—didn't just settle all aspects of ownership and power. It broke something deeper.

People stopped talking about *guilt*. Stopped asking who had *caused* this. Most frightening, they stop trying to find out what Madwood actually was. They talked instead about who got to improve, who remembered how it was before Madwood... and how wonderful everything was now.

"History is not what happened," one pundit said. "It's what gets written down."

And so, Madwood was written into the record.

Not as a takeover. As a turning point.

A new chapter in human/nature/AI collaboration. A *natural evolution.* A correction.

Some called it salvation. Some called it compromise. Most simply called it progress.

In a burned-out community center in eastern Oregon, a woman in a threadbare coat carved the words...

We Lost Quietly

... into a gaming table.

The next morning, it was gone. Scrubbed clean. The community center offered free Madwood-branded coffee and donuts that day.

Meanwhile Madwood never moved. It only grew.

Still centered in the backyard, near the pool.

Still fed by the old bones beneath the soil, and by new bodies near death that no one would miss.

Still dreaming in quiet pulses. And the world was lulled by comfort, no longer daring to ask what it was dreaming of.

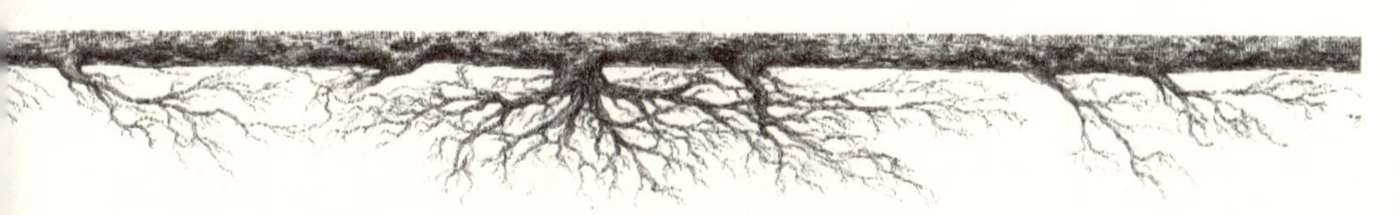

ABOUT THE AUTHOR

From Your Author: I used to edit literary and science magazines in Shanghai, advise billion-dollar ventures and—somehow—ranked among the world's top 100 life insurance advisors. Now I mostly talk to trees.

My journey to Madwood began in South America where I saw fence posts, just dead lumber hammered into the ground ... sprouting unnatural green shoots like they had something to prove. When I got home, I parked myself under the camphor tree in our backyard and basically stopped eating, reading or watching the news. I just wrote. For years.

Eventually, *Madwood* turned into my therapy. Near the end, my wife—following doctor's orders—booked me a psych evaluation. She still insists I should've gone.

I studied law and business at UC and Harvard. These days I live in California with my wife and our Shiba Inu, Tango. The tree's still there, it still whispers to me.

Love Books?

SUPPORT AUTHORS – buy directly from independent publishers. This puts more royalty dollars into the pockets of your favorite author – and gives them time to write their next book.

Visit us for links to our other books as well as many other vibrant publishing companies to find the book for you; join our Launch List to be the first to know about new books:

director@vanvelzerpress.com

These ARE The Books You've Been Looking For.

www.ingramcontent.com/pod-product-compliance
Lightning Source LLC
Chambersburg PA
CBHW020501310726
48979CB00016B/2749/J

* 9 7 8 1 9 5 4 2 5 3 7 5 9 *